THE GREEN MAN

by
HAROLD M. SHERMAN

I0616871

ARMCHAIR FICTION
PO Box 4369, Medford, Oregon   97501-0168

THE GREEN MAN

The original text of this novel was first published by Ziff-Davis Publishing

For more information about Armchair Books and products, visit our website at…

www.armchairfiction.com

Or email us at…

armchairfiction@yahoo.com

EARTH'S FIRST VISITOR FROM OUTER SPACE!

How would we actually receive a visitor from another planet? Try to imagine if one came to the United States in the year 1945. How would he be received by the government, the people, and the rest of the world in general?

Here is a tongue-in-cheek tale about Earth's first extraterrestrial visitor. A strange green man from a planet a trillion miles away with a prophetic message for all the people of earth—to be delivered to during halftime at a Notre Dame football game!

CAST OF CHARACTERS

NUMAR

This strange but eloquent visitor from a distant galaxy came to our world with an important message for the people of Earth.

PROFESSOR BAILEY

This famed astronomer's life changed forever when he happened upon an alien visitor on a lonely mountain road where his car had broken down.

BETTY BRACKEN

She was a dizzy dame and a movie star hopeful. She wanted all the publicity the Green Man could afford to her, but more than that she wanted a young flight lieutenant who looked like Clark Gable!

MRS. BAILEY

She was appalled that her learned husband could be taken in so easily by a fakir claiming to be a man from outer space.

HARRY HOPPER

This energetic young flight Lieutenant was willing to sacrifice anything, including his military career, to save his fiancée from the Green Man.

SAM SCHWARTZ

A Hollywood agent, his aim was to be the first person to sign an alien from outer space to a major studio movie contract.

SID ALEX

Another Hollywood agent, his aim was to make sure that Sam Schwartz was not the first person to sign an alien from outer space to a major studio movie contract.

SENATOR ALFRED HOOLIHAN

His sagging approval rating could be helped tremendously if he could convince the Green Man to accompany him through the halls of Congress.

CHAPTER ONE

THEY say anything can happen in California.

But Professor William Roscoe Bailey did not think it could happen to him—not to a world-renowned astronomer who had spent a lifetime with his feet on the ground and his head in the stars.

These stars were far removed, by cosmic distances, from those of the Hollywood variety. Millions of them could be seen only through the great telescope at Mount Wilson Observatory. To Professor Bailey they outshone in brilliance and glamour the entire constellation of stars and starlets that could be seen through the eye of a movie camera.

That was one of the troubles with the people of this earth—they were enamoured of the wrong kind of stars. One look at the heavens on a clear, cool night like this held more thrills for the Professor than an unobstructed view of Dorothy Lamour in a sarong.

Tonight, for instance, September 15, 1943, had been the Annual Meeting of his astronomical society at which the good professor had read a paper entitled, "Are Other Planets Inhabited?" It had proved to be the sensation of the evening.

"I contend," the Professor had stated, "that there may be millions of other worlds containing forms of life and intelligent creatures far beyond our present evolution. In time to come, through our development of rockets and control of atomic energy, we may be able to build spaceships and explore, not only the moon, but planets like Mars and Venus. This will no doubt lead to the discovery that conditions necessary to life here may not be required for the type of life evolving on other worlds. You gentlemen of science must then be prepared to revolutionize or to scrap your previous theories."

The Professor's address had led to spirited controversy and the furor he had caused was still on his mind as he drove down the mountain in his car with his wife, Nellie.

"What do you think, dear?" he asked, a bit timidly.

"About what?" said Mrs. Bailey.

"About the possibility of life on other planets?"

"I don't think much of it," said his down-to-earth spouse. "If you want my frank opinion, I don't think you helped your reputation, giving a talk like that. They probably think you're a little batty."

Professor Bailey almost steered his car off the road.

"But, Nellie, I'm as certain that other planets have life on them as I am that I'm sitting right here beside you."

The car motor suddenly coughed, sputtered and stopped. They were rounding a steep decline on the road to the valley below, Professor Bailey applied the foot brake and grabbed the emergency. The car lurched and came to a standstill on a precipice overlooking the twinkling lights of the entire San Fernando Valley.

"William! For goodness sake!" said Mrs. Bailey. "Get your mind off those stars and pay attention to what you're doing or we won't even inhabit this planet."

PROFESSOR BAILEY had no mechanical inclinations. He fussed with the starter but the motor wouldn't respond. He got out of the car, lifted up the hood and gazed helplessly at the inert mass of metal.

"It's no use," he announced. "I wouldn't know what's gone wrong in a million years. You sit right there, Dear, and I'll find some place along here with a telephone. I only hope there's a garage open this time of night."

Professor Bailey put the hood down and took a pocket flashlight from the car compartment. The night air was chilly.

"Better turn your coat collar up," admonished Mrs. Bailey, "and don't get off the road. You know what a poor sense of direction you have."

The Professor nodded and looked up at the stars. They seemed to be laughing at him.

"I don't know why this had to happen to me," he said, ruefully. "Just make yourself comfortable. I'll get back as soon as I can."

Playing his flashlight before him, the Professor continued down the winding and perilous road that led from Mount Wilson Observatory to the towns far below.

Ah! There was a light—a kind of luminosity—but it was off the road, quite a distance. The Professor hesitated. Should he venture that far off the highway? He peered about him. This was the only light in evidence, the only sign of habitation. There seemed only one thing to do and Professor Bailey did it. He found himself pushing through underbrush and clambering around shadowy cliffs, keeping his eyes, the while, on this spot of light ahead.

"Heavenly days," he muttered to himself. "It's further away than I thought. I doubt if these people will have a telephone line after I get there. Now where am I and how can I get back to the road?"

The Professor looked about him, squinting through his eyeglasses. He was not far from a clearing of some sort but he was turned around. Let's see—the road was over here? No—it was over there. Hold on—that couldn't be right. Now, wasn't this distressing!

There wasn't any sense in standing still. It was too cold for that. If he could only retrace his steps, get down this embankment.

A stone turned under the Professor's heel and he got down—head first!

HE LAY on his back and saw all the stars of the universe. He felt strangely dazed and tried hard to get his bearings.

There was the North Star in its same old place. Very reassuring, or was it? What in the name of the spiral nebula, Andromeda, was this? That huge silver cigar, glowing at both ends, which was coming down out of the sky!

It was just above the treetops now—and it was going to settle in that clearing. The thing was making a strange humming sound. It was about the size of a small submarine.

"What won't those airplane companies build next?" the Professor wondered. "I never saw anything like this before—not even in Buck Rogers."

The silver cigar was making a vertical descent now, like an elevator. If he wanted to see it land, he'd have to climb up on that rise of ground. There it was—hovering over the clearing as daintily as a humming bird. Its motors—if that's what they were—gave forth a musical sound—a kind of a singing whir.

Suddenly it was silent. The thing had come to rest so easily and quietly, he couldn't detect the slightest jar.

"Must be some secret testing place," thought the professor. "Guess I wasn't supposed to see this. Well, I'm here anyhow and I'm just going to get a closer look."

He pressed forward toward the clearing, picking his way by flashlight.

Yes, there it was—there was that big silver thing. But its sides were quivering and pulsating as though it was alive and breathing! Or perhaps it was the perspiration on the good professor's glasses. No, he'd wiped them off and looked again—and the thing was still inhaling and exhaling. Funny business. No flying crew in evidence. No sound. Just a silver monster, relaxing on the ground, gasping for breath after her flight through space.

"Well, this beats me," said the professor, "I thought I'd seen everything but..."

He hadn't seen everything. The underbelly of this silver spindle opened as though some unseen force had pulled a zipper—and a white-robed figure stepped out.

"Greetings," said this presence, in a voice as mellow-toned as any radio announcer's.

"How do you do?" said the Professor, a bit doubtfully. "Who are you?"

The figure advanced toward him and now he saw that it did not appear to be exactly human. The face was long, with an abnormally high forehead, and the skin seemed to be a pale green in color.

"I—I'm sorry," said the Professor, backing away. "I—I mean—what are you?"

The strange being smiled. "I travel from planet to planet. They call me Numar."

Professor Bailey rubbed his chin nervously and glanced about him.

"If you don't mind, I—I think I'll be going…"

"And I," said this presence, "am going with you."

The tone of voice was still mellow but persuasive. On closer examination, this being could be a member of the human family—a circus freak of some sort. But what should he be doing out here on a mountainside, dressed in a white robe, and coming to earth in a new-fangled airship?

"You won't want to be going with me," said the Professor. "My car—it's broken down…"

"Yes, I know," smiled the figure. "I observed you as I was nearing the earth and a little ray from my aerial vessel stopped your motor. You see, my friend, while you have been studying the stars, you, yourself, have been studied—and, from afar. I'm sure that you'll now be pleased to learn you've been selected to help me perform my mission on this earth."

A sudden feeling of panic seized Professor Bailey. To think that a little matter of stargazing would get him into anything like this.

"There must be some mistake!" he expostulated. "I haven't done anything to deserve this. I don't even believe this is possible. You're really somebody from the Douglas Airplane Factory, aren't you? Please take off that mask and tell me what's going on here!"

An expression of tolerant amusement brought a brighter green glow to the face of the strange personage.

"I have been en route to your planet for the past three months of your earth time," he announced. "This is but a day where I came from—straight through what you call 'the Milky Way.' I am a resident of the planet, which sounds in your tongue something like, Tal-a-May-a."

"Incredible!" said the Professor. "I must have fallen off a cliff and knocked myself unconscious. My poor wife—she's sitting in the car, waiting for me to return. I fear I'm lost and out of my mind—and if I ever return to consciousness I still won't know where I am."

"You are a bit bewildered," said the Voice. A pale green hand reached out and took the Professor reassuringly by the arm. "But I know the way back to your car. Come, let us go together."

The Professor gave a last look toward the clearing. Yes, it was still there—that silver-cigar shaped thing—only it wasn't breathing any longer. It hadn't been, since this being had stepped out of it.

"See here!" demanded the Professor, getting a sudden thought of great penetration, "if you actually came from another planet, how is it that you speak our language?"

"On my planet of Talamaya, we have a record of all your languages here—and I mastered your tongue before I set forth on this little journey."

"*Little* journey?"

"Yes, a mere trifle of a trillion or so miles. I'm en route to planets much farther distant."

"Please," begged the Professor. "I'm used to astronomical figures, but if you're who you say you are—what aid can a mortal like me be to you?"

"Professor Bailey," said the white-robed figure as they walked along. "You may consider yourself a poor mortal but in the eyes of the people on this earth and your fellow scientists, you are accepted as a man of science—a world authority—and you are to act as my host during the time I remain on your planet."

The Professor gasped. "You mean—I'm to introduce you to my friends—and even—to my wife?"

"Your wife by all means. We're approaching your car now. It's just around the next bend."

"Now, hold on—I've been pretty good-humored about this so far— but I still can't…well, it's unbelievable! It isn't happening! I don't know what's the matter with me—but if you think my wife will fall for this!"

They stepped out onto the highway and into the glare of the car headlights. Professor Bailey now had his first good opportunity to examine the being who had taken him in tow.

Yes, the texture of his skin was certainly green and his features, except for the elongated head, might have been that of any man's. A headdress was drawn so tightly about the face that one could not see the color of the hair, if any. Eyes were exceedingly dark, almost black-hypnotic in expression. The figure of this being was perhaps six feet tall, well proportioned and powerful.

"With a physique like that he could be a football player," thought the Professor. "And the way he grips my arm—he's *real* all right. But, if he's who he says he is—what am I going to do with him?"

As if in answer to these thoughts, the Professor's white-robed escort spoke.

"I perceive you still doubt. But I am able to offer you proof. Do you recall that I told you I had stopped the motor of your car?"

The Professor gulped and nodded.

"Well, you'll find that it will operate all right now."

"If it does," said the Professor, "that'll be proof enough for me." Then, after a moment's reflection, "Only I hope it doesn't."

When they reached the car, a startled Mrs. Bailey looked questioningly at her husband.

"Hello, dear," said the Professor, interested in checking his motor, "I couldn't find a telephone but, I—well, this is Mister…a…Mister…?"

"Numar," obliged the white-robed figure.

"Numar," repeated the Professor, opening the rear car door and gesturing. "Here—climb in—you can have the back seat to yourself." Then, to his wife, as he hurried around and slid in behind the wheel, "Mister Numar says he's from the planet Talamaya—wherever that is— but I told him I wouldn't believe that unless…"

The Professor put his foot on the car starter. The motor instantly responded.

"Oh, good heavens! He *is* from the planet Talamaya."

"What on earth are you talking about?" demanded Mrs. Bailey, finding her voice for the first time. "Who is this Hollywood actor and what's he doing so far from the lots?"

"He's not a Hollywood actor," said the Professor, in hushed, awestruck tones. "And don't let him hear you say that. You see how this motor's running? Well, there wasn't anything wrong with it. He just stopped it from miles up in the air, so I'd get out of the car and go for help and come to the place where he was landing in his spaceship. It's all very extraordinary."

"Yes, very," said Mrs. Bailey, "and if you expect me to believe that, you must be Mr. Ripley."

"Dear, you've just got to believe it." The Professor set the car in gear and resumed his trip down the mountain. "You're a witness to the fact that I didn't get the car fixed—and yet—here we go…"

"The motor was probably overheated. It would have started up just the same if you'd never met this man. Where are you taking him?"

"Darling—he's to be our house guest."

"Who says so?"

"He does—he told me we were picked out of all the humans on this earth to sponsor him. It's supposed to be our mission or something…"

"Well, of course—now I understand everything. He's some ismic leader or cultist who's escaped from an institution. We'll have to find out which one—and return him…"

Professor Bailey drove in silence for some distance. What could he say? He stole apprehensive glances through the rear view mirror to see if his "other world companion" was still with them. He was. What to do…what to do?

"If I'd come from another planet, I'd certainly wish to be treated right," thought the Professor. And then the enormity of this situation began to crowd in upon him.

If Mister Numar had really come from the planet of Talamaya—or ANY planet—it was the biggest news story in the history of the world! Why, it was much more important and exciting than if he, Professor William Roscoe Bailey, had discovered a new planet or galaxy. This news would chase the world war off the front pages and give everybody something big and sensational to think about. He must have been dazed, actually stupefied, not to have realized this at once. Here he was, Professor Bailey, world-renowned astronomer, most favored among men. Fate had selected him to play a tremendous role and now it was clear to the Professor why he had been selected. When a man of his reputation introduced this heavenly visitor to the world, Numar would be accepted for what he was. No doubt Numar had come to earth for some great and, as yet, unrevealed purpose. Beings of his stature didn't go shooting a trillion miles through space on a whimsy.

"Darling," said the Professor, as he reached their home, "you've had complete faith in me for the past thirty years and you must not lose it now. We're in on the ground floor of one of the greatest things that's ever happened on this earth."

"Oh, stop talking like a Hollywood ad."

"But, my dear," he expostulated, "don't you see—if I present this space traveler as my discovery to the world, it will make me more famous than having a star named after me."

THE Bailey home was a modest bungalow type with a spare bedroom overlooking a little rose garden, and the mountains beyond.

"This is your room and the bathroom's right off here," pointed Mrs. Bailey, in her best Frigidaire manner. "No doubt you'll want to freshen up a bit after your trip."

Numar nodded and smiled.

"And I wish you'd remove that green paint or dye and stop pretending you're somebody from out of this world," she continued, in spite of rib-jabbings from her husband. "I'm onto you, even if Mr. Bailey isn't!"

"Please pay no attention to her," begged the Professor. "My wife's always been a skeptic. When I wrote my paper on the size and frequency of sunspots, she told me I ought to be examined by a lunacy commission. Even when my theories were accepted by the Astronomical Society she said that most astronomers were just a bunch of nearsighted old bags."

"Now, William—I didn't say *bags*."

"Well, whatever it was, dear, it wasn't very complimentary. And the way you're acting, what do you suppose Mr. Numar is going to think of our civilization?"

Mrs. Bailey wasn't in the mood to uphold the dignity of the human race.

"I don't care what he thinks. As for me—I'm tired and I'm going to bed."

Professor Bailey coughed apologetically.

"That's a woman for you," he said. "I presume you have them where you came from?"

Numar bowed. "Oh, yes—woman is everywhere in the universe."

The Professor looked a trifle disappointed.

"But on our planet," Numar added, "we have nothing you would recognize as sex."

"Oh bosh and tither!" snorted Mrs. Bailey. "You'd be just as much a man as my husband if you'd take off that flowing robe and put on pants!"

The mysterious visitor eyed Mrs. Bailey with an expression of infinite patience.

"Pants," he explained, "have not evolved on our planet. Both sexes dress as I am attired."

"You see, William—it's just as I surmised. This masquerader is some fanatic who's trying to start a new cult. He's attached himself to you because he feels, with your scientific endorsement, he can attract a big following. If you sponsor him, you'll be ruined."

The Professor wore a pained expression.

"I'm sorry to have to take issue with you dear—but I believe in Mister Numar—and so long as I do, I'm willing to risk my reputation. You go to bed and let me worry about this matter."

"All right—but don't say I didn't warn you."

Mrs. Bailey stepped inside her room and slammed the door.

CHAPTER TWO

PROFESSOR BAILEY didn't sleep well that night. He tossed and turned on the couch in the living room. No use in going to bed with his wife and continuing the argument. Besides, it had been a fatiguing and nerve-shocking evening. But what was he to do on the morrow? How would be best to break the news of this momentous event to an unsuspecting world? The professor dreamed and saw thousands of skeptical, scoffing fellow humans, each of whose faces resembled that of Nellie, his wife. He was trying to get away from them all when he was awakened by someone pounding on the front door.

"Who is it?" he asked, half asleep, fumbling with the lock.

"Jamison," said a voice.

"Oh, good morning, Ed. I got to bed late last night, I…"

"Say, Will—do you know what's going on in your backyard? There's a funny looking geek out there parading around in a white robe—and he's absolutely green!"

"What? Oh…oh, yes, I know…"

"Did you hear what I said? The man is green."

Professor Bailey's tone was slightly irritable. He never liked being waked up. "Certainly he's green. That's his natural color."

"His natural color? What do you mean?"

"Just what I say. He's from another planet. Just arrived last night. They're *all* green up there."

"Oh come on…don't be handing me anything like that, Professor. I've lived next door to you too long. What kind of a scientific experiment is this?"

Professor Bailey was shivering in his pajamas.

"No experiment—no experiment at all. Do you mind if I slip into my bathrobe?"

Mr. Jamison stepped in the door, leaving it ajar.

"Listen, Will, my kids are out talking to that man now. They've been asking him what movie outfit he's with. I think myself he's some kind of a Yogi. But his green skin—that's what gets me. Never saw anything like it. How'd he get colored up like that?"

"I haven't the slightest idea," said the Professor, fastening the bathrobe around him. "Some difference, most likely, in his skin pigment. You'll have to ask him."

"Now, just a minute, Will—just a minute! Are you expecting me to swallow your story that this guy's from another planet?"

A look of defiance came into Professor Bailey's face.

"I don't care whether you swallow it or not—it's the truth."

"Well, I like that!" Mr. Jamison towered over the Professor. "I came over here as a friend to find out what's going on and you try to tell me this green man is from another world. Well, I don't believe it. This is too early in the morning for me to let anyone spoof me—and if you've turned into a practical joker at your age, you ought to be locked up. Good day."

A CONCERNED Professor Bailey now started for the rear of the house but collided with his wife as she came down the stairs.

"What on earth is all the commotion?" she demanded, pulling on her dressing gown. "I've just looked out the back window and there's a crowd gathering. Most all the neighbors in the block and people I never saw before."

"It's Mister Numar," said the Professor. "He's out there."

"William. You've got to get rid of that man. If you don't he'll get you in terrible trouble!" Mrs. Bailey's eyes flashed something akin to fire.

Professor Bailey saw that it was hopeless to remonstrate with her. "Nellie," he said, persuasively. "There's too much at stake here for us to be in disagreement. I've just had a most distressing thought. Perhaps the reason Mister Numar is up early and pacing about in our yard is because he's hungry. I stupidly neglected to offer him any food last night."

"But how would I know how to feed a man from Mars?" retorted Mrs. Bailey.

"He's not from Mars—it's Talamaya."

"Well, wherever he's from. I don't suppose they ever heard of toasted cornflakes up there. You'd better go out and ask him what he wants. It's hard enough getting a meal for a mortal man like you!"

"Oh, stop it," said the Professor, but he softened when he saw a twinkle in his wife's eye.

BY NOW, every foot of the Bailey backyard fence was taken up by spectators—men, women and children of all ages. They were standing on each other's toes and stretching their necks to get a better view of this figure in white with the skin of green. The personage, himself, did not seem to mind onlookers. He had stopped his pacing and was seated on a bright red garden chair, idly examining a rose bush.

"I tell you, he's not human," a scholarly appearing man was insisting. "I studied anthropology in school and there just isn't any Homo Sapiens with a head shaped like that…"

"Oh, they can make a man up to look like anything in Hollywood," said a woman. "But I can't understand what this freak's doing on Professor Bailey's premises."

"I know what he's doing," spoke up Ed Jamison, who had just rejoined the throng. "I've been in to see the Professor and he claims this bird arrived here last night from another planet."

"Oh, yeah?"

"How'd he get here?"

"The Professor didn't say. He got peeved when I doubted his word. I'll have to admit, though, I've never before seen a human being who was green."

"Me, either. He does look different. Can he talk?"

"I don't know. Let's find out." Mr. Jamison put one hand to the side of his mouth. "Hey, Mister! Hey, you!"

The white-robed figure looked in the direction of the voice.

At this moment, the rear door of the Bailey house opened and the Professor appeared. He had his tie in hand and was just fastening his collar. The size of the curious multitude stunned him.

"My goodness me!" he exclaimed.

"Come on, Professor—tell us what it's all about!" shouted someone.

A chorus of voices joined in the demand. The Professor hesitated as the white-robed figure walked over and stood beside him. Finally, as everyone waited expectantly, he cleared his throat.

"Well, there's very little to say, at present—except that Mrs. Bailey and I are happy to have, as our houseguest, this distinguished personage from a far off planet. Mr. Numar arrived unexpectedly last night. I haven't, as yet, had a chance to find out just why he came but I hope to be able to make an announcement to the press on his behalf soon. Just now I imagine Mr. Numar is terribly hungry because he hasn't eaten a mouthful of food since he landed, so if you'll please excuse us…"

The Professor took his celestial visitor by the arm.

"I shall be glad to join Mrs. Bailey and yourself for what you call breakfast," smiled Numar, "but, as for me, I never eat."

"You never eat?" gasped the Professor.

"Did you hear that?" cried a voice in the crowd.

"Never," repeated Numar. And then, for the information of all within ear range, he explained: "On my planet, we derive such nourishment as we need from the air and water. That's why I've been out here in the garden since your sunrise—getting my fill of air for the day. And now, if I may have a glass of water, I'll not require anything more for the next twenty-four hours."

A hum of surprised comment went the rounds.

"Can you imagine that…a guy who can live on air and water!"

"Not me—I'll take fried chicken."

The white-robed figure with the green complexion turned toward the house with Professor Bailey.

"How did you sleep last night?" the Professor was asking.

"Sleep?" said Numar. "I never sleep."

This was enough to set tongues wagging furiously. Was this strange being who he claimed to be or was Professor Bailey the unwitting victim of a clever hoax?

"DARLING," said the Professor, as they placed Numar in the guest chair at the breakfast table. "It's not going to be difficult to feed Mr. Numar. All we've got to supply him is plenty of air and water."

"After I've prepared ham and eggs and toast and coffee and rolled oats?" said Mrs. Bailey.

"It's all completely lost on him," said the Professor. "He's just informed me. They don't eat on his planet."

"I suppose the next thing he'll be trying to tell you is that he hasn't any stomach at all..."

Numar smiled. "That is correct, Mrs. Bailey. We Talamayans possess an organ more resembling a generator. It takes the elements from the air and water and converts them into electrical energy, which furnishes us with all the power we need to sustain life."

Mrs. Bailey sniffed her incredulity.

"William, how much longer are you going to stand for this kind of nonsense? Mr. Numar was up early this morning. He probably went down the alley to the Hamburger Tavern and had his fill. But no man is going to be my house guest and turn his nose up at my food!"

Professor Bailey controlled himself with difficulty.

"My dear," he said. "Don't be ridiculous. You can't feed a man food who has no stomach. It just isn't being done."

"I desire only a glass of water," said the mysterious visitor.

"Oh, very well!" snapped Mrs. Bailey. She got up from the table and flounced into the kitchen, turning on the water tap.

"You mustn't mind my wife," apologized the Professor. "She doesn't even like relatives dropping in unexpectedly. As it is, I'll have to eat your share of ham and eggs and toast, even if it kills me."

Numar's green countenance expressed amusement. "It must be an odd sensation to have a stomach," he said.

"Not nearly so odd as not having one," said the Professor. "I don't see how you're going to get very far on a mere glass of water."

Numar patted his host's arm reassuringly and the Professor jumped.

"Oh!" he exclaimed, "what was that?"

"I'm sorry," said Numar. "I forgot for a moment where I was. You see, I'm charged with electrical energy. I must remember to insulate myself before touching anyone."

Professor Bailey nodded, his eyes agleam with scientific interest.

"That's amazing, Mister Numar! You must let me take you to the University—put you under tests—let my fellow scientists see you demonstrate your powers."

Before Numar could answer, Mrs. Bailey appeared with a pitcher of water in one hand and a glass in the other.

"If water is all you'll have," she said, "you don't need to stop with a glass full. This is fresh from the city reservoir and there's plenty more where it came from."

She filled the glass with a flourish and set pitcher and tumbler before her green-complexioned houseguest.

Numar raised the glass to his lips. "You are kind, Mrs. Bailey. But you creatures on this planet have not yet discovered the enormous power in a drop of water. When you do, you will eat less and drink more."

"I thought so," said Mrs. Bailey. "Now it commences to come out. You're one of those food cultists who travels around getting people to go on special fasts and diets. You're pretty clever all right, but I can see through you."

Numar made no reply but took a long draught of the water. A sudden look of revulsion came over his face. He began to choke and reached for a napkin.

PROFESSOR BAILEY, alarmed, jumped up and whacked him on the back. He found himself catapulted against the wall, in a sitting position. "What on earth!" his wife was exclaiming.

"My dear Madam," said Numar, his countenance a paler shade of green. "What did you put in this water?"

"Nothing!" said Mrs. Bailey. "William! Get up off the floor. What's the matter with you two, anyway?"

"Nellie," said Professor Bailey, getting shakily to his feet. "I've just been struck by lightning. Don't ever touch that Mister Numar or you may be electrocuted!"

"Stuff and nonsense!" denounced Mrs. Bailey, now thoroughly aroused. "What's the matter, Mister Impostor? Did that water go down your windpipe?"

"That water," said her unwelcome visitor, "is not pure."

"Of course it's pure," retorted Mrs. Bailey. "What do you suppose the city puts chlorine in it for?"

"Chlorine?" said Numar. "So that's what it is."

"You don't need to worry, Mister Numar—that chlorine's killed all the bacteria."

"And it almost killed me," said Numar. "We have no bacteria on our planet. My organism will not assimilate chlorine. I'm sorry to trouble you but I'll have to have spring water."

"You appear to operate much like a battery," observed the Professor, helpfully. "How about distilled water?"

"I believe that would be just the thing," said Numar.

"Good," said the Professor. "I'll have our drug store send over some bottles." He left the dining room to telephone the order.

Mrs. Bailey sat studying her strange houseguest. "If you're putting up a front, it's a mighty slick one," she admitted. "'I can't figure out what your game is just yet—but I'm warning you not to carry this thing too far." As Numar sat, saying nothing, she eyed him with growing suspicion. "This could be a Hollywood stunt to advertise a new picture. But if you take advantage of my poor husband this way, you'll regret it the rest of your born days."

"Mrs. Bailey," said the personage in green. "You must believe me when I tell you I was not born on this planet. I came here for a purpose, as your distinguished husband has informed you, and he has been chosen, of all humans on earth, to assist me. You can make it easier for him and for yourself if you will be good enough to cooperate."

Mrs. Bailey took hold of the arms of her chair as a feeling of uncertainty and bewilderment assailed her. "No," she said—more to herself than to anyone else. "I mustn't let myself come under his spell. He's hypnotized William and now he's trying to get me. Oh, this is terrible! What am I going to do?"

PROFESSOR BAILEY came hurrying back into the room. "Your distilled water is coming right over," he announced. "I ordered an extra bottle for the battery in my car. It's run down, too."

"Thank you, Professor," said Numar. "Now, please take care of your own organism. That extra supply of ham and eggs will give you the energy you need because we have a strenuous day ahead of us."

Professor Bailey took up his knife and fork as dutifully as a small boy acting on orders of a parent. His wife poured twice too much sugar in her coffee and sat stirring it, with her cheek muscles twitching.

"Of course, Mister Numar," she said, "you can change your mind and eat any time you wish. I should think you'd get tired posing like that. And if you really intend drinking that distilled water, I think you ought to have your head examined."

Her unwelcome houseguest bestowed a tolerant look upon her. "I think you would do well to get some nourishment, too," he suggested. "I can foresee that this is not going to be an easy day for you, either."

Mrs. Bailey gasped in exasperation. She felt momentarily squelched. How was she going to save her husband and herself from this self-assured impostor? The Professor had been religiously attacking his ham and eggs. The two ate in uncomfortable silence, feeling the eyes of their visitor upon them.

"Here, Mister Numar," said the Professor, finally. "So stupid of me. Wouldn't you like to read our morning paper?" He picked up a copy of the *Los Angeles Times.*

"No, thank you. I know all the essential things that are taking place on your planet. Very few of them are reported in the paper. The rest do not matter."

Mrs. Bailey gagged on a swallow of coffee. "I suppose you know what's going to happen next," she taunted.

"I do," said Numar. "Your door bell's going to ring."

He had no sooner spoken than the doorbell did ring—a long, vigorous, continued ringing. Professor Bailey jumped up.

"It's the boy from the drug store with your distilled water," he said. "He should know better. I'll give him a good piece of my mind…"

The bell kept on ringing.

"For mercy's sake!" said Mrs. Bailey, getting to her feet. "He must think someone is dying for that water."

The Baileys rushed to the door together. It was not the boy from the drug store. It was a bundle of feminine dynamite, one hundred twenty pounds of blonde beauty, exploding joyously in their faces.

"Hello, Uncle William…hello, Aunt Nellie…surprise! I knew you'd be glad to see me! I just flew in this morning from New York. Warner Brothers has promised me a screen test. Isn't that swell?"

UNCLE and aunt were almost too dumbfounded to speak.

"Why, Betty Annabel Bracken!" exclaimed Mrs. Bailey.

"Yes, it's…er…swell about the screen test," said Professor Bailey, eyeing his stunning niece apprehensively. "But your arrival here, at this time, is a trifle awkward…I might even say—unfortunate…"

"Why, what's the matter?"

"I think, Nellie—you'd better explain," said Professor Bailey, "while I get back to our guest."

"Oh, my goodness!" said Betty. "Do you have other relatives or friends visiting? If that's the case, I'll go to a hotel."

"No, dear," said Mrs. Bailey. "We've got something worse than that. We've got a gentleman here from another planet…or at least so he says…"

19

"Why, Auntie—you're spoofing!"

"No, I'm not, dear…oh, excuse me, that must be his distilled water."

A young man was coming up on the porch with a package.

"Whose distilled water?"

"The man from Mars."

"Package for Professor Bailey," said the boy, edging in between the niece and the door. "Six bottles of—"

"Yes, I know," said Mrs. Bailey.

"Just take them in the dining room to Mr. Bailey."

"Okay." The boy passed through between the two women but came out again almost immediately, eyes bulging.

"Gee, Mrs. Bailey—I never seen a guy like that before. Is he real?"

"That's what I want to know," said the professor's wife.

A cloud of dust marked the delivery boy's path from the house.

"Why, Auntie—this is utterly fantastic!" said Betty, stepping in and depositing her suitcase. "I'm bursting with curiosity. When did this 'space traveler' arrive—and how come—and everything?"

"Well, Betty," said Mrs. Bailey, "it happened like this. Our car broke down last night in the mountains. Your uncle went to get help and came back with this mysterious character who calls himself Numar."

"You don't say. What's he look like?"

"You'll see for yourself in just a minute. I've a strong suspicion he's a humbug."

"But, Auntie—how could a man like Uncle William—one of the world's greatest astronomers—be taken in?"

"Oh, Betty—it's always easy to fool a scientist. They're looking so hard for the truth that they can't ever see anything false."

"You mean—Uncle actually believes this man is from where he says he is?"

"I'm afraid he does. And if he goes on record publicly—he'll be the laughing stock of this world."

Betty's big blue eyes became even bigger. "Why, Auntie—we can't permit this. Isn't there something we can do?"

Mrs. Bailey bit her under lip and considered. "Yes, there is…" she said, suddenly. "Something you can do…Betty—you're an actress. You can help me expose this fakir."

"Oh, Auntie, I'd love to. But how?"

Mrs. Bailey took her niece confidentially by the arm and whispered in her ear. "Most every man, whether he's a fake or not, is susceptible to sex appeal. If you could only pretend to fall in love with this Mister Numar and lead him on—I think it wouldn't take long to solve his mystery."

"I think you're right," said Betty, chuckling softly. "Besides…it might be kind of fun. Where is he, Auntie…lead me to him."

THE arrival of the distilled water had relieved Professor Bailey a great deal. It was quite a responsibility caring for his unearthly visitor, especially since some of his internal workings were so at variance from the human.

"Feeling better, now?" he asked, solicitously, after Numar had imbibed a full glass of the distilled liquid.

"Very much," smiled the green man. "I'll function perfectly now for the remainder of the day. By the way, your niece is a most charming and attractive young woman."

Professor Bailey stared. "How do you know? You haven't seen her yet…"

"Oh, yes—I intercepted her thought as she was coming here from the airport, intent on surprising you. I took a good look at her then. She's a very clever girl—very!"

"Well, I—I'm glad you think so," said the Professor. "I was a little afraid…you see…we only have one guest room."

"Oh, I can just as well stay in your study. In fact, I'd prefer it. A bedroom is entirely lost on me. I can read some of your books of science while you sleep."

The Professor regarded Numar, wonderingly. "Do you really mean it when you say you don't sleep?"

"I wish I could, sometimes," said Numar. "It seems to me it would be a delightful experience."

"You don't eat and you don't sleep," pondered the Professor. "You live on air and water. You look almost like a human and yet you're not human. Your body stores electrical energy like a powerhouse. You say you've come a trillion miles through space. This is almost too much for my brain cells. I won't feel right until I can have some of my fellow scientists examine you. Do you mind if I call a few of them over?"

"You needn't call them," said Numar. "They'll be over soon enough—and so will a host of others."

The Professor looked alarmed. "Oh, I hope not. My home is so small and I've always lived here so quietly. I confess, Mister Numar, that I'm kind of at a loss exactly as to how to entertain you."

Numar reached out his hand to give his host another reassuring pat but the Professor pulled back just in time. "If you don't mind," he said, "I've already been shocked enough."

Numar smiled. "You would have felt nothing," he said. "I had remembered to insulate myself."

There was a slight commotion at the door. It was Mrs. Bailey.

"Mister Numar," she said. "My niece has just arrived from New York."

"Yes, dear," said the Professor. "He already knows it."

"Oh...then you've told him," surmised Mrs. Bailey. "She would like to meet you, Mister Numar." Then, with a touch of sarcasm, "She says she's never met anyone from another planet before. May I bring her in?"

NUMAR arose from the table and stood his full six feet. But for the exceedingly high forehead, he made a striking figure, his countenance and long tapering fingers appearing almost as though they had been cut from green marble.

"I should be delighted."

"That's most gracious of you," said Mrs. Bailey. "Then may I present Miss Betty Annabel Bracken?"

Making a dazzling entrance on cue, Mrs. Bailey's niece swept into the room. She stopped short in front of the white-robed figure, a bit taken aback by his poise and presence. "How do you do?" she finally managed, and held out her hand.

Professor Bailey got to his feet, almost knocking over a chair. "Now, now, Betty...I wouldn't if I were you!"

But it had already happened. Numar had taken her hand in his and was holding it.

"Well, I never!" said the Professor, and sat down again.

"Auntie's been telling me about you," said Betty, as Numar said nothing, only looking at her from the depth of his black eyes. "Have a nice trip here?"

"Quite uneventful, thank you."

"You call traveling billions of miles uneventful?"

"One gets accustomed to it, in time."

Betty squirmed, uncomfortably, and withdrew her hand. "My, I don't think I ever would. Why, I just finished flying from coast to coast...that's three thousand miles, you know."

"Yes, I know—and it took you twelve hours. Can you compute how long it would take me, traveling as I do, with the speed of light?"

"Whew! That's a sixty-four dollar question for Uncle William," laughed Betty. "I'm no good at figures."

"I think you are," said Numar, eyeing her. "Very much so."

"Why, Mister Numar!" gasped Betty. "You sound almost human."

The tension was broken, or perhaps increased, by the ringing of the doorbell.

"Well, who do you suppose that is?" said the Professor. "Excuse me, please." He left the room, looking a trifle annoyed.

"Won't you sit down?" invited Numar, gesturing toward a chair as Betty remained standing staring at him.

"That's the most remarkable makeup!" she exclaimed. "I don't see how you did it."

"Me, either," said Mrs. Bailey.

"Makeup?" repeated Numar. "What do you mean by makeup?"

"Why, your face, your eyes, your long head line, those hands—everything. It's wonderful—and that shade of green. I've never seen anything like it. It's even uncanny!"

"You earth people are so amusing," said Numar. "Everything you can't understand you think is unreal or artificial. I am not made up. This is the way I really am."

Betty's eyes widened. "You mean you're green like that all over?"

"Why, certainly. Aren't you white all over?"

Mrs. Bailey hurriedly got up to clear the breakfast dishes. "I think we'd better change the subject," she said.

CHAPTER THREE

PROFESSOR BAILEY was having his troubles at the door. He was confronted by the chief of police and two burly officers of the law.

"Professor," said the chief. "I can hardly believe this about you. But I've had several reports that you are harboring a suspicious looking character here."

The Professor's indignation rose like the mercury in a thermometer. "Who told you?"

"Several neighborhood complaints. See that crowd gathering outside?" The chief thumbed over his shoulder. "Somebody said we should look for a green man in a white bathrobe. Is anyone answering that description here?"

Professor Bailey nodded. "I'm afraid there is."

"Well, lead us to him."

"Now, Chief—don't be too hasty. There're a few things I should tell you about this…er…personage. In the first place, he's not human…"

"He's not *what?*"

"He doesn't belong to our species. He's not of this world."

"So that's what *he* thinks. I get you. Then it's the nut house for him."

"Oh, no!" The Professor was horrified. "You don't understand.

Mister Numar arrived here last night by spaceship from the planet Talamaya."

"Talamaya. Never heard of it. Spaceship? Say—what're you talking about?"

"Talamaya's a trillion or so miles from here," said the Professor, helpfully. "Mister Numar can tell you more about it. I haven't had time yet to..."

"Professor, if I didn't know you, I'd say you were headed for the nut house. Lemme smell your breath. Did you go on a planetary bender?"

"I'm perfectly sober—and sane—I hope," said the Professor.

"Well, show us this fugitive from a distant planet and we'll soon tell you!" ordered the chief.

"Follow me, gentlemen. Oh, you don't need to draw your guns. He's not dangerous...at least, he hasn't been up to now."

Mrs. Bailey and Betty had been trying to trick the mysterious visitor into some statement that would reveal him to be what they presumed him to be an ingeniously camouflaged human being, but, thus far, no luck. They were certainly not prepared for the dramatic entrance of this blue-coated trio.

"Stand where you are. Don't move! We've got you covered," said the chief.

Numar stood looking into the muzzles of three revolvers.

"Whom do I have the honor of addressing?" he asked.

"Chief of Police Andrews and two officers of the law," introduced the Professor.

"The law," said Numar, and smiled, "Quaint custom-upholders of the law. On my planet, we haven't had a police force for the last ten million years."

"CUT out that kind of talk!" barked the chief. "Where do you come from and what are you doing here?"

"Talamaya is my home planet but I'm on an extended tour of the universe. I've stopped here to deliver a message to you earth people. When I've done that, I'll be on my way."

"This sounds like double-talk to me. Professor—I'm going to have to take this gent to the station for a questioning. We'll wash that green paint off him, too. Don't worry...we'll get the goods on his skin game."

"If you do," said Mrs. Bailey, "I wish you'd let us know what it is. We haven't been able to find out."

Numar, apparently undisturbed, turned aside to Professor Bailey.

"You still believe in me?" he asked.

"Well, yes," said the Professor. "After what I've seen—unless my senses are tricking me."

"That's fine," said Numar. "Then, if I'm to accompany these courageous representatives of law and order, would you mind coming along and bringing a bottle of distilled water? It might be a bit difficult for me to convince these gentlemen that I really need it. And I shouldn't like to have to cause them any trouble or inconvenience."

The Professor picked up a quart bottle, which the chief immediately snatched from him.

"So that's what this guy has been drinking," he said. "Looks like wood alcohol to me. Sure, we'll take this along—for evidence."

"Well, Mister Numar," said Mrs. Bailey. "I can't exactly say I'm sorry to see you go. You've certainly upset this household no end since you attached yourself to the Professor last night. But I must say, you seem to be a gentleman. I hope things don't go too hard for you."

"Oh, Auntie," said Betty. "We're going to the station house with Mister Numar. I wouldn't miss this for the world!"

"You're going, I'm not," said Mrs. Bailey. "I've got these dishes to do and the day's marketing. We've still got to eat whether Mister Numar does or not."

"All right, you," said the chief. "Get moving…"

"You first, gentlemen," said Numar, nodding toward the door.

"What do you mean *us* first?" snapped the chief. "You're under arrest. Lay hands to him, boys."

The bluecoats advanced upon Numar who raised his hands. "I'd advise you not to touch me," he said, quietly.

"So would I," said the Professor.

"Oh, you would, would you," roared the chief. "Well, just for that, put the handcuffs on him!"

Each officer grabbed an arm and each officer, just as quickly, turned a backward somersault.

"You see what I mean?" said the Professor.

"What's the matter with you men?" demanded the chief.

"You try handcuffing him," said the first officer to regain his feet. "I feel like I've been kicked by a mule."

"Now, gentlemen," said Mrs. Bailey. "I've had enough of this kind of business. If you want to wrestle with Mister Numar, please take him outside to do it."

The chief held the handcuffs and looked testily at the green man. Numar smiled and extended his hands, with wrists together.

"You would like to try?" he asked.

"Now, that's more like it," said the chief and touched the handcuffs to Numar's wrists.

THERE was a blinding flash, like a short circuit, and the chief of police of La Canada, suburb of Los Angeles, in the state of California, came down on the top of the Bailey breakfast table.

Only Numar remained unmoved.

"You see what I mean?" said the Professor, again.

"You first, gentlemen," said Numar, and nodded toward the door.

The chief and his two police officers needed no further invitation. They were only too glad to precede their prisoner who walked serenely after them, but turned at the doorway to extend his apologies to a speechless Mrs. Bailey.

"I regret very much this had to happen," he said. "But, fortunately, you had gotten your nourishment out of the meal. I suggest you rest up while we are gone. There is still a strenuous time ahead."

"Good heavens!" moaned Mrs. Bailey. "Don't tell me you have any intention of coming back?"

PROFESSOR BAILEY was proud of his little house and yard. He had spent much time fussing with the front lawn. There was a young avocado tree, which he counted on for shade in his declining years. Then there was a lemon tree that had three green lemons on it, ready to pick. The hedge that lined the walk was the professor's pet. He trimmed it himself once a month and chased stray dogs from it.

Now, as Professor Bailey stepped out onto the front porch behind the three police officers and Numar, he suffered his greatest shock of the day. It looked as though every man, woman and child in town was parked in his front yard. Boys had shinned up his avocado tree and were hanging to the groaning limbs.

"Look!" they shouted. "There he comes! There's the green man!"

The crowd pressed forward, straddling the hedge in many places and trampling it. The turf of the lawn had already been scruffed up. The patrol car by the curb had proved a strong magnet. But the word-of-mouth of the neighbors had done the most damage.

"Stand back, everyone!" ordered the Chief. "This man is a dangerous character. Don't anyone touch him. He's got some kind of an infernal machine on him. It's liable to kill you outright!"

The curious mob backed away and tramped the hedge some more.

"Please, my good people!" appealed the Professor. "Watch what you're doing! Boys, get down out of that tree."

"Aw, gee, then we can't see," said the smallest. "Gosh, is he gonna explode or somethin'?"

It was no use. The only way to disperse the crowd was to get Numar away from there as quickly as possible. The police had made a lane for him down the sidewalk to the car and were waiting for Numar to join them. Betty appeared on the porch and took the Professor's arm.

"Uncle William," she said. "I'm going with you…"

"No, dear," said the Professor. "Police stations are no place for a girl like you."

"Just the same, I'm going," declared Betty. "You're not going to face this ordeal alone."

Professor Bailey had learned through years of experience not to argue very much with a woman. Besides, he had more pressing things on his mind. Numar was descending the steps and walking with an undeniable majesty toward the patrol car. People pressed as close to him as they dared and the bigger boy in the tree reached down to touch him as he passed. This was his instant undoing. He let loose a surprised howl and landed in the crowd, taking three elders to earth with him.

"Good work," said the Professor, in an undertone to Numar. "He shouldn't have been up in my tree, anyway." Then to the awe-struck crowd, "Keep away, everybody! Didn't you hear what the Chief said? This man is dangerous!"

THE way the spectators began to leave the Professor's yard brought joy to his heart until he saw the ruin they left behind. Mrs. Bailey was standing on the porch surveying the same sorry spectacle.

"You people ought to be ashamed of yourselves," she called after them. "You can see better freaks than this at any dime museum. Now go on home!"

But no one paid any attention. They were all in the street, jamming around the patrol car and trying to look through the small high windows.

"Goodbye, Auntie!" cried Betty, as Chief Andrews helped her into the car. "Don't worry about Uncle. I'll take care of him for you."

The siren sounded a warning and the car scattered the crowd in front of it. Then those who had autos of their own ran to them to follow the police car to the station.

Ed Jamison, next door neighbor, ambled up the sidewalk, kicking crumpled empty cigarette packages and chewing gum wrappers out of his way. He stooped to pick up a broken piece of the hedge and eyed Mrs. Bailey who had sunk down upon the porch railing, her head against a post.

"Well, Mrs. Bailey," said the man most responsible for this impromptu gathering. "What do you think?"

"I think," said Mrs. Bailey, eyes blazing, "it's a hell of a note."

With that she got up, choked back an angry sob and went into the house, slamming the door.

THE hangers-on at the police station, the idly curious, the court attendants, the police captain and his aides were accustomed to the usual routine happenings of an average day. There was the constant parade of drunks, wife-beaters, sneak thieves, Tom-the-peepers, con men, street walkers, vagrants and traffic violators. But never in the history of this or any other police station had an officer ever brought in a man who claimed to have come from another planet. Here was one case where a man didn't have to bite a dog to make news. The moment Numar was arraigned before the incredulous magistrate on charges of disturbing the peace and misrepresentation, the police reporters ran for the telephone booths to call their papers.

"Gimme the managing editor's desk, quick! Hey, Chief…send your feature writers…send photographers…send everybody. There's a guy been picked up out here who claims he came a trillion miles through space to visit the earth…no…I'm not kidding!" Well, how can I tell? Sure, he looks different—he's green for cryin' out loud! And besides, Professor Bailey claims he's the real article…yeah, the astronomer. He's not going to go off the deep end for nothing. Well, if it isn't true, it's great. You get the pitch, Chief. He's a cosmic globetrotter!"

The stampede was on. Every staff man and woman the Los Angeles newspaper offices could spare jumped into a car and went speeding to the modest La Canada police station to take part in perhaps one of the greatest interviews of all time. If it was a hoax it still had huge news value.

The courtroom was packed. "Where is he? Where's Professor Bailey? Who's got the dope? What's the low-down? Let's see this superman!" they shouted.

The magistrate had lost all the hair on his head, otherwise it would have been standing on end. He was a nervous little man and he had just come from the anteroom where this visitor from space was being examined. His face was wet with perspiration.

"Now, just a minute. Be calm everybody…this doesn't happen every day. I confess I'm in quite a daze myself. The Chief's getting his story now."

"Is he on the level?" asked a man from the Herald-Express.

"He says he is," replied the magistrate. "I wouldn't know. But if he is, he doesn't belong in this police court. He ought to be in the mayor's office, getting an official welcome."

"That's right," laughed a woman feature writer from the Times. "This is a swell place to welcome a visitor from another world."

THE door to the anteroom suddenly opened and Chief Andrews came out, followed by the court stenographer, Professor Bailey and Betty Annabel Bracken.

"Hello!" cried a photographer. "What's that dame doing in this setup? Did this guy from another planet come to see her?"

"Oh, no," denied Betty, impulsively, "I'm just Professor Bailey's niece. I came out here for a screen test and found that my uncle was entertaining this Mister Numar."

"That's swell, baby!" called a reporter. "That gives us a great sex angle!"

"Oh, but I don't want..." said Betty, trailing off.

Professor Bailey squeezed her arm. "Betty, dear, you'd better let me do the talking. I've had to deal with reporters before. They're a bad lot."

"Yes, uncle," she acquiesced. "But I can't help it if I'm photogenic."

"Now, ladies and gentlemen of the press," the Chief of police of La Canada, Charlton K. Andrews, was saying. "I'm about to produce for you what may be the sensation of the ages. I wouldn't exactly want to go on record as stating that I believe this man's story but I haven't been able to shake it yet. This is the most baffling case in my long history of crime detection as head of the police department in this great city..."

"Bring on the green man! Cut out the introduction! Let us judge him for ourselves!" came a chorus of shouts.

But Chief Andrews was not to be denied his big moment. He had been a flatfoot for many years and some citizens had even accused him of having a flathead but he was smart enough to sense that this might be his one chance for immortality. Never before had he been honored by such a distinguished representation of newspaper people. He intended to make the most of it.

"As I said before, I'm going to let you see this person who calls himself 'Mister Numar.' I'm going to let you talk to him and see what you can get out of him. But I'm warning you, he's got some electrical apparatus hidden on him and he's refused so far to let me search him. No, don't laugh! This gentleman may be a fakir but we can't be too sure. That's why we've got to go slow. I'm here to testify that I just touched this man and it knocked me down. So don't any of you people get too near him. I'm holding him on suspicion till I find out more about him."

"You ought to be a spieler in a sideshow," joshed a reporter. "Trot out your electrical robot."

The Chief stepped to the door and motioned inside. "Okay, Mister Numar. You can come out now."

THE Professor and Betty were standing on the raised platform near the magistrate's bench. Beneath them every seat was filled in the little courtroom and newspapermen and women and photographers packed the aisles. Outside a crowd lined the corridors and extended into the street. There was a moment of curious suspense as all awaited the appearance of this purported being from another planet.

Numar's entrance was impressively slow and stately. He was met by a popping barrage of exploding light bulbs as photographers took their first pictures. He advanced to the edge of the platform and smiled down at this earth's most skeptical, sensation-sated type of audience.

"My greetings to you," he said, and stopped. They waited expectantly for him to say more, eyeing him critically all the while—but he did not speak.

"Well, how about it?" called a reporter. "What have you got to say for your self? What's your racket?"

Professor Bailey stepped forward, "This is not the right procedure to use in interviewing such a rare and distinguished personage. It is ignominious enough for Mister Numar to be held here in a police station when he should be associating with the finest men and women of our earth and receiving the highest honors within our power to bestow."

"Can we quote you on that, Professor?" fired a reporter.

"Yes," said Professor Bailey, with a staunchness which surprised himself. "You may."

Numar was studying the array of faces before him with the interest a scientist takes in guinea pigs. He did not seem to mind the air of jocular skepticism that prevailed. They had come with the evident intention of putting him on the spot. Now that they were in his presence, they quite obviously didn't know how to do it.

"I will answer ten questions at this time," said Numar, graciously. "Perhaps you newspaper people would like to get together and decide what you would most prefer to ask me."

There was an immediate hubbub, much cussing and discussing among those assembled. Finally, a group of reporters emerged, a representative of each Los Angeles paper and the news services.

"I've been appointed spokesman," announced veteran reporter Steve

Hines of the Herald-Express. "We've got a list of questions here we'd like to fire at you."

Numar fixed his black eyes upon the interviewer and smiled pleasantly. "You may proceed."

Reporter Hines opened his collar at the neck and got ready for action. His colleagues had their pencils and notepads ready to record their impressions of whatever might be said.

"Let's see now—the first thing we'd like to know, Mr. Numar, is where is your planet of Talamaya located?"

"Beyond the reach of your present telescopes," Numar answered. "Up in what you call the Milky Way."

A boisterous laugh boomed out from somewhere in the back of the courtroom. Numar looked soberly in that direction. The laughter ceased.

"Well, of course, that's not so very definite," said the interviewer. "And there's no way we can really check it out."

"Yes, that is unfortunate that your scientific instruments should be so undeveloped on this earth. However, I can hardly be held responsible for that."

"Well, tell us—how did you get here?"

"By spaceship."

"Spaceship, eh? What was the motive power used?"

"Electro-stellar-magnetic."

Someone whistled and a murmur ran through the courtroom as pencils scribbled.

"Where did you land upon arrival?" continued reporter Hines.

"In the mountains—not far from Wilson Observatory."

"That's quite unusual," speculated the interviewer. "Why did you choose this remote place for landing rather than one of our airports?"

Numar was standing erect on the platform, his arms folded across his chest, looking down at his interrogator.

"Because there were magnetic properties in the mountains that I needed for landing purposes." Then, with a friendly glance toward the professor, Numar added, "And because I wished to make contact with Professor Bailey who was nearby."

All eyes sought out, the Professor who bowed, a bit self-consciously, Betty took his arm and put her head against his shoulder, with a "my hero" expression. It impressed one of the photographers who snapped a picture. Betty acted annoyed in a pleasant sort of way. But Numar easily held the center of the stage.

"Where is your spaceship now?" the veteran Hines was asking.

"In the mountains, where I landed," said Numar, simply, "awaiting my return."

This caused a ripple of comment and an excited woman reporter jumped up on her chair. "Oh, Mister Numar—that's thrilling! Will you let us see and examine this aerial vessel?"

Numar, amused, turned to reporter Hines and inquired: "Was this one of the ten questions you wished to ask me?" His quiet authority and demeanor was something a hardboiled newspaper fraternity had not, heretofore, encountered.

"Why, yes, it was I mean—it is!" stammered Hines, as everyone nodded in assent.

"I am sorry," said Numar. "You will not be permitted to see or examine my spaceship. Its construction is beyond your comprehension. Inspection of it would only confuse and discourage you in your evolution. For this reason, it has been rendered invisible."

CHIEF OF POLICE ANDREWS had been sitting on the arm of the magistrate's chair. "Can you imagine that?" he whispered. "If that guy's a fake, he's got the world's greatest line!"

"He certainly knows all the answers," said the magistrate. "It will take a pack of Philadelphia lawyers to pin anything on him."

It was apparent that the newspaper people did not like Numar's evasive remarks about his spaceship. They had been given some fancy runarounds before but this was being done so smoothly and easily that over half their allotted questions had been asked and they had gotten nowhere.

"Do you expect us to believe your last statement?" demanded interviewer Hines, in a tone of exasperation.

"No," smiled Numar, "but I'm just as confident you can't refute it."

Hines jerked off his tie and threw it on the floor. "Come on, now, Mister Numar. Let's quit shadow boxing and get down to cases. We're all hard working people. We didn't come out here on a wild goose chase— or did we? If you're really a bird from another planet, what is your purpose in coming here?"

"That's the first sensible and significant question you've asked me," said Numar. "I came here to deliver a message of great importance to you earth people. At the proper time I intend to present this message over every radio station in the land and from Chicago."

"Chicago!" Every person in the room rose up. "Why Chicago? What's the matter with Los Angeles? Why can't you deliver your message here?"

"Because," said Numar, and now he had everyone hanging on his words and what he was saying was being relayed out into the corridors and down into the street. "Because," he repeated, "Chicago is destined to be the new capital of the United States and the commercial center of your world. It will eventually be the headquarters for the Peace League of All Nations. I'm interested in the future of your planet, not its past. Therefore I shall address the people of Earth from Chicago!"

AT last, this mysterious personage had said something specific. At last he had given these self-exalted members of the press something they could hang their hats on. To be sure, there was no proof whatsoever that he was who he said he was or that he had come from where he said he had. But, if this green man, fake or not, really intended to say something to the human race from Chicago or Timbuktu, this was a story worth headlines in any newspaper. After all, the scientists would probably get hold of this Numar person soon enough. Let them worry about whether he was genuine or not.

"I believe," said Numar, as pencils scratched furiously, "that you are entitled to one more question."

Interviewer Hines excitedly consulted his notes. "Oh!" he said, "oh, yes...here it is, Mr. Numar. Can you answer this? How long do you intend to stay on earth?"

Numar smiled. "That," he said, quietly, "will be determined by developments."

It is a wonder that some reporters were not killed in the rush to grab all available telephones and call their stories in to their papers. A few remained behind with photographers to pose Numar in company with different individuals.

"Chief Andrews," directed one camera man. "We'd like to get a shot of you putting the handcuffs on Mister Numar. We want to run a picture with the heading, 'Police Chief Captures Man From Another Planet'..."

"It's a cute idea," said the Chief, "but I'm not going to put any handcuffs on that man. I'm not even going to stand too close to him. Not after the shock I got today."

The magistrate stood up. "Oh, now Charlie. I don't think Mister Numar would object. Let me get in this picture with you." He reached out and took Numar by the arm.

"Look out!" cried the Chief.

But nothing happened.

"I'd be delighted to pose with you gentlemen," said Numar.

The magistrate chummily retained his hold of Numar's arm but Chief Andrews kept his distance.

"Well, I'll be damned," he said. "I can't understand this."

PROFESSOR BAILEY and Betty stood off at one side watching proceedings.

"Uncle, this is terrible," said Betty, "taking Mister Numar's picture with people like that! You're the one who ought to be photographed with him."

"Hush, dear," said Professor Bailey. "I'm not seeking any notoriety. My front yard is ruined now. I'm just afraid of what's going to happen next."

"I'm not," said Betty. "And I think you're just plain foolish if you don't take every advantage of this great opportunity. I would, if I were in your place. Why, just think, Uncle...whoever is photographed with Mister Numar will get his picture all over the world."

"Yes, I've thought of all that," said the Professor. "But I'm not so sure now that I—"

"All right, Professor, you're next!" called the cameramen. "That's all, Chief. Move over, Judge. Give the Professor a break."

Professor Bailey raised his hand, protestingly. "Now, gentlemen, I appreciate this, but if it's just the same to you..."

"Go on, Uncle!" said Betty, giving him a push.

"Snap it up, Professor!" directed the cameraman. "We gotta be getting back to town with these to catch the first editions. We want a shot of you shaking hands with that guy."

Professor Bailey looked up at Numar apprehensively. "Is the...er...current turned off?" he whispered.

Numar nodded, amused wrinkles showing in his face, and held out his hand. The Professor took it, gingerly, an awesome expression on his face. Flash light bulbs exploded.

"That's great," said a cameraman. "That's a honey! Professor, you looked then like you'd just discovered a new star."

"I hope you don't use it," said the Professor, uneasily. "I never take a good picture, anyway, not even when I'm posing with Nellie."

The photographers consulted one another. Betty tried to catch their eyes. She didn't have much trouble because they were just getting ready to turn their attention to her.

"Now, Baby, it's your turn. You know the newspapers can't get along without sex appeal. We can always get the picture of a pretty girl in the paper when we can't get anything else. So we want a shot of you kissing this man from the Milky Way."

THIS was more than Betty had bargained for. Numar's face remained green but hers turned red.

"Why, the very idea!" she exclaimed.

"Come on, doll. You don't object, do you, Mister Numar? Don't they kiss on your planet?"

"No, they do not. This is going to be a new experience for me."

Betty felt her knees go weak. Professor Bailey gave her a little shove. "Go ahead, dear," he said, a bit impishly. "Remember—you said this was a great opportunity."

"Gee…gosh…" said Betty, under her breath. Then, to Numar: "Do you really want to try it?"

Numar nodded and held out his arms. The Professor had a moment of sudden panic.

"On second thought," he said, "I guess you'd better."

But Betty was advancing toward Numar, her eyes fixed upon his, like someone walking a tight rope. Numar's arms clasped about her.

"You—you don't have to do this if you don't want to," she said, uncertainly.

"I think this will be very interesting," said Numar.

The photographers pointed their cameras and lifted their flash bulbs.

"That's the way," directed one of them. "Pucker up your lips, Mister Numar. What's it gonna be—a Clark Gable or a Charles Boyer?"

Numar looked aside, inquiringly. "I don't understand," he said.

"Oh, those names are movie actors," explained Betty, nervously. "They've each got a technique all their own."

Numar smiled down at her. "I suppose, after all, this is quite an individual proposition."

"Yes, I—I suppose so," said Betty.

Chief Andrews nudged the perspiring magistrate. "I wouldn't be in that guy's arms for a million dollars…"

Professor Bailey moaned to himself: "I don't know what possessed me. What will Nellie say to this?"

The cameramen were growing impatient.

"Hey you two…cut the conversation and give us some osculation. Come on…relax. Don't act like you're taking poison. Let's see some love-light in your eyes. Act like you meant it. Maybe this'll get you your screen test."

This was all Betty needed. She shut her eyes as the green lips of Numar descended upon hers.

The room had filled with other spectators and some reporters who had returned from phoning in their flash stories. They broke into whistles of applause as the clinch was held and camera shutters clicked.

"Okay, you can break now," called the cameramen. But Numar's lips were still pressed against Betty's. "Hey, break it up. Cut! Will Hays won't like this."

BETTY disengaged one arm and began to gesture frantically in the direction of Professor Bailey.

"Oh dear...oh my," said the Professor, dancing around the two. "Something must have happened. Chief! Somebody! Do something! Maybe she's being electrocuted!"

"Don't touch 'em!" warned the Chief.

Betty's imploring gestures continued. Photographers hastily reloaded their cameras and shot more pictures.

"This is the hottest thing since Rudolph Valentino," said one of them.

"Not good for a first kiss," another chimed in.

"Mister Numar!" begged Professor Bailey. "Perhaps you don't know, but on this planet, there's a limit to such things."

Betty was now growing wild. She had gotten both arms free and was waving them behind her.

"Phone the electric light company!" yelled the Chief. "Something's gone wrong with this guy's electrical apparatus. He's got a hold of her and he can't let go!"

There was pandemonium in the courtroom. This wasn't funny any longer. It was a field day only for the photographers who kept on shooting.

"My, God, how she can take it?" wondered one of them.

"You mean—how he can dish it out," said another.

"Get a pulmotor!" cried the Chief, now beside himself.

"Get an ambulance!" shouted somebody else.

The clock on the wall had been ticking off not seconds, but minutes. All marathon osculation records had long since been broken.

The officer in charge of the police radio came rushing upstairs. "Chief!" he cried, "there's been a bank robbery and my radio set's gone bad. I'm getting powerful interference."

"There it is!" said the Chief, pointing at the embraced couple. "That's what's doing it. Don't anybody touch them until the circuit's broken—"

"Well...how am I going to contact our radio cars?" demanded the officer.

"One thing at a time," said the Chief. "We're in worse trouble here."

Professor Bailey had waited, praying ardently that this greatest of all clinches would be broken without injury to either party. But now it was high time something was being done.

"I'll just have to risk it," he decided. "It may be the death of me but those electrical forces have got to be grounded."

SO saying, he courageously took hold of a radiator pipe with one hand and grasped one of Betty's hands with the other. There was a crackling flash of blue flame and Numar and Betty shot apart. The Professor landed in a sitting position on the platform, with Betty on top of him. Numar staggered back, almost fell, and leaned against the bench for support. The magistrate had tipped over in his swivel chair trying to get out of the way, and Chief Andrews only escaped by a mad leap in the opposite direction.

"Betty, are you all right?" asked the Professor.

Betty was looking dazedly around. "Man…how that guy can kiss!" she blurted out. "Just like an electric shock. I could feel a million little needles running through me. I just couldn't get away. And right there at the last, when you grabbed my hand, that photographer should have been more careful. His flash light bulb went off right in my face."

"That wasn't a flash light bulb," said the Professor. "That was a flash of electricity when I broke the circuit. I can still feel it in my joints."

The two were still sitting on the floor, surrounded by a pop-eyed crowd.

Numar, looking a pale green, came over to them. "I'm sorry," he said. "I had no idea my system would react this way. I temporarily lost control of my magnetic forces. I hope, Miss Bracken, it was not too great an ordeal for you."

"Well," said Betty. "It was one I'll never forget."

"Nor shall I," said Numar. "I now have a new custom to take back to my planet."

"If you feel like standing," the Professor suggested to Betty, "I believe I would like to get up off the floor."

Numar extended his hand to help Betty to her feet. "No thank you," she said, and scrambled up by herself.

"Don't you touch anybody else," ordered Chief Andrews. "I'm going to put you under lock and key and have some electricians search your person. You must have yourself all rigged up with electrical gadgets. As long as you're walking around like this, you're a menace to the public."

"A search will avail you nothing," said Numar. "Besides, I will not permit it."

"We'll see about that," snapped the Chief. "You're not going to buck me after all my years in this department."

CHAPTER FOUR

THE officer in charge of the police radio had run back to his instrument in the room below. Now he excitedly reappeared. "Say, Chief—the radio—it's working all right again. Car number ten has picked up the trail of the bandits. They're in a high-powered car going east on Highway 66."

"That's good," said the Chief.

"No, it's bad," said the officer. "They're being outdistanced. But they've got the license number. It's 9W-7448."

"Would you like me to stop the bandits' car for you?" asked Numar, showing sudden interest.

Chief Andrews was startled. "What was that? What did you say?"

"I said," repeated Numar, "that I'd be glad to stop the bandits' car if you like. I feel somewhat responsible for the bandits getting away since I interfered with your radio."

"But how can you stop their car?" demanded the Chief.

"He can do it," assured Professor Bailey. "He stopped *my* car when he was coming in for a landing in his spaceship."

"May we go downstairs to the radio room?" requested Numar.

"Sure, sure," said the Chief. "Make way, everybody—clear the room—how did all of you people get in here anyhow?"

There was a general rush for the stairs and the same crowd tried to jam into the small radio room as the officer in charge sought to make contact with Car Number Ten.

"Car Ten," he called. "Hello, Jake...you still on their tail? Come in."

There was a slight sputter of static, then Jake's voice was heard. "Yeah...but they're getting away from us. We can't keep 'em in sight much longer."

NUMAR was standing just behind the radio operator. He faced the east and a distant look came into his eyes. Professor Bailey and Betty were nearby in company with the Chief. A small coterie of reporters and photographers had attached themselves to Numar on regular assignment. They were competing now with every member of the police department on duty at the station, including the janitor, for an opportunity to witness this mystery man's latest gyration.

"Don't press too close" warned the Chief. "This guy's as full of juice as a high voltage line. If that secret apparatus he's carrying stops that car, I'm going to turn him over to the FBI as a dangerous alien."

Numar was apparently concentrating. "9W-7448," he was repeating under his breath. His green eyelids were closed, concealing his piercing black eyes. "Oh, yes," he said, suddenly. "I see the car now. Three men are inside of it. One in the back seat has two satchels full of bank money. Speedometer reading is 78 miles per hour." Numar stopped talking, eyes still closed, and put out his right arm with pointer finger extending as though touching something.

The radio officer was keeping contact with Car Number Ten. "Hello, Jake. How you making out now?"

"They're slowing down," Jake reported. "Something's happened. Maybe they're running out of gas. They're pulling up beside the road. Now they're jumping out of the car. Looks like they're going to shoot it out. Stand by! We're closing in…"

Numar remained motionless but his face wore an interested expression as though he were seeing what was taking place. His features relaxed into a smile. He opened his eyes. "The bandits threw down their guns," he informed.

"We've got 'em!" came Jake's excited voice over the short wave. "It was a cinch—they tossed their guns in the ditch. We've recovered the loot, too."

"Just a minute," broke in Chief Andrews. "Ask Jake, how come the bandits stopped their car and gave up?"

This question was repeated and there was a temporary silence on the radio.

"Tell the chief," said Jake's voice, "the motor went dead. They don't know what the hell went wrong with it. They've got a tank full of gas."

"Well, that's the dangdest coincidence," said Chief Andrews, "that I ever ran into. At least I hope it's a coincidence. If it isn't…" The Chief began to look alarmed. "Professor, on second thought, I think I'll release this human dynamo in your custody. You're responsible for him from now on. Take him away with you."

"But what will I do with him?" asked the Professor.

"That's your affair," said the Chief. "You found him, didn't you?"

Numar now stepped forward. "Chief Andrews is right," he said, "We have finished our business here. I have been interviewed by the press and stories of my arrival will soon appear in the papers. I suggest we return to your home and await further developments."

Professor Bailey appeared greatly distressed.

"Just a minute!" said a man in the crowd. "I'm a talent scout for MGM I'd like to put you under contract."

NUMAR eyed the important appearing gentleman. "What's MGM?"

he asked.

The gentleman's face turned purple. "You—an actor—and you don't know MGM? Brother, do you need an agent?"

Numar seemed entirely unimpressed.

"You're kidding, of course," said the man. "Everybody's heard of MGM."

"I should say they have," said Betty, "although *I* came out here to take a screen test for Warner Brothers."

The talent scout eyed her up and down. "Well, you might have something at that. I came in on the tail end of your clinch. Are you and your boy friend working together? I'll put you both under option."

Betty's eyes glistened. "Oh, Mister Numar!" she exclaimed. "Did you hear that? We can be in pictures! Isn't that thrilling?"

Numar shook his head. "I doubt very much," he said, "if my services would prove satisfactory. But I foresee a great future for you."

"You do!" cried Betty, delighted. "I could kiss you for that!" She started impulsively toward him.

"Now, don't start that again!" bellowed Chief Andrews. "Get out of here, the lot of you. What a day...I'm going to make application to retire on a pension."

The talent scout followed Professor Bailey, Betty and Numar to the street, as did the crowd.

"Your name and address, Miss?" he requested.

"I'm Betty Annabel Bracken, she gave answer. "You can reach me at Professor Bailey's. He's my uncle."

"That's fine," said the man. Then, turning to Numar. "Where are you stopping, sir?"

"Where Miss Bracken is," smiled Numar.

"Great grief," said the Professor, "what am I in for now?"

An empty taxi passed by and the Professor hailed it. Anything to get away from this curious throng which had been dogging their footsteps and growing in size. The taxi driver missed Professor Bailey's signal but Numar raised his hand and pointed toward the cab. It stopped half way down the block, in the middle of the street. The driver jumped out, raised the hood, and began tinkering with the motor. Traffic piled up behind him and car horns commenced an impatient honking.

"Your cab is waiting," observed Numar.

The Professor, startled, gave Numar a knowing look. "Oh...oh yes," he said, "Come on, Betty." He took her by the arm and the two with Numar made their way toward the stalled taxi. "Let us through, please!" called the Professor as they proceeded. "Don't touch Mister Numar, anybody, or you'll get shocked. Let us through to that cab."

THEIR way was barred by an emaciated looking middle-aged man in a wheel chair. He was being pushed by a stout-armed, stout-figured nurse who shouted at Professor Bailey.

"Let us through, yourself! Do you think you're entitled to the whole street?"

The invalid cupped a hand to his ear. "What's that, Miss Pratt? What'd you say?"

The crowd parted and the figure of Numar loomed suddenly in front of him. The sight of a green man in white flowing garments was too much for the wheel chair occupant. He thrust out his hands, instinctively, to fend off this apparition, and thereby received the shock of his life. It was such a shock, in fact, that his body, stimulated as it had not been in years, rose out of the wheel chair. He suddenly found himself standing on the sidewalk.

"Look!" he cried, to all around him. "Look...I've been cured! I can walk!" He took a few faltering steps and his nurse collapsed in the wheel chair.

"Holy smoke!" shouted an eyewitness. "That green man's a healer..."

"It's a miracle," the former invalid kept quietly repeating to himself. "I've been paralyzed for eight years—and now look! I can walk...*I can walk!*"

"For heaven's sake!" gasped the Professor. "Keep moving, Mister Numar! Once this word gets around, everybody will be wanting to touch you. We've got to catch that cab!"

Reaching the taxi, Professor Bailey jerked open the door and pushed Betty inside.

"Hurry, Mister Numar, hurry!" he begged.

As Numar climbed in, the cab driver looked up from under the hood. His face was smeared with grease and he had a screwdriver in one hand.

"I can't take you people!" he shouted, irritably. "Can't you see my car's broke down?"

There was the sound of a police whistle down the block. Chief Andrews and two officers were pushing through the mob to find the cause of the traffic jam.

"I think," said the Professor, in a mild tone to the driver, "if you'll get back in your cab, you'll find it will run all right."

"Oh, you do, do you?" roared the driver, slamming down the hood.

"Push that taxi over against the curb!" yelled the approaching chief of police. "Professor...what are you doing out there? Now what are you up to?"

"It's all right," reassured the Professor, getting in the cab. Then, to the irate driver who had slid into his seat behind the wheel. "Try your starter. See if it works."

The driver touched the starter with his foot. The motor turned over at once. He shifted into gear and shot off down the street.

"Well, I'll be a monkey's uncle..." he said.

But Chief Andrews was using more colorful epithets as he got caught in the back-wash of the crowd and the snarl of untangling traffic, which was hot on the Professor's trail.

"My, it's almost time for lunch," said the Professor, drawing a breath of momentary relief. He reached for the bottle in his pocket. "Mister Numar, will you have some more distilled water?"

"I think I will," said Numar, taking the bottle. "After my experience with Miss Bracken, I feel strangely depleted."

HOME may have been the place of refuge for the common man but the happy, timeworn phrase, "a man's home is his castle" no longer applied to Professor Bailey's domicile. It was a place of siege by all and sundry, for notoriety had descended upon him with the clinging persistency of a California fog. He hadn't built a better mousetrap, he had hardly opened his trap at all, and yet the world was beating an ever more widening path to his door. Not only the front, but also the back.

As for Mrs. Bailey—she had been brought up to believe that "a woman's place is in the home" but she now fervently wished it might be anywhere else. When Professor Bailey returned home, bringing his white-robed and green complexioned friend with him, Mrs. Bailey took him aside to give him a piece of her mind which he had not had before.

"William...Roscoe...Bailey..." she said in a low voice, her teeth gritted. "What in the name of common sense and sanity do you mean by this? Why didn't you leave this monstrous fraud with the police? You're getting yourself in so deep you can never get out. And what's more, you've gotten Betty involved. That girl's so excited she can hardly talk."

"I don't agree with you there," said Professor Bailey. "Betty never wants for something to say and she usually says it just when it will do her the most good."

"Why, how can you talk about my sister's child in that manner?" said Mrs. Bailey.

"My dear," said the Professor, his expression pained and apprehensive. "You don't know your sister's child. She's so movie-struck she will do anything to get in pictures. And that girl knows the value of publicity. I may as well warn you that you're apt to be shocked when you see the afternoon papers. Betty put on what amounted to a kissing exhibition with Mister Numar for the photographers!"

"She did what?" asked Mrs. Bailey, unbelievingly.

"You see," explained the Professor, "Mister Numar had never kissed anyone before."

"For pity's sake!" exclaimed Mrs. Bailey. "How disgusting! And you let her do it?"

"Well, it all happened so suddenly," said the Professor, lamely, neglecting to mention that he, in a weak moment, had urged Betty on. "I really didn't think she'd go through with it."

"You mean to say the papers are going to print pictures of her kissing that green-faced baboon?" demanded Mrs. Bailey.

"I presume they are," said the Professor. "And I might describe them, in advance, as being extremely torrid. In fact, some unfortunate complications developed. This kissing experience almost wrecked Mister Numar. Once he'd started kissing Betty, he couldn't let go."

MRS. BAILEY was getting more horrified by the minute. "Don't tell me! Where was all this going on?"

"In the police station."

"The police station...of all places! Oh, this gets worse and worse. And to think that I—" She was going to say that she'd encouraged Betty to make love to Numar, but decided it best not to incriminate herself.

"The reason Mister Numar couldn't let go," said the Professor, " was on account of his magnetic forces. They seemed to have a strong affinity for Betty. If it hadn't been for me, the two of them might have been electrocuted."

"Oh...so you're in these pictures, too," said Mrs. Bailey. "Well, why didn't you say so in the first place. That's what you're really worried about. A man in your profession! I don't want to hear any more. The front doorbell is ringing, so is the telephone, and someone's pounding on the back door! I'm not going to answer any of them. I'm going upstairs, lock myself in my room, and leave you to get out of this mess yourself!"

"Now, Nellie!" called the harassed Professor. "Won't you listen to reason?"

"*Reason!*" she exclaimed, as she ran upstairs. "Just look at the crowd outside. Try your reasoning out on them!"

The Professor crept to the front window and cautiously peeked out. What he saw was enough to strike fear and concern in many a stout heart. It looked like all the lame and the blind in LaCanada and neighboring communities had been assembled in the yard and street. Numar was supposed to be in the study. He could hear his wife upstairs talking in a loud voice to Betty. The ringings and the poundings on doors continued. He could hear feet shuffling about on his porch and faces began to be pressed against windowpanes.

Seized with a sudden feeling of panic, Professor Bailey rushed to the telephone. He placed the receiver against his ear.

"Hello," said a voice. "Is this Professor Bailey's residence?"

"Yes it is," said the Professor. "Please get off the line. I want to call the police." He jiggled the phone and disconnected the party, then hurriedly dialed the police station. "Give me Chief Andrews...tell him it's Professor Bailey..." He waited, with growing tension, until the Chief's voice came on the wire.

"What is it now?" asked the Chief.

"Send the riot squad!" begged the Professor. "My house is surrounded! I don't dare go to the door. People are trying to get in. I guess they think Numar's a miracle man. Hurry, Chief...I can't hold out much longer!"

"All right," said Chief Andrews. "We'll get there as fast as we can. But if this keeps up, we'll have to have a bigger police force!"

THE Professor hung up the receiver and began barricading his front and back doors with furniture.

"Hey, Professor Bailey!" insistent voices were calling. "We know you're in there. Answer the door! We want to talk to you. Let us in!"

The Professor retreated to his study, a little room on the first floor on the rear right of the house. There he found Numar seated, in his easy chair, quietly reading one of the Professor's own books, entitled: "Astronomy Made Simple."

Numar looked up and smiled. "This book is properly titled," he said. "Of course you earth people cannot be expected to know much about the universe as yet."

"Mister Numar," said Professor Bailey. "I'm sorry to interrupt your reading but we seem to be facing a serious crisis and it's all because of you."

"Yes," said Numar, "it always happens this way."

"What do you mean?"

"I always cause a stir when I arrive on any new planet. I can never foretell what kind of a stir. That depends upon the nature of the inhabitants."

The clamor outside was becoming more and more audible and

insistent.

"Well, I don't know about life on any other planets," said the Professor. "But I think you should know, Mister Numar, that the human creature is still highly superstitious. I'm afraid even now those people out there have gotten the idea that you're a great healer."

Numar put the book aside and stood up. "But I'm not," he said. "We have no need of healing on my planet. These bodies of ours are constantly replenished by magnetic currents derived from air and water."

"Just come with me and take a look out the front window," said the Professor.

As they stepped into the hall and walked toward the living room, telephone and doorbell were ringing. The Professor took the receiver off the hook as he passed.

"You see how easily our conveniences can become a curse," he remarked.

Numar observed the heavy davenport propped against the front door. Someone was turning the doorknob as well as ringing the bell.

"You see what I mean?" said the Professor. "That would be quite disturbing in time."

Numar nodded, with an expression of amused sympathy. But when he stood behind a window curtain and looked out, his face sobered. Pressed to the front of the crowd were men, women and children in pitiable states of physical distress. Some were blind, some were on crutches or canes, some were in wheel chairs, some were in arms, but all reflected some condition of invalidism or injury. Behind and around these surged a sensation-seeking, curious crowd. But just at this moment the attention of all had been captured by an incredibly frail little man who stood beside an empty wheel chair.

"AS GOD is my judge, folks," he was saying, "I didn't know who this man was. I just saw him coming toward me in his white robes and I reached out and touched him—and look what happened to me!" He lifted each thin leg in turn and raised his equally thin arms. "Anyone want to buy my wheel chair?"

There was a mixture of laughter and applause.

"No," said a man on crutches, "All we want is a chance to touch this man like you did."

"That's all!" shouted a chorus of others.

"You say this man's from another planet?" queried a woman who looked to be arthritic. "I'll be willing to believe it if he helps me."

"Sure--he must be from another planet," said a lame woman next to her. "You can't touch any human and get cured. Most humans would give you something worse."

Professor Bailey looked sidewise at Numar. "What are we going to do with these people?" he asked. "Maybe there is something to what you did for this man. Our medical science is now curing different types of cases with electrical shock treatments."

"Yes," said Numar. "A few might benefit by contact with the currents which pass through my body—but they would get the same results from the treatments you speak of."

"But how are we going to convince them of that?" asked the Professor, pointing out the window, "Just listen to how they are talking."

The voices of those outside and around the porch could be plainly heard.

"How much does he charge to let you touch him?" a nervous-appearing woman who had elbowed her way forward was asking.

"Nothing, I guess," said a little bent-over man with a crook in his neck. "At least not yet...but he may have to if people keep coming like this..."

"Well," said the woman, decisively. "We've got to him first. He ought to let us touch him for free."

"Do you hear that?" said the Professor. · "You'd better go back in my study and hide till the police come. Get in the closet, if necessary. Please hurry! It sounds like they're going to break the door down!"

"I will do as you request," said Numar, quite calm and undisturbed. "Don't worry too much, Professor. Things always turn out all right."

"That's easy for you to say," the Professor called after him. "But you haven't lived on this planet as long as I have. You should see what happens at a bargain sale. And these people have the same look in their eyes right now!"

BETTY came running down the stairs. "Oh, Uncle! You must open the door! That MGM talent scout is out there. I just saw him. He's lost his collar and tie trying to get through the crowd!"

"If I ever open that door, I'll lose more than that," said the Professor. "You get back upstairs with your aunt."

"Oh, Uncle, isn't this thrilling! I wonder if they saw my pictures in the papers?"

"Yes," said the Professor, irritably. "I suppose this whole crowd's come out here to get a sample of your kisses."

"Uncle William, you're a horrid old man!" said Betty. "Why this telephone receiver's off the hook. No wonder I didn't get my call from

Warner Brothers! How do you expect I'm going to get anywhere in pictures this way?"

"Damn you and the picture industry!" exclaimed Professor Bailey. "I'm losing my home and my reputation and my sanity—all at the same time."

The telephone started ringing. Betty leaped for it.

"Hello...what's that you say...trouble?" She eyed the Professor. "Yes—plenty. Oh—on this line, you mean? Well, it's all right now. Thank you, operator...please do." Betty turned to her uncle, holding the receiver to her ear. "The operator said she had over fifty calls—some of them very important—and I'll bet at least half a dozen were from Warner Brothers. If I miss my chance getting into pictures just be-cause...oh...hello! Yes...who? *Who?* The Los Angeles Chamber of Commerce? Are you sure you have the right number? Professor Bailey? Oh, just a minute." Betty motioned to Professor Bailey and held out the receiver. "It's President Hammond of the Los Angeles Chamber of Commerce," she said. "Please don't stay on the wire long. Operator says there's another call waiting."

"You stay away from that door," warned the Professor, as he took the phone, "and keep an eye out for the police."

Betty busied herself with her makeup. "There're photographers out there, too," she said.

"Hello," said Professor Bailey into the phone. "Yes...yes? Oh! You've just seen the papers. Chicago? That's right. Mister Numar *did* say he was going to deliver a message in Chicago. Well, now, Mr. Hammond—I am loyal to Los Angeles but there doesn't seem to be any-thing I can do...yes, I see your point...well, I'll speak to Mister Numar. No, I can't call him to the phone...he's very busy just now...we're all busy. Excuse me, Mister Hammond. I hear the police siren. The police are coming. Thank you very much for calling...goodbye." The Professor put the receiver down, leaving it off the hook.

CHIEF of police Andrews had arrived in a squad car with three of-ficers. He made a lane through the crowd and delegated his men to get the people off Professor Bailey's front porch.

"What's going on here?" he demanded.

"We're waiting to see the green man," said a self-appointed spokesman who had been ringing the doorbell. "He's got wonderful healing powers. All you have to do is touch him and you're well!"

"I touched him once," said the Chief, "and I haven't felt right since. You people are nuts. Now, go on. Get away from here! Go home—and let Professor Bailey alone!"

"No, no!" came a chorus of shouts from the crowd. "We're not leaving till we see the green man!"

Chief Andrews had a rolled up newspaper in one hand. He left his three officers to hold the crowd in check and banged on the Professor's front door. "Open up! Let me in!"

The door opened to admit him and closed quickly behind as some of the crowd evaded the police officers and dashed up on the porch.

"You see," said Professor Bailey, moving the davenport back across the door. "You just got here in time."

Chief Andrews laughed. "You don't need that thing blocking the door, now I'm here."

"I'm not so sure," said the Professor.

"Now, Uncle," said Betty. "I have perfect faith in Chief Andrews." She gave him a commending look. "Chief, did you notice that MGM talent scout? I think you could safely let him in."

"You can't safely let any of that mob in," said the Professor. "Now, Betty, I'll thank you to keep out of the way."

"Why—I'm only trying to help!" said Betty.

"Like you did at the police station," said Chief Andrews. "Trying to steal the limelight! Where do you come off at, posing with Mister Numar? You certainly look pretty in the paper, you do." He slapped the rolled copy of the Herald-Express with the back of his hand.

"Oh!" cried Betty, reaching out and snatching the paper. "Have you got a copy? Oh, let me see it. Thank you very much!" She already had it unrolled and was scanning the front page.

"Oh, Uncle—here it is." She read the bold headlines. "Mystery man arrives from another planet. A green man named Numar, guest of Astronomer Bailey, claims to have traveled here in mysterious spaceship. Has message for world to deliver from Chicago. Police are investigating claims... Why, there's a two-column story about it. And it says here there is a full page of pictures on page six." Betty was all thumbs as she tried to find the page.

"Now you're really going to see something," said Chief Andrews. "You're going to see what an ass you made of yourself—and what we all did, for that matter!"

Professor Bailey looked disturbed and bewildered. "Oh, did the pictures turn out as badly as that?"

"I'll say they did!" fired the Chief. *"Numar's not in any one of them!"*

CHAPTER FIVE

"WHAT'S that?" The Professor looked over Betty's shoulder as she reached page six. "Oh, my goodness…oh, my dear! Great heavens—good grief!"

"Why, Uncle!" gasped Betty. "How could this happen? Why, there's just blank spaces where Mister Numar's supposed to be. How could he do a thing like that? Why didn't he photograph?"

"That's what we all want to know," said Chief Andrews. "Look what the paper says about it." The Chief pointed to the main heading and a paragraph over the pictures. It read:

MAN FROM ANOTHER PLANET—WHERE IS HE?

Our photographers swear they snapped him in all these pictures but the elusive Mister Numar didn't show up on the negatives. Yes, we are doubting our own senses, too. Here's a case where seeing isn't believing. Numar appears to be the most baffling trickster and escape artist since Houdini. The police are investigating but his real identity is still unknown.

"Now look what they say about this picture," said the Chief. He pointed again, and the dazed Professor Bailey and Betty read:

WHAT'S WRONG WITH THIS PICTURE?

LaCanada's Magistrate Taylor and Chief of Police Andrews look as though they are proud and happy to be posing with Mr. Numar—but their distinguished guest from another planet has pulled the good old disappearing act. What a cruel prank to play upon two unsuspecting upholders of the law.

"Well, I never!" said the Professor. "Never in my born days. This is very unusual…very…"

"It gives me goose pimples," said Betty. "Oh, look, Uncle. There you are, standing all alone, with a silly expression on your face, looking at nothing."

Professor Bailey stared at the photograph in utter disbelief. He shook his head from side to side as he read the editorial comment about it.

HELP US SOLVE THE MYSTERY

In this photograph, the eminent astronomer, Professor W. R. Bailey, who would not be party to a hoax (or would he?) is here supposed to be shaking hands with his visitor from the planet Talamaya. But, where is this visitor? From the look on Professor Bailey's face and from the blank space beside him, Mr. Numar is still seemingly millions of miles away—and the good professor is merely shaking hands with himself.

"'THIS is all completely beyond me," said Professor Bailey. "I can't comprehend it."

"Nobody can," said the Chief. "But you haven't seen anything yet. Just get a load of little Miss Sex Appeal and what this Numar did to her."

The lower half of the page contained six striking action photographs and when Betty got a glimpse of them she began shrieking.

"Oh! Oh! Oh! Oh, how could he? Why, that's terrible! Just look, Uncle. He's ruined me...simply ruined me. I...I can never look the world in the face again!"

The Professor *was* looking. He removed his glasses, rubbed them briskly and put them on again. He saw the same thing, only more of it.

"Just a minute, now, Betty. Don't jiggle the paper so. Let me see what it says. Here—let's read it together."

They scanned the lead comment and the descriptions under each picture.

GENTLE READER—WE CALL UPON YOU TO STUDY THIS SERIES OF AMOROUS CONTORTIONS.

In these pictures, screen aspirant Betty Annabel Bracken is supposed to be introducing the "green" Mr. Numar, visitor from Talamaya, a planet a trillion miles from here, to the good old human art of kissing. The photographers swear that Numar sizzled and burned like an overdone steak and couldn't let go of Miss Bracken until Professor Bailey grounded his electrical charges through an innocent radiator in the room. But again—WHERE is Mr. Numar? And what is Miss Bracken doing— osculatory acrobatics by herself?

LET US ATTEMPT TO INTERPRET THESE PICTURES FOR YOU.

These photographs graphically depict Betty Bracken in what appears to be a romantic embrace.

In picture No. 1, her head is tilted back, lips puckered and eyes closed, with just the proper expression of awe on her face. But do you see anyone kissing her? If you do, please write or wire us at once.

Picture No. 2: Betty's face is registering surprise and fear. She seems to be trying to pull away from something—yes, something apparently shocking.

Picture No. 3: This reveals Betty obviously NOT enjoying herself too much. Her lips look slightly mashed as though there is some pressure against them. She is bending backward from the waist—probably about to execute a back-bend.

Picture No. 4: In this shot, Betty is definitely signaling for help with one hand behind her.

Picture No. 5: Betty now has two hands behind her and is waving them semaphore fashion. The letters she is spelling out are undoubtedly S O S.

Picture No. 6: Professor Bailey to the rescue! He has grabbed one of Betty's hands and she and the Professor are sailing through space as though propelled by some invisible force.

QUESTION: Where was the man from that other planet who was supposed to have been kissing Betty all this time? Was she in reality just kissing the atmosphere and had everyone been hypnotized by the mysterious Numar? Could be—say the scientific experts. There must be an explanation! Do you have one? The eye of the camera doesn't lie—or does it? The cameramen swear they hadn't been drinking—but they're probably out drinking now…

"I'll never get over this," sobbed Betty, "not as long as I live! These pictures will go all over the world!"

"I thought that's what you wanted," said the Professor.

"This isn't funny, Uncle William. Hollywood won't look at me now. Nobody will!"

"My dear girl," said Professor Bailey, "I'm afraid you don't know human psychology. If these pictures don't attract attention to you—none ever will."

BETTY stopped crying at once and took another look.

"Well, just the same," she compromised, "I think we should sue Mr. Numar or something. That was a very ungentlemanly thing for him to do."

"I suppose the other papers, when they come out, will be just as bad, if not worse," Professor Bailey said, aside, to Chief Andrews.

"You can count on that," said the Chief. "There's only one explanation for what happened. We were hypnotized—the whole gosh-darned bunch of us. And that goes for the photographers, too. We just thought we were posing with Numar. He was probably sitting off to one side, just having a big laugh at our expense."

"That sounds quite likely," said the Professor, greatly pained. "Dear, dear! This is getting more and more complicated."

Professor Bailey," queried the Chief, point blank. "On the level now, just between us, who is this fellow, Numar, and what are you trying to put over with him?"

"I give you my word," said the Professor. "I don't know any more about him than you do but I did see him land in his spaceship." He hesitated a moment as a sudden disturbing thought struck him, and then added, "Or at least I think I did."

"That's just the point!" emphasized Chief Andrews. "This nonsense has gone on long enough. It's high time we were getting hold of this Numar and putting the heat on him. I don't enjoy being made a fool of any more than you do."

Betty had been looking out the window. She now began tapping the pane and gesturing.

"What are you doing?" called the Professor.

"It's the MGM talent scout," explained Betty. "He's arguing with the police officers. He's got his coat off now. Uncle William, if you don't let him in, I'm going out to see him. That's no way to treat a man of his importance."

Betty ran to the door and began to tug and push at the davenport.

"Chief," said the Professor. "You have my permission to do your duty."

"It's a pleasure," said the Chief. "Now, young lady, you sit down on this davenport with your back to the door and forget Hollywood for five minutes. Your uncle's got enough on his mind without having to worry about you." He turned Betty around and gave her a compelling push. She sat down and stayed there.

ANGRY shouts now came from outside and it was evident that the crowd, steadily increasing in size, with many newcomers waving newspaper accounts of Numar, was on the verge of getting out of hand.

"Where is Numar?" demanded the Chief. "We'll have to do something and do it quick."

Professor Bailey rushed to the study and found Numar sitting quietly, eyes fixed on the ceiling, with a trance-like expression in them. The Professor called but got no response. He ran over and reached out his hand to touch this strange houseguest but thought better of it.

"Numar!" he shouted. "Wake up! I thought you never slept…"

Numar's eyes moved; the glassiness began to disappear. He straightened up and looked at the Professor.

"I have not been asleep," he said. "I have been in a higher state of consciousness—communicating with my planet, Talamaya. Some important work is awaiting me there when I return from my trip—a hundred years from now."

"Oh, stop it!" said the Professor, greatly perturbed and annoyed. "That kind of talk isn't going to get you anywhere on this earth. There're several hundred human creatures outside and more coming every minute who want to communicate with you right here and now. And they won't take 'no' for an answer."

"Very well," said Numar, rising. "I'm at your service."

Chief Andrews met them in the hall. "What I could say to you wouldn't look good in print," he flung at Numar. "But we can't go into that now. Your public is calling. They're demanding a personal appearance." The Chief eyed Numar's figure, suspiciously. "Are you really here—or aren't you?"

Numar smiled. "I'm very much here."

"Well, you'd better be. And no more shennanigans! Those people out there are expecting to touch you and get cured of everything from falling dandruff to housemaid's knee."

"I've already explained to Professor Bailey," said Numar, "that I have no healing powers. However, I do possess certain magnetic forces."

"I know what you possess," said the Chief. "You possess some new-fangled electrical machine which you've hidden somewhere under those flowing robes. We'd find it soon enough if you'd let us search you. But I'm advising you now to junk that apparatus before you cause any more trouble."

"I can control these electrical forces, by an effort of will, so no one can feel them," said Numar.

"Then you get busy and do it," ordered the Chief. "Go out there and let some of these fanatics touch you. When they don't get shocked—then maybe they'll go away and leave you alone."

THERE were sounds of scuffling on the porch and a banging on the door.

"Here they come," said Betty. "Can I get off the davenport now?"

"Unlock that door, Professor. Give me a hand with this davenport. Yes, Miss Bracken, you can get off. How do you think we can lift this with you on it? Remember, Numar, no funny business. I'll go out first and try to calm 'em. You come after me, and for the love of Pete—don't turn on the juice!"

Professor Bailey turned the key in the lock and the door swung inward. One of the police officers who had been guarding it sat down heavily with two men and two women on top of him.

"Hold on, everybody!" called the Chief. "Numar's coming out to see you."

A cheer went up from the crowd.

"Well, it's about time!" shouted a disgruntled soul.

"But you folks'll have to line up," the Chief directed. "No rushing or stampeding. Clear the porch, everybody! Get back! You'll all get a chance to see him."

Even with this reassurance, people fought to get some front position or vantage point as the Chief called for Numar. At his appearance, there was a mighty surge forward.

"There he is! Let me touch him first. That's no fair, I've been waiting longer than you have. Stop pushing! Oh, I'm being crushed! Touch me, Mister Numar! Touch *me!* I want to be healed. Let me through to him. I know he'll cure me!" These and many more utterances came from the throats of the frenzied mob.

Numar was caught in the human swirl and carried bodily off the porch despite the Herculean efforts of the three police officers and Chief Andrews, who were being badly mauled.

Professor Bailey watched this unbelievable spectacle from his porch, feeling as helpless as an eyewitness of a tornado. These pent-up feelings and desires of the lame, the halt and the blind had to be satisfied. Each of them feared they would somehow not be given opportunity to make personal contact with this mysterious personage whose curative touch had earlier healed the man in the wheel chair.

Mrs. Bailey watched the scene from her upstairs window and called down, anxiously, to her husband. "William! Don't stand there...do something! If you don't, there won't be anything left of Mister Numar. Look! They're trying to tear his robe off!

Numar was certainly in the thick of it. He was apparently putting up no defense, permitting himself to be buffeted about. His face, however, had an indescribable expression. One couldn't tell what he must be thinking. After the first mad rush had spent itself, those who had touched him began to compare notes.

"I didn't feel anything, did you?"

"Not a thing. And I've still got my rheumatism."

"My back isn't any better, either."

"Where's that guy in the wheel chair who said Numar had cured him?"

"I don't believe he did."

"Hey, you! What kind of a game is this?"

THE frail little man, singer of Numar's praises, who had offered to sell his wheel chair, was now surrounded by angry, disappointed, sick and weary men and women.

"You told us we'd feel an electric shock and be cured. Well, we haven't—and that never happened to you. You've been imagining things!"

"But I did feel something," the frail little man of the wheel chair protested. "You've got to believe me. I did feel it...and it cured me...I couldn't walk and it cured me!"

His statements fell on deaf ears. Disillusionment and bitter disappointment showed darkly in many faces.

"That green man's a faker," charged a hunchback on crutches. "He's probably paid you to testify for him. He ought to be arrested..."

"Yeah—he's a phony if I ever saw one. He and Professor Bailey ought to be locked up for perpetrating a fraud."

Numar had remained standing in the dead center of this human turmoil. His flowing robe was still intact despite the hysterical efforts his former worshippers had made to tear it from him. This, in itself, was unusual but not so much, perhaps, as the fact that he had not yet uttered a word. He faced the wrath of his accusers with a quiet poise and dignity, which seemed strangely out of character with their charges.

At this moment an automobile pulled up at the curb and a man and woman jumped out. The woman was carrying a three-year-old daughter in her arms.

"Oh, I hope we're not too late..." she was heard to say.

Her husband took her arm and piloted her through the sullen crowd. They had eyes only for the white-robed figure. As they came into his presence, the anxious mother looked up at him.

"Oh, Mister Numar! We read about you in the paper—that story about how the invalid in the wheelchair touched you and was cured."

"That's true!" said a voice, nearby. "I'm that man, lady. As God is my judge."

The woman was oblivious to the murmurs of skepticism and indignation that swept through the group surrounding her.

"Then, Mister Numar," she appealed, "perhaps you would touch my little girl and make her well again. She hasn't been able to move her right arm or leg since she was taken sick a year ago. My husband and I have taken her everywhere and spent all our money—but it's no use."

The blue eyes of the little girl were gazing up into Numar's deep black ones. He smiled down at her with a look of great warmth and tenderness.

"You're green!" said the little girl.

Numar put out his hand and stroked her right arm, gently.

"Oh!" exclaimed the child, "That tickles!"

She pulled her arm away.

"John!" cried the mother. "Oh, John—did you see that? She moved her arm. I—I can't believe it...she moved her arm!"

The child never took her eyes off Numar's. "Tickle me some more," she said, and laughed.

NUMAR'S green hand passed lightly down, in a stroking motion, over her slender right leg.

"That tickles, too," said the child. "Oh, my—how it tickles!"

She jerked her leg and kicked it free from Numar's touch.

"You see?" cried the frail little man of the wheel chair, facing his accusers. "You see?"

"You are all right now," said Numar to the little girl. "You will always be all right."

The mother set her daughter's feet upon the ground. Numar knelt on one knee and held out his arms. The child took two tottering steps and threw her arms about his neck.

"I like you," she said.

Numar lifted her up and patted her head and said: "You are going to grow up and be a big girl and make your father and mother very happy." With this, he gave her back to the mother's arms.

Neither parent could speak, but tears of deepest human gratitude shown from their eyes.

A spell had fallen upon all who had witnessed this little miracle but now the spell was broken by a professional appearing man, pushing forward. Numar had just turned away and was walking toward the house when confronted by this gentleman.

"Just a minute, you," said the man. "I'm from the Medical Society. I just saw your performance. I don't know what kind of treatment you used, but do you have a license to practice medicine?"

Numar's black eyes examined his challenger.

"License?" he repeated.

"Yes," said the man. "You can't treat people for illnesses or physical disability in this state—or any state—unless you're a recognized doctor or practitioner."

"Who says he can't?" said the hunchback on crutches. "I've just seen what he did, too—and if he can heal people by touching them, I say he ought to have a right to do it."

The man from the Medical Society turned upon Numar's newfound supporter who was now backed by many who had lost faith in him a few minutes before.

"My dear sir. The Medical Society doesn't recognize any such healings as genuine. How do we know this man wasn't just putting on an act? How do we know that little child was actually paralyzed in her right arm and leg? That's the trouble with you invalids. Just because you can't get cured by your doctors, you start running after these, quacks. This green man here isn't mysterious to me. I've seen his type before. He's just got a new twist on an old wrinkle, that's all. If any of you people believe his cock and bull story about coming from another planet, you're crazy!" The man from the medical society paused and gave a curious look at Numar. "Incidentally," he said, "Where *did* you come from?"

Numar did not reply. Instead, he mounted the steps to the porch.

"Hold on, here," said the man. "I'm not through with you yet."

He reached out and grabbed Numar by the arm. It was as though he had touched a live wire. He leaped high in the air and let out a yell.

The crowd laughed.

"Serves you right," taunted a cripple. "You had no license to touch him."

But this humor was totally lost upon the representative of the medical society.

"Arrest this faker!" he demanded of Chief Andrews. "I know how he operates now. He's got an electrical contrivance—and he just tried to kill me!"

"You'll have to swear out a warrant," said the Chief. "But if you'll take my advice, you'll let well enough alone."

A PERSPIRING gentleman, coat over one arm and tie and collar in hand, dodged past the police and reached Numar on the porch.

"Remember me?" he asked. "My name's Sid Alex. I'm the MGM talent scout. You're terrific, Mister Numar. Absolutely terrific! I've been trying to get to you for the last half-hour. You'll go great in pictures."

"Have you seen the newspapers?" asked Numar, quietly.

The talent scout laughed. "Yeah—that's a good trick! What a publicity stunt! You keep on pulling that and you'll have the whole country ga-ga. Then let us bring out a picture of you so the public can really see you for the first time—and we'll clean up."

Numar shook his head. "The public will never see my picture," he said. "I appreciate your interest—but I do not photograph."

The crowd had pressed around the porch and those within earshot gasped their amazement. The talent scout looked at Numar, uncertainly.

"Listen, brother," he said, in a low tone. "That's a great line to hand out to your public. But you're not kidding me. Don't keep playing so hard to get. We'll pay your price."

Betty suddenly stuck her head out the upstairs window.

"Yoo-hoo!" she called. "Here I am, Mister MGM. Did you want to see me?"

The talent scout glanced up at her and Numar stepped quickly into the house. The door was shut and locked behind him.

"Hey, Mister Numar!" he called. "Don't do that to me!" Then, looking up at Betty he said, "Yes, young lady, I do want to see you. I've got a real business proposition to make. You get Mister Numar to sign with me, and I'll put you in pictures."

"Oh, that's wonderful!" cried Betty. "You leave it to me!"

"Can I come in and talk to you?" asked Mr. Alex.

"Well, not right now," said Betty. "You just wait around outside and I'll let you know, soon as I get things arranged."

"For anything as big as this, I'll wait all night!" he waved. "You go to it."

CHIEF ANDREWS was compelled to give the home of Professor Bailey continued police protection. The services of two officers were required, one guarding the front of the house and the other, the back. Long after Numar had made his appearance and then retreated behind locked doors, a constantly changing crowd of people came and went outside. With nightfall this crowd still persisted as later editions of the Los Angeles papers carried further stories and photographs.

Controversy waxed hot and hotter. Was Numar, the mysterious green man, actually a traveler from another planet or was he a colossal mountebank—perhaps one of the most ingenious of all times? There were as many different opinions as there were people who had seen or had any contact with Numar. These now numbered some hundreds, and increasing numbers of curious men and women were seeking a chance to see Numar and judge for themselves.

Most baffling of all was the inability of photographers to capture Numar's likeness on a film. They had peppered away at him from all angles but when they brought their negatives from the dark room, only a blank space remained where Numar should have been. This violated all the known laws of physics. What the human eye could see, the camera should have been able to photograph.

A series of pictures had been taken of the young couple who had brought their three-year-old daughter with the hope he could cure her. When Numar had reached out his hand to touch the arm and leg of this child, these scenes had been shot. The pictures revealed the little girl reacting to something and actually moving her right arm and leg but Numar was conspicuous by his absence. Even more sensational were pictures snapped when the overjoyed mother had set the feet of her little girl upon the ground and the child had held out her arms and taken several faltering steps toward Numar. He wasn't there at all, although the expression on her face indicated she was seeing someone.

But the picture that aroused the most excited comment was one made of Numar as he had lifted the child in his arms and was handing the little girl over to her mother. In this picture, the three-year-old daughter was in mid-air with no seeming means of support. This looked so much like trick photography that the cameramen on the different papers had gotten together and signed affidavits, testifying that these published pictures had been reproduced exactly as they had been taken.

"We have no explanation for this phenomenon," said the editors. "We believe it to be a feat of magic, but if so, none of the country's leading magicians know how it is being done. Of course, the possibility of hypnotism should not be ruled out. Even so, it is a type of mass mesmerism more extensive and amazing than any heretofore demonstrated.

"It is a known fact that the fakirs of India who perform the disappearing rope trick, employ hypnotic methods to make their audiences see what they do not see. This has been proved by people who have snapped pictures of the rope being tossed in air and the Hindu boy climbing this rope, finally vanishing in space. When such pictures have been developed, they have shown the fakir to be seated cross-legged upon the ground, with no rope or native boy in sight. The 'scene' has taken place only in the observer's mind.

"In this case, however, the cameras caught the little girl in mid-air, indicating that she had actually been lifted up by Numar who managed to keep himself invisible! What technique Numar uses has not yet been discovered."

PAPERS carried the statements of several prominent physicians with respect to the two persons Numar had apparently cured by a "laying on of the hands." These doctors made it clear, if Numar possessed some electrical apparatus, as was surmised, that the sudden surprise and shock occasioned by contact might have proved effective. This did not necessarily mean that Numar had any supernatural powers or that he was not a native resident of this planet.

Dr. Cochrane of the Medical Society, referred to Numar as, "a shameless charlatan who is trading upon the sentiment and gullibility of desperate and earnest health seekers." He went on to declare, "It is to be lamented that so distinguished and respected a scientist as Professor Bailey should have been taken in."

Both United and Associated Press news services put the incredible story of Numar on the wire to newspapers throughout the country. It created an instantaneous nationwide sensation. Dispatches were cabled and sent by wireless abroad. Worldwide interest was immediately so great that editors clamored, in every tongue, for more information about this mysterious green man.

Here, at last, was apparently a real "man from Mars" story. The fiction of Buck Rogers and his spaceship had become fact. What the comic strips had predicted had come true. What reasonable doubt remained as to Numar's actually being a man from another planet only served to heighten the mystery and the interest. The two greatest news stories of modern times had been Lindbergh's flight to Paris and birth of the Dionne quintuplets. But Numar's alleged arrival on earth from a planet a trillion miles away was the new Pulitzer Prize winner. No story of crime or passion, war, world peace or taxation could compete.

"Tell us more!" was the cry that went up on all sides. "If he can't be photographed, what's he look like? Is the body of the green man different from ours? Does he really live on air and water? How does he generate his power? Can't somebody find his spaceship? What does Numar think of us? Tell us every move he makes. When is he going to speak in Chicago? We want to know!"

CHAPTER SIX

BIG HANK MORRISON, publicity director of the University of Chicago, was sick at heart. His institution had yielded to the hues and cries of its alumni and restored the venerable game of football to the school's sport curriculum. For some years brawn had been discarded for intellect, but now, brawn had been invited to participate once more in the cultural life of Chicago University. After all, the revenue from such games as football and basketball had paid many professors' salaries in numerous colleges and why shouldn't the University of Chicago enjoy the fruits of such physical labors? Perhaps it had been wrong to place undue emphasis upon brain over brawn. The great athletes of the country usually became leading insurance, stock, and automobile salesmen, if not movie stars or radio sports announcers. Could any mere intellectual hope for such post graduate success? This was the false reasoning that had brought football back to the campus of Chicago University.

Why, then, should Big Hank Morrison be sick? He was seated in his office, leaning his double chin on one pudgy hand and staring glumly at the season's football schedule, now half played. Standing beside him was Robert M. Hutchins, University President.

"It's murder!" moaned Hank. "We should have stuck to tiddlywinks. Our boys need more seasoning. This is too much to expect. We haven't scored a single touchdown all season. And next Saturday, we take on Notre Dame. There won't be anyone at Soldier Field but the ushers. How can I ballyhoo a slaughter like this?"

"I know," said the president. "It's to be expected. No matter how good our team might become. We shouldn't have let those alumni line up such a schedule."

"Well, we're in it now and we're losing our shirt," said Hank, shifting his double chin to the palm of his other hand. "There's no sense in playing the game. The score's bound to be about thirty to nothing—and it won't surprise me if our gate is near zero."

"The gate is what worries me," said the president. "The cost of maintaining a losing team is appalling. And booking this game with Notre Dame at Soldier Field was frightfully bad judgment."

BIG HANK MORRISON got to his feet, which was, in itself, a major operation. He exerted himself still further by walking to the window overlooking the campus. There he leaned his three hundred pounds on the windowsill.

"I wish I could think of some way to pack that field with spectators," he said. "Our team can't perform miracles even with Notre Dame as an opponent...but if we could get some extra added attraction...wait a minute!" Big Hank rumbled back to his desk and picked up the evening paper. "I've got it!" he cried, and pointed to the streamer headlines.

MAN FROM ANOTHER PLANET TO SPEAK TO EARTH PEOPLE FROM CHICAGO.

"This'll do it!" he cried. "Every Notre Dame game is broadcast from coast to coast—and this green man says he's coming to Chicago to deliver a world message."

"I don't seem to get the connection," said the president.

"Connection!" Big Hank hit the desk with his fist. "The connection is perfect. What better opportunity can he get than appearing before a crowd of a hundred thousand people and saying what he has to say on the radio between halves!"

A little bell began ringing in the president's mind.

"I see," he said. "But what makes you think a man with the background Numar's supposed to have would even consider such...?"

"Where can he ever get a bigger listening audience?" retorted Big

Hank, reaching for the phone. "Someone in every family listens to football. I'm sure the sponsors of Green's Vitamin-plus Spinach won't object. I'm going to try to get this Numar on the phone and make him a proposition."

"But if he should turn out a fake?" asked the president.

"After the stir he's already caused," said Big Hank, "he'll still be the biggest draw in the country. Everybody will want to hear and see him. We'll fill Soldier Field to overflowing."

The President of Chicago University sat down and looked speculatively into space.

"Yes," he said, half talking to himself. "I believe you're right. We could recoup our season's financial losses in one afternoon. Besides, such a feature would be consistent with our progressive attitude in education. It's entirely appropriate that we should welcome a being like this from another planet. I might even introduce him to the radio audience myself."

"Now, you're talking, Mr. President," said Big Hank, who then picked up the phone. "Long distance, get me the home of Professor W. R. Bailey in LaCanada, California." Turning back to the president, he said, "It'll be a round-the-world hookup. This game is being broadcast to all the boys in the service. I'm telling you, if we can put this over, I've had the brainstorm of the century!"

IN NEW YORK CITY, Clifton Fadiman put aside his set of the Encyclopedia Britannica.

"I can't find any record," he said, addressing a number of employees in his private office, "of any being from another planet ever having landed on this earth. If this Numar is really the first, he should be written up for our new edition." He paused thoughtfully for a moment. "Why, what's the matter with me? He should be our next guest on the *Information, Please* program!"

Mr. Fadiman crumpled a list of possible guest stars, which included the names of Wendell Willkie, Clare Booth Luce, Dorothy Thompson, Eleanor Roosevelt, John L. Lewis, and Thomas K Dewey. He filed this list for future reference.

"This Numar's the talk of the country," he continued. "He's put all our local celebrities in the shade for the time being. He would be terrific on *Information, Please*. Think of all the ground-breaking questions we can ask him!"

Fadiman reached for the phone.

"Sorry," the operator finally reported. "Professor Bailey's line is temporarily disconnected."

Undaunted, the country's leading exponent of literature, culture and intellectualism wrote out a telegram. It read as follows:

Numar,
Visitor from the Planet Talamaya,
c/o Prof. W. R. Bailey,
LaCanada, California

Will you and Astronomer Bailey appear as guests on our *Information, Please* program this week in New York? We will furnish plane transportation. Your answers to our questions can enlighten the world. We'll pay you each five hundred dollars, along with a set of Encyclopedia Britannicas. For your information, we have one of the highest Crosley ratings on earth and can promise you a big listening audience. Please wire acceptance to Clifton Fadiman, Box "57 Varieties," New York City.

IN WASHINGTON, D. C., Alfred B. Hoolihan, famous isolationist Senator, was in need of something to restore him to public favor and the national limelight. Since extolling the virtues of "America First," he had been consigned to political oblivion with entry of the United States in the world war and participation in international affairs. But reading the account of Numar's arrival on earth gave Senator Hoolihan a tremendous inspiration.

"I may have been blind to the global trend—but I can see now," he said, "that the next step forward in civilization is going beyond the mere international. It's going to be interplanetary. There's a day fast approaching when our good neighbor policy will be extended to neighboring planets...and my being the first to advance this idea in Congress will establish me, once more, as a man of vision and foresight."

The Senator pondered deeply for a moment.

"I know what I'll do. I'll go before the Senate and propose that this visitor from the planet Talamaya be invited to address Congress in a joint meeting of the two houses. This green man should also be taken to the White House to meet the President. And of course, I'll go along as his personal escort. This will give me an excellent opportunity to mend my political fences. How can I be accused any longer of isolationism when my policy now takes in the entire universe?"

BACK in LaCanada, California, overburdened telephone and telegraph operators wished wearily and fervently that this visitor from another planet had picked some other place to land. Phone calls and telegrams, even radiograms from abroad, were coming in at a rate beyond their capacity to receive. Old Uncle Joe, seventy-year-old Western Union boy, had gone to bed with hot water bags on his legs to soothe the aching muscles occasioned by thirty-seven trips to and from Professor Bailey's home, carrying stacks of wires each time. In fact, the current supply of telegraph blanks had been used and messages now were being written out on yellow copy paper. Jim Taber, retired telegraph operator, had been called back on duty to help decipher the rush of messages, variously addressed to "Numar," "Man From Other World," "Unearthly Visitor," "Green Man," "The Power Invisible," "Super Man," "Space Traveler," and the like.

Communications were from many known as well as unknown humans from every walk of life. These hundreds of telegrams and recorded phone calls were piled high on the Baileys' dining room table and overflowed upon the floor. They were being opened and sorted by Betty who was now putting her former stenographic training to good use.

"You see, Uncle," she said, "If you'll just let me, I can really be quite helpful. Mister Numar needs a secretary the worst way…someone he can trust—like me. He's getting some perfectly wonderful offers—but I don't want him to accept any until he talks to MGM. And, speaking of MGM, the talent scout is outside right now. He's gone off and had dinner and come back again. Won't you let me bring him?"

"No!" said the Professor. "Mister Numar has stated emphatically that he will have nothing to do with pictures. What messages are those you have in your hand?"

"Oh," said Betty, referring to a packet of several dozen wires. "These are the pick of the lot—what seemed to me most important. If Mister Numar wants to, he can certainly make a lot of money while he's here."

"What good would our money do him on his planet?" asked the Professor.

"That's right. I hadn't thought of that," said Betty, "Well, maybe he'd like the publicity, anyway. He must want something. Everybody does."

MRS. Bailey had resigned herself to a life of continuous pandemonium. She felt almost as though she was barricaded against the world, which was apt to break in upon her any moment. But perhaps tonight would bring an end to all this nonsense and the exposure of Numar. Three of her husband's most respected and most distinguished scientific friends were coming over to interview this self-announced earth visitor. Surely such prominent authorities as Dr. Edward Kruger, biologist; Jeffrey Larabee, electrical engineer, and Professor Horace Weldon, astronomer and physicist, would not have any wool pulled over their eyes. Their reputations meant too much to them. They should be able to see through the clever practices of this artificial green man and save her husband from any further embarrassment.

"William," said Mrs. Bailey. "The first sensible thing you've done is to let these authorities see Numar. Once they've passed judgment on him, you won't have to sponsor him like you've been doing. I think Mister Numar will be glad to perform another magical trick and put on a disappearing act."

"Nellie," said the Professor, "you just don't believe in anything, do you, unless it's as plain as the nose on your face?"

"You leave my nose out of this," said Mrs. Bailey. "You've been looking at the stars for so long that you need somebody to help keep your feet on the ground. I'm doing the best I can!"

NUMAR, himself, seemed glad to give an audience to Professor Bailey's fellow scientists. He greeted them graciously as they were escorted inside the house by the police officer on duty.

Dr. Kruger, the biologist, was a man of perhaps sixty, reserved and coldly calculating. Mr. Larabee, the electrical engineer, had reached the three-score-and-ten mark and retained an energetic, penetrating interest in his work. Professor Weldon, the physicist, had gained fame in astronomy as an avocation. He belonged to the school that believed there was only one substance in the universe, expressed through an infinite variety of forms. He was the youngest of the three men at fifty-five, and towered over them physically with his six feet, six inches.

The three scientists made an interesting appearing group as Professor Bailey closed off the living room so that they could be alone with Numar. The first few moments were extremely awkward as each caller tried to avoid staring at the Professor's houseguest.

Numar seemed to sense this self-consciousness for he said, pleasantly. "I am accustomed to this kind of interview, gentlemen. It may help you to know that I am as interested in studying you as you may be in studying me."

Dr. Kruger laughed. "Yes, of course! It ought to work both ways."

"You'll have to pardon us, Mister Numar," said Mr. Larabee. "Talking to a man from another planet requires a little mental adjustment. I have a great many questions I'd like to ask you but I want to be sure they're intelligent."

Professor Weldon eyed Numar, critically. "I suppose you're prepared for us to query you pretty frankly," he said.

"I am," replied Numar, "and I will answer everything I permissibly can."

"What do you mean…permissibly?" demanded Dr. Kruger.

"I mean," said Numar, quietly, "That there is certain knowledge you human creatures are not supposed to have on this earth until you have reached a greater evolution. I am forbidden to give you any such knowledge should you chance to ask me."

The three scientists exchanged consulting glances.

"Will you let us examine you physically?" asked Dr. Kruger.

Numar smiled and shook his head. "Sorry. I must refuse."

"Then you place us at a disadvantage at the very outset," said Dr. Kruger, bluntly. "We are naturally curious and anxious to learn all we can about you."

"That's true," said Mr. Larabee. "We understand you have strange electrical powers. As an engineer, that particularly interests me."

"The green pigment of your skin," said Professor Weldon. "That's most extraordinary. I hope you realize, Mister Numar, that much depends upon the report we make about you to the public. If you really have a message to deliver to the world, our endorsement can mean a great deal."

Numar nodded. "I appreciate that. I can explain this much. This apparel that I seem to be wearing is a part of my being while I am on this journey. It is a protective covering and has high vibratory qualities. For this reason, it cannot be removed."

"So that's it," said the Professor. "I wondered why they didn't tear that robe off you in the rush outside. Well, well, well…fancy that!"

"You gentlemen may examine my hands if you like," said Numar.

THE three scientists stood up and advanced toward Numar, eagerly. He arose and extended his hands to them.

"Look out!" warned Professor Bailey. "You're apt to get a shock!"

"No," said Numar. "I am controlling these forces. They will feel nothing."

Dr. Kruger and Mr. Larabee took hold of Numar's right arm while Professor Weldon examined the left. They exclaimed almost together.

"He's green, all right. A different feeling to his flesh, too. Extremely firm. Notice the fingernails. You can't see through them. They are a darker green. He seems to have a higher body temperature. Strange, there aren't any veins showing. He doesn't seem to have pores."

These comments had come, one on top of the other.

"It's possible, of course," said Dr. Kruger, "that this is some unusual green dye which has been applied so skillfully, almost like a veneer, that we can't ordinarily detect veins or pores. However, if this green dye is coated over the entire body, you gentlemen realize that no human could live. You will note the same green texture in the face. Why, even his lips and teeth are green. It hardly seems probable that any man would go to such extremes to perpetrate a fraud. I've certainly never seen anything like this."

"Nor I," said Mr. Larabee. "Perhaps we can judge him best by checking on these electrical forces he's supposed to possess. Would you object to letting us feel something, Mister Numar?"

"Now, Jeffrey," said Professor Bailey. "You don't know what you're asking. You're not as young as you used to be. Better be careful. Your system may not be able to stand it."

"Fiddlesticks!" said the seventy-year-old electrical engineer. "I've felt some good, heavy shocks in my time." He turned to Professor Weldon who was holding Numar's left hand. "How about it, Horace? Would you like to have Mister Numar—?"

"Very much!" said Professor Weldon, tightening his grip.

"And you, Edward?" asked Mr. Larabee, turning to Dr. Kruger who had Numar's right hand.

"Certainly," said Dr. Kruger. "I'm here to go as far as Mister Numar will permit."

"There's room for you here, William," proposed Mr. Larabee. "You can take hold of Numar's left arm with Horace."

"No, thanks," said Professor Bailey. "If you don't mind, I'll just step over here out of the way." He moved over toward the door and put a chair between himself and the group. "I wish you'd take my word for this," he added, apprehensively. "You're going to feel something, all right."

Mr. Larabee gave Professor Bailey an annoyed glance. "William," he said, "I'm disappointed in you. Any true scientist must investigate at first hand." He turned back to the group. "Now, is everybody ready?" he asked.

"Ready!" chorused Dr. Kruger and Professor Weldon.

"Now, Mister Numar," said Mr. Larabee, "would you mind...?"

PROFESSOR BAILEY hid his face in his hands. He had scarcely done so when three men, past middle age, left the floor of his living room and flew in three different directions. Dr. Kruger came down with a crash on the piano keys. Professor Weldon thudded against the bookcase and brought scientific volumes raining down upon his head. Mr. Larabee landed on top of the davenport and disappeared from sight between it and the wall.

Numar stood, quiet and composed, in the center of the room. An awful stillness followed.

"You see what I meant?" said the Professor.

Professor Weldon untangled his long frame, sat up on the floor and rubbed several bumps on his head. "You shouldn't put such heavy books on those higher shelves," he said. "It's dangerous!"

Dr. Kruger had slid off the piano, looking scared and sheepish. "Your piano may need tuning," he said.

Mr. Larabee's head now appeared from behind the davenport. "What power!" he exclaimed. "I don't blame you, Professor. Once is enough."

There was a rap on the door. It was Mrs. Bailey. "What on earth is going on in here?" she asked.

"Nothing, dear," said the Professor, "Just a little scientific experiment."

"Well, it sounded like the house was coming down," said Mrs. Bailey. "Why, look at this room—those books on the floor! Why, Mr. Larabee— what are you doing behind that davenport?"

Mr. Larabee looked foolish. "Well, upon my soul—how did I get over here?"

Mrs. Bailey went out and shut the door.

The Professor turned to his three fellow scientists. "Let's see now— where were we?" he asked.

"The question is—where are we?" said Dr. Kruger. "I'll feel that jolt for days. If we could get beneath that man's robe, I'm sure we'd find an electrical device of some sort. Possibly a new invention."

"I'm not so certain," said Mr. Larabee, as he straightened the davenport. "That didn't feel like any shock I ever felt before. I'm about ready to believe…"

"Now, don't be too hasty," said Professor Weldon. "We've got to think this thing through. I'm inclined to believe with Edward. It seems too incredible…"

"What's the matter with you two?" demanded Mr. Larabee. "You know that animals give off electricity. Take the electric eel, for instance. Take our own brains—we've already proved they give off electric impulses. Why couldn't a man from another planet have a power like this?"

"Well, it defies all known laws of biology," said Dr. Kruger.

"Yes—and physics," said Professor Weldon.

"But not of electricity," said Mr. Larabee. "No, gentlemen, I'm prepared to state that this Numar is the genuine article. I can't explain how he generates his power but I certainly can testify to it."

DR. KRUGER and Professor Weldon looked worried.

"Do you realize what you are saying?" they asked. "Are you willing to risk your professional reputation?"

Mr. Larabee fairly bristled. He shook an agitated finger in the faces of his two colleagues. "Bah! for you and your reputations!" he said. "Did you feel this electric shock, or didn't you?"

"It may have been hypnotism," said Dr. Kruger.

"That's true," said Professor Weldon.

"It *must* have been hypnotism. Maybe his skin isn't green at all. Maybe he's got everybody hypnotized. Maybe we'd better be getting out of here!" Professor Weldon started edging toward the door.

"That's a good idea," said Dr. Kruger. "I've got another appointment, anyway."

Mr. Larabee stood his ground. "What kind of scientists are you?" he demanded. "You didn't come here with open minds. You'd decided beforehand that Numar was a fake. Now that you've found out differently, you don't dare admit it."

"We're entitled to our opinions," said Professor Weldon. "Good night, William." He started to go through the door, forgot to stoop and produced another lump on his head. "My advice to you is to get rid of this person as fast as you can."

"Yes," said Dr. Kruger, as he followed Professor Weldon out the door. "This association is doing you no good. No good at all."

"Mister Numar," said Mr. Larabee, facing Professor Bailey's silent houseguest. "I apologize to you for my fellow scientists. That's the trouble with us human creatures on this earth. We get so steeped in our own little egos and little knowledge that we think we know it all. I don't wonder that you aren't permitted to tell us much. Most of us refuse to believe even when we *do* see."

Numar nodded, understandingly. "That was true of my species millions of years ago," he said. "This attitude will change in time."

"I hate to look ahead that far," said Mr. Larabee. "It hurts my brain." Then, turning to Professor Bailey, "Well, William, all I can say is—I admire you for being a martyr to science. Some day—when we are traveling by rocket ship to the moon and distant planets—perhaps your name will be remembered and revered. But don't expect any recognition in your lifetime."

Mr. Larabee shook Professor Bailey's hand.

"Good night, dear friend. And goodbye, Mister Numar. I hope you don't think too unkindly of us humans."

Numar smiled. "I knew what you were like before I came here," he said.

"You did?" said the country's most esteemed electrical engineer. "Then, if I may ask—why the hell didn't you stay away?"

CHAPTER SEVEN

THERE was a ladder resting against the side of Professor Bailey's house just under the guest room window. The figure of Betty was at the window, stealthily giving instructions to the man below.

"It's the only way I can see you," she called down. "You'll never get in the house."

"You're sure we won't be detected?" asked the man.

"No," assured Betty. "My aunt's gone to bed with an ice pack on her head and Uncle's tied up with those scientists and Mister Numar."

The man started climbing the ladder. "I've done lots of things to get talent in my time," he said, "but never anything like this."

"Isn't it thrilling!" said Betty. "It was awfully nice of that policeman to help you with the ladder."

"Wasn't it?" said the MGM talent scout. "I helped him—with ten bucks!"

"Oh, well," said Betty. "I suppose it's all in the business. That's what's so wonderful about this country. Everybody helps everybody else."

The talent scout reached the window ledge and looked down. He swayed and caught himself. "It makes me dizzy to be up high," he said. "Let's talk fast, Miss Bracken."

"Why, I'll talk just as fast as you want me to," said Betty. "What shall I say?"

"First," said talent scout Sid Alex, "did you get Numar's consent about him going into pictures?"

"Well—no," said Betty, "not exactly—but he's given his consent to about everything else."

Mr. Alex took a good hold of the ladder. "What do you mean by that?"

"Well," replied Betty, "He's going on the Sackswell Coffee House Hour tomorrow night in Hollywood with Frank Morgan—and right after the show, he's taking a plane for New York City with Professor Bailey."

The talent scout braced himself, unsteadily. "What's Numar going to New York for?"

"Clifton Fadiman sent for him," said Betty. "He's going to be on *Information, Please.*"

"And then what?" demanded the man from MGM.

"Oh, then," said Betty, "he's going to Washington to talk to Congress and see the President…oh, Mr. MGM…you almost fell!"

Mr. Alex leaned heavily against the ladder. "Ye Gods!" he said, "What publicity! The man will be a world sensation. I've got to sign him up. Is he coming back to the coast?"

"Yes," said Betty, "but he's stopping off in Chicago first to attend a football game."

"Football? What the hell does he know about football?"

"He doesn't have to know anything. He's just making a speech between halves. They've promised him the greatest radio hookup in history."

"When was all this arranged? Who managed this?"

BETTY rolled her eyes. "Well, I guess I helped some. I opened up the telegrams and picked out what looked good to me and went in and read them to Mister Numar—and he told Uncle William to wire these people that he'd be glad to accommodate them."

The talent scout groaned. "And I've been hanging around here for hours trying to get a look-in," he said. "And you call yourself a friend of mine?"

"I'm awfully sorry," said Betty, "but pictures are the one thing Mister Numar doesn't go for. I think he must have taken a bad photograph at one time."

"Just the same," decided Mr. Alex, "I'd better stick close to him in case he changes his mind. If any other studio should grab him before us, my name would be mud."

"Oh, we wouldn't want that to happen," said Betty.

The ladder began to shake from below. MGM's talent scout clutched the windowsill to steady it. "Hey!" he called down. "What's the idea? Let go! Stop it!"

"It's another man," said Betty. "It's so dark down there, I can't make out…"

"Is that Miss Bracken up there?" cried a voice.

"Why yes," acknowledged Betty, surprised. "Who are you?"

"My name's Schwartz from Warner Brothers," said the voice. "The New York office just wired me to look you up. Why didn't you report for your screen test?"

"Oh, Mr. Schwartz!" exclaimed Betty. "Come right up!"

The ladder began to tremble under his added weight. "Thank you," said the voice. "I don't mind if I do."

"Well, I do mind!" said the aggrieved Mr. Alex. "You stay away from here, Sam. I got here first."

"Why hello, Sid, old boy," said the Warner scout. "Fancy meeting you here."

"My…" said Betty, "I wish I could invite you both in but I guess you know what's been going on here. I suppose, Mr. Schwartz, that you saw my pictures in the papers?"

"Yeah. But that guy making love to you didn't photograph so good. My company's interested in him, though. I got orders to sign you both up."

"Now, wait a minute!" said MGM. "You can't muscle in here!"

"We can't, eh?" said Warner. "We got a line on this lady first. We gave her a letter promising a screen test if she'd come to Hollywood."

"Did you sign her on an option?" asked MGM.

"No, not yet," admitted Warners.

"Did you pay her fare here?" asked MGM.

"No," said Warners.

"Then she's in the open market," said MGM. Mr. Alex risked freeing one hand to reach in his pocket and pull out a contract form, which he extended to Betty. "Here, Miss Bracken—take this and sign it."

"Don't you do it!" commanded Mr. Schwartz, standing on the rung below Mr. Alex. He waved another contract form. "You can't trust MGM. They hire you on a seven year contract and you sit in a hotel room for seven years, manicuring your nails."

"Says you!" retorted MGM. "Just fill in that blank space, Miss Bracken. Put yourself down for two hundred a week to start."

"Two hundred a week!" howled Mr. Schwartz. "Yoi! Yoi! What a cheapskate. A girl with your sex appeal? Just fill in that blank space on our contract. Put yourself down for two-twenty-five to start."

BETTY held the two contracts in her hands. She was silhouetted against the desk lamp behind her. The pupils of her eyes were learning things. She hesitated—a perfect piece of timing.

"All right—make it two-fifty," said MGM.

"Two-seventy-five," said Warners.

"Now listen," said Sid, in a low voice. "You know, Sam, that she's not worth it."

"Who are you kidding?" said Sam, in Sid's ear. "D'you think I'll let you get the inside track to Numar?"

"Three hundred you get!" said MGM. "But not a cent more."

"All right," said Betty, impulsively. "I'll take it!"

"But I'll give you three-twenty-five," offered Warners.

Betty, pen in hand, looked puzzled.

"No you don't" said Mr. Alex. "You've accepted. You belong to MGM."

"That's a lot of baloney!" said Mr. Schwartz. "You don't belong to anybody till you sign on the dotted line. And if you come with Warners, I'll put you in a picture with Errol Flynn!"

"Oh, you will!" said Mr. Schwartz. "Well, we'll go you one better— we'll put Miss Bracken in one of our pictures where we use every star on the lot."

"Well, after all," said Betty, philosophically, "money isn't everything."

As she signed the MGM contract, Mrs. Bailey walked into the room.

"Why, Betty Annabel Bracken," she said, "I thought you were talking in your sleep. What are you doing up?" Mrs. Bailey was flimsily attired in a plain dressing gown, her hair caught up in a coil on top of her head.

"Oh, Auntie!" cried Betty. "You've just walked in at the biggest moment of my career!"

Mrs. Bailey started as she saw the heads of two gentlemen peering over the window sill from the top of the ladder. "Why?" she gasped. "Who are these men? What are they doing here?"

"They're talent scouts," said Betty, brightly. "The man higher up is from MGM and the other one—you can't quite see all his face from where you are—is from Warner Brothers. They're both awfully nice people—but I'm signing with MGM."

Mrs. Bailey was thunderstruck. She placed a hand to her pounding forehead. "There's too much in this house to watch," she said. "I can't keep an eye on your uncle and on you, too!"

"You don't need to worry, Mrs. Bailey," said Mr. Alex. "We'll take care of your charming niece. We'll make a star out of her in time."

MRS. BAILEY came over where she could get a better view of the two men on the ladder. "This is a strange way to do business," she said.

"Well, we didn't want to bother you people," explained MGM. "You've had such a busy day." Then, turning to Betty, "Miss Bracken, how would you like to make the trip East with your Uncle and Mr. Numar? I think you could probably help them a great deal and keeping your picture in the papers won't hurt you, either. We'll be glad to send you along and pay all expenses."

Betty's face registered delight. "Oh, Mr. MGM I think that would be wonderful. Don't you, Auntie?"

"No!" snapped Mrs. Bailey. "I don't approve of it at all! A young girl like you running around the country without a chaperone…"

"But, Auntie—I'll have Uncle William," Betty protested.

"Uncle William!" repeated Mrs. Bailey, scornfully. "If the way he took care of you at the police station is any sample, you wouldn't be safe with him for a minute."

"Mrs. Bailey!" called Mr. Schwartz, in dulcet tones. "May I suggest something?"

Mrs. Bailey stared out at the face in the shadow. "What is it, young man?"

"From where I'm standing," said Mr. Schwartz, shifting his feet on the ladder rung, "You look like a very attractive, sensible, motherly lady to me. I don't suppose you get away from home very much. Have you ever been to New York?"

Mrs. Bailey drew a wistful breath. "Why, no—I haven't," she said. "The nearest I ever got was Buffalo, when we were married. But my husband's been to New York several times to meetings of his Astronomy Society."

"Well, there you are," said Mr. Schwartz. "Did anyone ever tell you, Mrs. Bailey, that you'd make a good type for pictures?"

"Mercy, no!" said Mrs. Bailey, blushing.

"It's the truth," said Mr. Schwartz, in his most convincing manner. "Miss Bracken, will you please hand that Warner Brothers contract over to your aunt?"

BETTY wonderingly obeyed instructions.

"Hold on, here," said Sid in a low voice. "Sam Schwartz…what are you up to?"

"You've made a deal," hissed Sam. "Now I'm going to make one." He looked at Mrs. Bailey and said, "Madam, Warner Brothers is willing to send you on this trip with your husband, along with Mr. Numar as a chaperone for your niece. We'll make pictures of you en route and when you come back to Hollywood…well…we may make an actress out of you."

"That's something I wouldn't want," said Mrs. Bailey. "But I would like a trip to New York."

"Well, you may change your mind later so we'll sign you up for the trip and pay you a hundred dollars a week," said Mr. Schwartz.

"You louse," said Mr. Alex. "You can't do this to me. If anyone's going to hire Mrs. Bailey, it's MGM. Don't sign that piece of paper, Madam! Sign *this* one from me. And put yourself down for *two hundred* a week."

"Two-twenty-five," said Warners.

"My God!" said Sid. "Do we start this all over again?" He looked at Mrs. Bailey. "All right, Madam—make it *two-fifty*." He passed up a contract form to the bewildered Mrs. Bailey.

"Don't sign it," directed Mr. Schwartz. "I'll pay you two-seventy-five."

Mr. Alex swallowed. "Three hundred!" he said, desperately.

"Mrs. Bailey!" called Mr. Schwartz. "That contract in your left hand is from Warner Brothers. I was the first one to see your possibilities. You can't turn me down. I'm making you my last offer: three—hundred—twenty-five...*per* week!"

"Why, Auntie!" gasped Betty. "That's more than MGM's paying me!"

"It is," said Mrs. Bailey, eyes blazing. "Well, I wouldn't sign with a company like that. Here—give me your pen."

"But, Mrs. Bailey," cried Mr. Alex, "You don't understand!"

"I think I do," said Mrs. Bailey. "I don't claim to be an actress at all but my niece here has spent several years at it and yet you only give her three hundred a week when Warner Brothers is willing to give me three hundred twenty-five with no experience whatsoever. No wonder people say such nasty things about Hollywood."

"Catch me," Sid said to Sam. "I think I'm gonna faint..."

"It's going to be a pleasant trip," said Sam. "Let's see now—who gets Numar?"

"Now, Betty," said Mrs. Bailey. "I think you'd better tell these gentlemen 'goodnight.' They can see us tomorrow and make whatever arrangements are necessary."

The ladder began to shake from below.

"Hey! What's going on up there?" said a gruff voice.

"It's a policeman," said Sam, looking down.

Sid chuckled. "Guess they've just changed the guard. You're first down, Sam. That'll cost you ten bucks!"

ON the wall above his bunk, in the quarters of Flight Lieutenant Harry Hopper, Kelly Field, Texas, there was tacked the photograph of a stunning blonde. She was not Betty Grable, nor Carol Landis, but to Harry she was all pinup girls softly molded into one. In other words, she had all the curves in the right places.

He had met her a year ago, on Broadway, when the two of them had been cast to play bit parts in a shoestring production dubbed "Never Too Early To Learn." Inspired, perhaps by the title, they had learned to love one another, even though they received their closing notice the night the show opened in New York.

"I just know you're going to take Clark Gable's place in Hollywood," she had said to him, with his stardom in her eyes.

"Darling," he said to her. "We'll go to Hollywood together. You've got everything Betty Hutton's got—and more!"

"Well, at least my name's Betty to start with," she had said. "And with you to spur me on, there's no telling to what heights I may climb."

"There's only one shadow that may cross our paths," Harry had said to her.

"You mean your relatives might object to our marrying?" she had asked.

"Not only mine, but yours," he had said. *"Uncle Sam!* I'd have been in the service long ago if it hadn't been for my football knee. My application's been in for aviation and they've called me for a new examination, next week. If I pass the physical, we'll have to postpone our Hollywood adventure."

"I could wait for you for ages and ages," she had told him.

And then had come his country's call…there was no more water on his knee. "Fit as a fiddle!" the examining physician had pronounced. "You're about as good as they come."

And Harry had gone, at once, to camp—leaving Betty to pursue her career alone.

IT WAS Harry's buddy and roommate who first called his attention to a remarkable coincidence. They had both received their wings together. Lt. Ted Macy was at present attached to the Commandant's staff at operational headquarters, while Harry was leader of a pursuit squadron. Both men were at present in advance training with ground strafing and combat tactics being stressed. The days had been hard and grueling under a blistering Texas sun.

Tonight the two young flying officers were propped up in their bunks, enjoying a few moments of luxurious ease before lights out. Ted Macy had a copy of yesterday's Los Angeles Herald-Express which one of the boys from that city had passed on to him.

"Strange thing about that man from another planet," said Ted, as he read the account. "What do you make of it?"

"I saw it in the San Antonio paper," said Harry. "I don't believe it. In the first place, no genuine visitor from another world is going to land near Hollywood. You can bet your bottom dollar that guy's an actor."

"Well, he's certainly got them all guessing so far," said Ted, turning the pages. "Holy smoke! Here's a full page of pictures and the guy doesn't even photograph. Wait a minute—what's this? Well, I'll be damned! No—it can't be…but it sure looks like…what did you say your girl's last name was?"

Ted was now staring at the picture Harry had tacked on the wall, comparing it with some pictures in the paper.

"Bracken," said Harry. "If you must have particulars—Betty Annabel Bracken. And for your further information, she hasn't written me since she flew to Hollywood."

"Well, then, here's the reason why!" said Ted, tossing Harry the paper.

The future Clark Gable of the screen did a "take" on this page, which registered the full range of human emotions. He histrionically portrayed surprise, horror, indignation, jealousy, anger, mortification, injured pride and finally—resolute determination.

"What the hell does she think she's doing?" he exploded.

"Looks like she's trying to imitate Ethel Barrymore, Betty Davis and Zasu Pitts—all at the same time," said Ted.

"It's pure corn any way you slice it," said Harry. "Pure corn! She needs someone to manage her—and she needs that somebody quick."

"Looks like she got roped in by this guy Numar," observed Ted. "I don't know about his being a green man, but she's sure a green dame."

"This never would have happened," said Harry, pacing up and down between their bunks, "if it hadn't been for this war and my going in the service. That's something else I've got against the Nazis and Japs. If I'd only gone to Hollywood with her, she'd have made out all right."

"What makes you think she isn't doing all right now?" said Ted. "Could you have gotten her any bigger publicity?"

"So that's what you call it," said Harry. "My girl making a jackass of herself in six scenes! How did they ever get her to pose like that? Get a load of that expression on her face…she looks like she's kissing a vinegar jug! You can't tell me Numar was ever even in those photos. Wait till I catch the press agent behind this!"

"Better not move too fast," counseled Ted. "You notice, don't you, that her uncle, Professor Bailey, is mixed up in this? He's a pretty famous scientist. Even I've heard of him. This all may be on the level."

"It can't be!" raged Harry. "I'm going to get a leave and go to Hollywood and find out what this is all about."

IT WAS too late that night to get action and early the next morning all men in Harry's squadron were called for maneuvers.

"This is a hell of a note!" said Harry, as he went on the field with Ted.

"I don't feel any more like flying than a submarine commander. I haven't slept a wink all night. The more I think of what's happened to Betty, the madder I get. Numar's the guy I'm going after. When I get through with him, he'll wish he'd never come to *this* planet!"

Harry climbed into his plane.

"Take it easy," said Ted. "Don't let it get you down."

Lt. Ted Macy continued on to operational headquarters. He was on duty in the observation tower with other officers and their chiefs of staff.

The maneuvers this morning were to be devoted to ground strafing. A pursuit squadron was to go out fifty miles over the desert and come in over a prescribed path, flying low. The observation tower commanded a vista of about twenty miles in every direction. Several miles distant toward the west, there was a little town. Its presence was marked by a tall brick chimney—about all that remained of an old factory site. The returning course led about a mile from this town, but when the planes were sighted coming in, one lone plane was seen to be off course, diving straight at the chimney.

The commandant caught this plane in his field glasses.

"It's Hopper!" he exclaimed. "He's certainly living up to his name. He came so close to that chimney, he dusted soot off the top. Look at the damn fool! He's circling and diving at it again. Good Lord!" The commandant wiped a dripping brow. "I thought that time he was going down inside to clean it out. What's up with that guy...anybody know?"

"I do, sir," said Lt. Ted Macy. "A blonde bomber. She's knocked him cuckoo. The guy's out there, flying blind. He's so upset he can't see straight. He's probably trying to take his feelings out on that chimney."

"Call him in," ordered the commandant. "Flag him down. Get him out of the sky! Oh...I can't look...did he miss her that time?"

Flight Lt. Harry Hopper overshot the field and came so close to the observation tower that everyone in it fell flat on the floor. He made a two-point landing and almost ground-looped, but he waved away the anxious ground crew and the approaching ambulance. Brought into the presence of the white-faced commandant, he was asked, when that officer had recovered his breath: "Lt. Hopper, explain yourself—if you can."

For answer, Harry went into the hip pocket of his flying suit and pulled out a crumpled page of pictures from the Los Angeles Herald-Express. He smacked this down on the desk of the commandant.

"That explains everything, sir," he said.

The astonished commandant eyed the photographs. "My God!" he said. "What's this?"

"Believe it or not, sir," said Harry, "that's my girl."

"She seems to be in bad shape," observed the commandant. "Oh…I see…she's supposed to be kissing someone. What's this? An invisible man? Someone from another planet? What rot!"

"You see, sir, what I'm up against," said Harry. "I'm in need of a furlough, sir—to attend to some urgent personal business."

"Well, your request seems justified," said the commandant. "I'll grant you a five-day leave, to take effect at once."

"Oh, thank you, sir," said Harry. "Would it be asking too much, sir, to let me go in my plane? I've got to get there in a hurry."

The commandant considered. "You really should be disciplined for the good of the squadron," he said. "But your record has been exemplary up to this time. I guess we can afford to overlook it. Take the plane—but keep in touch with the army air command wherever you are."

"Thank you again, sir," said Harry, saluting. "I'll come back a new man, sir."

"If you don't," said the commandant, eyes twinkling, "Heaven help that chimney!"

CHAPTER EIGHT

FIRST reaction of the world-at-large to the startling news story of an earthly visitation by a being from another planet was one of skepticism and incredulity. Those not actually on the scene could not conceive how the reporters and photographers could have been "taken in." The only portion of the news report that gave more serious minded readers pause for thought was the eminent Professor Bailey's identification with this green man, Numar.

Many people remembered how Professor Bailey, some years before, had announced discovery of a new star in the constellation, Capricornus, and had endured the scorn and ridicule of his fellow astronomers for some months, until they had eventually and somewhat shamefacedly substantiated his findings. There was just the remote possibility that Professor Bailey was right again, and had not been hoodwinked as was being widely suggested.

While the people of the planet Earth were embraced in an atmosphere of war, news of Numar's alleged arrival from the planet Talamaya, with an important message for human creatures, had reached Germany by circuitous routes.

"He can't be a god," a noted German authority was quoted as commenting. "He doesn't speak German. And, besides, he's not an Aryan."

The reaction in Russia was of interest. "Numar's visit to a capitalistic country is to be regarded with suspicion," said an important Russian official. "If this being were genuine and if he had a real message for the masses on this earth, he would have landed at the Kremlin in Moscow."

In Japan, Emperor Hirohito was silent but someone very close to His Imperial Majesty was recorded as saying: "No Super Being can come to our earth without permission of The Son of Heaven. The fact that this gentleman is said to be green reveals to us that he, like so many other delightful hoaxes, has been...made-in-America."

The people of China had greeted the news of Numar's arrival with their age-old complacency. "Why disturb one's venerable tranquility as to whether this honorable personage is genuine or not? In a thousand years, you may know the answer."

John Bull in England found this report of an interplanetary visitor more difficult to swallow than American brewed tea.

"It is the kind of hocus pocus," said George Bernard Shaw, "that one might expect from our naive American cousins. They have been in the business of fooling themselves since they took the country from the Indians. This green man, I venture to say, is going to turn out to be an Irishman."

Australia, home of the boomerang, freely predicted that this elaborate prank would boomerang against its perpetrators. "We know too much about wool in this country," said a prominent Australian sheep raiser, "to let our American friends pull this kind over our eyes."

In South America, a new revolution was blamed on Numar's arrival. In Egypt, it was intimated that this was what the Sphinx had been waiting for all these years. And, in South Africa, when the news reached one of the cannibal tribes, their chieftain was reported as rubbing his stomach and saying, "Green man...yum...yum..."

PROFESSOR BAILEY was quite perturbed over these world reactions. The fact that his old friend and fellow scientist, Jeffrey Larabee, had made a public statement declaring that he considered Numar genuine and the possessor of absolutely amazing and incomprehensible magnetic powers, had hardly offset the public condemnation of Dr. Edward Kruger and Professor Horace Weldon. These latter two gentlemen, world authorities in their respective fields of biology and physics, had told of their "shocking" experience and had gone an record as saying that they were not qualified to judge "ingenious tricks of magic." The extreme gullibility, of Professor Bailey was inferred. However, despite this, he had somehow found the courage to stand by his strange house guest and even to agree to accompany him on his local trip to the Eastern Seaboard of the United States.

"I may be hypnotized," the Professor said to himself. "I may not even be in my right mind, but I have been with this Numar for the better part of two nights and two days. In all that time I haven't seen him take a bite of food…and he's actually apparently living on air and this distilled water. I'd like to see even my wife do that. If he's not from another planet, then he's the strangest freak of nature ever born on this earth."

The Professor was packing some clean shirts and several changes of ties in his bag, preparatory to the plane flight he and Numar were to make, following the Sackswell Coffee House radio broadcast that late afternoon. He had only been up in a plane once before and that was the time he had cooperated with the United States Army in taking pictures of a total eclipse of the sun. The Professor had been compelled to wear an oxygen mask on that flight and was so busy with his cameras that he was hardly able to realize he had been off the ground.

"I'll be glad to get up in the air again," he said to himself. "And I guess Numar will, too. It's about the only place left where we can get away by ourselves. I still haven't had a chance to talk five minutes to him alone."

There were many important questions of universal significance that Professor Bailey wished to discuss with this space traveler, once given the opportunity. It was hard for the Professor to think of an alien being of Numar's profound accomplishments, actually present here on earth, but with no one taking an intellectual approach toward him. Why, the whole world should be sitting humbly at his feet, only too willing to listen and learn. But, instead of this, what was the public doing?

DEMANDS and offers for Numar were coming in, not only from radio programs, picture producers, football promoters and self-seeking politicians—but from museums, carnival operators, county fairs, circuses, conventions, luncheon clubs, women's organizations, firemen's and policemen's benefits, charity shows, booking agents, vaudeville managers, and a bewildering host of others, not forgetting and including a request for a personal appearance at a state hospital for the insane.

The "thumbs down" given Numar by two such outstanding scientists as Dr. Kruger and Professor Weldon had been sufficient to chill all other scientific interest. At the mere suggestion that any other scientist of repute should interview or attempt to examine Numar, these distinguished gentlemen registered expressions of holy horror.

"It's quite a problem," said Professor Bailey, as he reviewed Numar's brief forty-eight hours on earth. "How am I going to get the people to take Mister Numar seriously? I have a feeling that they are going to make sport of him wherever he goes. I'm really astonished that he has promised to appear with Frank Morgan and that sophisticated *Information, Please* group. Of course, he might be treated a little better in Congress, but I doubt it. As for his planning to address the world between halves of a football game—well, I suppose Mister Numar knows what he's doing, but—if he doesn't—I sadly fear for the consequences."

There was a rap on the Professor's door and Mrs. Bailey poked her head in. "What are you doing?" she asked, "making a speech?"

"Was I talking out loud?" said the Professor. "Oh, dear me. What did I say?"

Mrs. Bailey came into the room. "Something you didn't want me to hear, I presume. You've been talking to yourself a great deal lately. You know what that's a sign of, don't you?"

"Well, Nellie, it's too late to worry about that now. This pair of socks has a hole in them and my best tie has a spot on it."

"Don't tell *me*," said Mrs. Bailey. "I'm not the one who's been wearing them!"

The Professor looked distressed and put them on the bed. "I wish I was like Mister Numar," he said. "He just wears what he's got on from one century to another, as far as I can figure out."

"Oh, stop talking in millenniums!" said Mrs. Bailey. "My head's reeling enough now, as it is."

THE Professor halted his packing and looked at her. "I regret having to leave you behind," he said. "I can't quite understand why I'm making this trip, myself. I know my reputation's probably gone forever but I'm in this thing now and it seems that I've got to see it through."

Mrs. Bailey sat down on the side of the bed. "William," she said, "what would you say if I said I was going with you?"

Professor Bailey dropped his shaving mug on the floor. "Why, I'd say, you're joking!" he said. "You fly in a plane? Why, you're afraid to look down from our attic window."

"Well, I guess, if I have to, I can shut my eyes," said Mrs. Bailey, "because, dear, you're not going on this plane trip alone."

A look of real alarm crossed the Professor's face. "Nellie, you're not well," he said. "Let me call a doctor."

She pulled him down on the bed beside her. "Now, William, calm yourself. It's all been arranged. I'm being paid three hundred and twenty-five dollars a week for making this trip."

It was a good thing Professor Bailey was sitting on the bed. "You're—what?"

"I'm going as Betty's chaperone," she announced.

"Betty!" fairly shouted the Professor. "How does she get into this?"

"Well, she's being paid three hundred dollars a week to go along."

The Professor put a hand to his throbbing head. "But, what for?"

"For Warner Brothers and MGM," she said.

The Professor threw up his hands. "Oh, this is too much! Nellie, I didn't think it was in you!"

"Neither did I," said Mrs. Bailey. "I'm really quite proud of myself."

The normally mild disposition of Professor Bailey was having a great strain placed upon it. "It's a good thing," he said, "that I'm not given to profanity. To think of my wife tying up with a picture company..."

Mrs. Bailey's own dander was up. "That's not any worse than tying up with Numar!" she said.

"Well," said the Professor, forlornly. "This is all quite beyond me. I may as well take things as they come." He looked at her, testily. "But it would help," he said, "if you'd mend this hole in my sock and take this spot off my tie."

Mrs. Bailey hesitated a moment, then picked up the articles mentioned. "I hate to think of doing this on my salary," she said. "But I guess, after all, I'm still your wife..."

THE Sackswell Coffee House Hour was broadcast from Hollywood at five in the afternoon. That meant seven o'clock, Chicago time, and eight p.m. New York time. Its program, starring the popular comedian, Frank Morgan, commanded one of the country's big listening audiences. A standard feature of the show had been presentation of a genuine authority in some business, art or profession who would be introduced to Mr. Morgan after Frank had told an impossible story of his own achievements in this field.

Tonight, the sponsors of Sackswell Coffee were patting themselves on the back. They had secured, on short notice, perhaps the freak attraction of all time. Numar, the man from another planet, was to be interviewed and then introduced to the show's comedian who would carry on from there. Mere newspaper and radio announcements that Numar was to appear on the program had the country by the ears. One didn't have to believe in him to want to hear him speak and to see the fun Frank Morgan would have at his expense. It promised to be an early evening high spot in radio dialing.

Seats for the broadcast were snapped up in no time, and a crowd of several thousand radio fans had gathered outside the broadcasting station in Hollywood an hour before the program was scheduled to go on.

It had been a hectic day for everyone in the Bailey household as preparations had been completed for the trip east, and additional telegrams and telephone calls had been attended to. Chief Andrews had succeeded in keeping Numar under cover although a curious throng milled around and about the Bailey residence, many people still wanting "to be healed."

It was with a feeling of great relief, therefore, that Chief Andrews welcomed the arrival of two big limousines with police escort at four p.m., one from MGM and the other from Warner Brothers studios. Each limousine contained, in addition to the liveried chauffeur, an important, aggressive appearing individual. Talent scouts Sid Alex and Sam Schwartz got out of their company's cars and stood glaring at one another.

"Well," said Sid, "I suppose you think you're going to take Numar in *your* car?"

"I certainly am," said Sam. "It's all been arranged with Mrs. Bailey."

"Nothing doing!" said Sid. "I've arranged everything with Miss Bracken. Besides, I don't trust you with Numar alone."

"And I don't trust you," said Sam. "So, it's mutual!"

"Let's toss a coin," proposed Sid, flipping one in the air. "Heads I win...tails you lose."

"Okay," said Sam. "Toss it again...hey...what did you say? Hold on, there...heads you win—tails *I* win..."

"Well, have it your own way—I was only trying to give you a break. Here we go." Sid threw the coin into the air, caught it deftly and turned it over on the palm of his hand. "Heads, it is. Tough luck, Sam, old boy. Numar rides with me."

"Wait a minute!" Sam reached out quickly and grabbed the coin, turning it over. "You chiseler! It's heads on both sides!"

"Well, what do you know," said Sid, unabashed. "It beats all—what the Treasury is turning out nowadays."

WHILE the two were still arguing, Chief Andrews emerged from the house, breaking a way through the crowd for Numar, with Betty walking brightly by his side, followed by Mrs. Bailey in her Sunday best, with Professor Bailey manfully bringing up the rear as he lugged two suitcases.

Numar hesitated between the two cars.

"This way, Mister Numar," said Sid, bowing in his most ingratiating manner.

"Over here," invited Sam.

Seeing his apparent indecision, the two men ran, as if with one thought, to assist Professor Bailey with his bags.

"Follow me, Professor," said Sid. "You're riding in my car with Mister Numar."

"No, Professor," said Sam, "you and Mister Numar are riding with *me*."

Each talent scout had one of the Professor's bags and raced back to his car with it, opening the door. Betty and Mrs. Bailey were forgotten for the moment. The Professor looked bewildered. Numar took him by the arm.

"Come," he said, "Chief Andrews is waiting." The two of them got in the police car, much to the Chief's astonishment.

"Get in, Miss Bracken," said Sid, dejectedly.

"Get in, Mrs. Bailey," said Sam.

"Get in, Chief," said the Professor, "we can't very well go without you."

Chief Andrews slid behind the wheel. "Will *I* be glad when I get you people out of town," he said.

The strange entourage got under way, led by two motorcycle policemen, who kept their sirens screeching. They were followed by the car with Betty and her MGM representative, Mr. Alex; then the car containing Mrs. Bailey, with her Warner Brothers' representative, Mr. Schwartz.

There were cheers along the way from some interested spectators, most of whom took them for a wedding party. But there was no happy marriage between MGM and Warner Brothers. For Sid and Sam, the honeymoon was over before it had begun. Betty and Mrs. Bailey were the pawns in a move to win big stakes—and Numar, the green man from the planet Talamaya—was the prize.

"WHERE in the sacred name of radio is Frank Morgan?" said Danny Dingle, director of the Sackswell Coffee House radio program. He ran nervous fingers through what remained of his hair and glanced exasperatedly at his wristwatch. Everyone else connected with the show—actors, musicians, announcers, sound effects men, engineers and those too unimportant to mention, were standing by. "He's forty minutes late. That doesn't leave us enough time to rehearse the show before we go on the air."

Danny turned to his secretary who had been trained to stay on his heels at all times.

"Miss Salamander—will you please park your gum for a minute and phone his home again? Try his ranch, his club, and begin on the Hollywood taverns. Maybe Frank's forgotten what day of the week this is."

"Maybe it's the crowd outside," suggested Miss Salamander, rolling her eyes and snapping her gum. "Maybe Mr. Morgan can't get into the station. You know what trouble Mister Numar's party had."

"That's an idea," said Danny. "Get on the loud speaker, somebody— and ask if Frank Morgan is in the crowd. Ye gods, if Frank's out in that mob, he'll be lucky to have any clothes left on him."

The loud speaker outside the building was turned on and an announcer's voice inquired: "Ladies and gentlemen, has anyone seen Frank Morgan? Please pass the word along. We're trying to locate Frank Morgan. Please help us, folks! If Frank Morgan's out there somewhere, he's needed at the studio right away."

There was a traffic jam extending for two blocks in each direction along Sunset Boulevard, from Vine Street.

"Frank Morgan!" went the cry, passed from mouth to mouth. "Anybody seen Frank Morgan?"

"Yes, I see him," said a fat little woman, standing up in her car and pointing. "There he is, over there. I've been seeing him for half and hour. What a thrill! I've never been so close to a Hollywood star in all my life."

The car containing Frank Morgan was surrounded...no...*submerged* by autograph seekers. They were standing on the running boards, sitting on the fenders and hood, and one of them had even climbed into the machine. With traffic at a standstill, this was a field day for them.

"Hey, Frank!" someone shouted. "They're calling for you at the station."

"Tell them to stop calling and do something," said Frank. "If you folks don't move, I can't move. Don't some of you have anything else to do? Don't you work anywhere? Don't you sleep? Are you all from out of town?"

The crowd laughed good-naturedly but nobody moved. They couldn't. The tie-up was up ahead, at the corner of Vine and Sunset.

"Morgan's been found," the announcer reported to Danny Dingle. "He's sitting in his car on Sunset, near Cahuenga."

"Well, tell him to abandon the car and get on up here!" ordered Danny.

"Ladies and gentlemen," appealed the announcer over the loudspeaker. "For those of you who came late, the Green Man is already in our studio. We can't let any more of you in. There isn't room. But it's getting close to our broadcast time and our star, Frank Morgan, still isn't here. He's down at Cahuenga and..."

This was all the further he got. There was a general crushing movement of all on foot in that direction.

"Hey, you people in cars!" cried the announcer. "Give Frank a break! Help the police clear a lane for him. Let him through!"

STANDING at a window overlooking Sunset Boulevard, in a small reception room adjoining the studio, Numar and Professor Bailey had been gazing down upon the scene below. They had been ushered into this room upon arrival and told by Danny Dingle that they would be called when all was ready for rehearsal. It was now a quarter to five and Professor Bailey was getting nervous but Numar showed no signs of concern. The two of them could hear the voice of the announcer as it came out over the loud speaker system, and watch the reaction of the crowd.

"I'm certainly glad we're out of that mob," said the Professor. "It's a frightening thing, Mister Numar, when we human creatures all take a notion we want to see something. Just look at them out there! And to think, you caused all this. Those cars are commencing to move now. I guess, since they've found they can't see you, they're letting Mr. Morgan through...yes...there he comes. Listen to them cheer him! That's the way we Americans are. Let a great scientist or inventor come down the street and he isn't even recognized. I wonder what you must be thinking of us?"

Numar smiled, thoughtfully. "You are creatures of great promise," he said.

Professor Bailey looked at Numar, doubtfully. "You think so?" he asked. "Sometimes, I wonder..."

EIGHT minutes before time for the Sackswell Coffee House Hour to go on the air, a breathless, disheveled Frank Morgan, minus his tie and a shirtsleeve, reached the studio.

"It's hell to be popular, but I love it," he said. Then, looking around he continued, "Where's that Green Man? I could kill the guy..."

"Never mind the Green Man now," said director Danny. "You glue your eyes on this script. You'll barely have time to give it a run-through before we're on. This show isn't timed or anything. I don't know where I'm at. I'm going in and see the Green Man now and get him set. Meet you in the studio. If you have a spare moment, pray for me."

Danny Dingle rushed from the rehearsal room to where he had

Numar and Professor Bailey in waiting. He carried a copy of the script in hand.

"I'm terribly sorry," he said, "but you're such a terrific attraction, Mister Numar...this crowd and everything...we won't have time for rehearsal. You ever been on a radio show before?"

"Not on this planet," said Numar.

"Oh...oh, yes...I forgot. Well, there's not much to it. Your lines are all written for you, Mister Numar. We got our data on you from the papers. I think you'll find it all quite accurate."

Numar took the radio script and turned its pages with his long green fingers.

"I see. My name appears here in several places."

"That's right," directed Danny. "You've caught on. All you do is read what's under your name. Don't read anything else."

"You don't wish me to say anything for myself?" asked Numar.

"Not a word," said Danny. "You'll mess everything up, if you do."

"But what if the words you have written, do not appeal to me?" asked Numar.

Danny pulled out a handful of his own hair. "Well, read it, anyway! You're getting paid for this, Mister Numar. Don't forget that! And you're getting a world of publicity, besides. You can write your own ticket after this. Come on, now. We've just got three minutes. Follow me. We're going out onto the studio stage. Come along, Professor. You can sit in the back."

Danny grabbed Numar by the arm, intending to pilot him. There was a sudden flash and he went skidding across the floor, landing in a sitting position against the wall.

"That damned rug!" he said, jumping up. "Somebody ought to tack it down."

As he reached for Numar's arm again, Professor Bailey stopped him just in time.

It was one minute to five when the harassed director of the Sackswell Coffee House radio program had his cast all assembled on the stage before an overflow studio audience. He took three aspirin tablets and clapped them in his mouth.

"These should be digitalis," he said to himself. "My heart's worse off than my head!"

Seated in the front row, beaming and waving at Numar and also at the Professor, was the girl who had come to crash Hollywood. She sat next to a glowering Sid Alex, who sat next to a contented Mrs. Bailey, who sat next to a glowering Sam Schwartz. The hands of the clock pointed to five p.m. and the red light flashed on.

"Ladies and gentlemen," said the announcer. "What is good till the last drip? One guess...Sackswell Coffee!"

COMMERCIAL statements, in this glorious day of radio, must be endured—but they can be passed over lightly on paper. Suffice it to say that the entertainment part of the program was eagerly awaited. More so, today, than at any other time in the long dripping history of Sackswell Coffee.

"And now, ladies and gentlemen," said announcer Pete Engle. "We have with us tonight—don't laugh—this is on the level...if it isn't, so help me...the most extraordinary, the most phenomenal, by all odds the most sensational celebrity of our time. He's actually standing beside me at this moment. Think of it, ladies and gentlemen—Numar, the Green Man, who has just reached us here after traveling a TRILLION MILES—yes, a TRILLION MILES through space, from the planet Talamaya!"

Numar, under Danny's direction, stood up, with his script, before a microphone. An usher held up a card marked, "Applause" and the goggle-eyed audience beat its palms.

"Well, Mr. Numar," said Pete Ellis, following the script, "I'll bet, after a long journey like that, you were glad to find even the Earth to land upon."

"Yes," read Numar, "This is the longest distance I have ever traveled for a cup of coffee."

"I suppose it would be unfair to ask what brand?" read Pete.

Numar looked up from the script. "Yes, it would," he said.

Pete Ellis looked frightened. Danny Dingle jumped to his feet with gobs of perspiration standing out on his forehead. "I told you to stick to the script!" he whispered excitedly.

"I do not like what is written," said Numar. "It doesn't make sense."

"This program's not supposed to make sense," said Danny, his voice rising. "We had Einstein last week. *He* read what was written. Who do you think *you* are?"

Danny's voice, in his excitement, had carried over the radio and the audience was roaring.

"Well, Mr. Numar, we'll pass on to the next question," adlibbed announcer Pete Ellis, hopefully. He read again from the script. "Now that you're here, what do you think of us?"

"I don't like this answer, either," said Numar.

"You've got to read your lines!" raved Danny, again in an excited whisper. "We can't produce a radio show this way. Give him his cue. He can't go on without the cue!"

A SECOND of silence on the radio is not golden. Every announcer is trained to fill in with something—anything—if things go wrong. If he even starts reciting the alphabet or counting from one to ten, it's better than nothing. Pete Ellis was almost at this stage now. He decided to make one more try to stay with the script.

"Mr. Numar," he read, "we earth people have often wondered—but we've never actually known—when you passed by the moon on your way here, did you notice if it was really made of green cheese?"

Numar laid his script down and stood, unspeaking. The audience howled and so did Danny Dingle but his howl was pitched in a different key.

"All right," said Pete Ellis to Numar, "if you want to play, I'll play, too!" He then tore up his script.

"Get Frank Morgan out here! Get him on the air, quick!" directed Danny. "Throw him his cue, Pete. Never mind Numar!"

"My gosh!" said Pete, groping on the floor through the torn pages. "Where is it?"

Danny handed Pete his own script and pointed with his finger. "There" he said.

The studio audience was rocking and so was the radio audience, from coast to coast.

"That's all very interesting, Mr. Numar," read Pete Ellis. "This has been a most informative interview. It must be wonderful to travel through space the way you do, living only on air and water."

This was Frank Morgan's cue. He came running to his microphone, script in hand.

"What's that, Jockey? Who's been living on air and water? What jail was he in? I usually get bread in mine...whoops! What am I saying? Where have I been? That *is* the question, isn't it? Jockey, I've just returned from the most amazing trip through interstellar space ever undertaken by man or insect. Pete, you may not believe this, but I've had a drink out of the Big Dipper..."

"Oh, Frank! How can you say that?"

"Well, it's written here...whoops! What am I saying?"

"The Big Dipper! Of all the impossible, nonsensical...you didn't even get anywhere near it—"

"I didn't?" said Frank. "But I even milked a cow in the Milky Way."

"Frank...be careful what you're saying. There's a man here who really came from the Milky Way—and you never drank milk in your life."

"Now, Jockey, don't interrupt my story...let's see—where was I? Oh, yes...I passed by Taurus, the Bull, and reached out and twisted his tail. Then I gave Venus a hug and kicked Jupiter in the pants."

"Frank...I'm trying to tell you something...you see that green man over there?"

"Green man?" asked Frank. "Oh, yes...green...what a misfortune. Well, there I was—sailing through space at the rate of a million miles an hour..."

"But, Frank, this Mr. Numar travels at the speed of light! That's one hundred and eighty-six thousand miles a second—or, roughly, six hundred and seventy million miles an hour."

"WHAT? You're joking?" said Frank, eyes glued to his script. "You can't travel that fast on hot air. I know—I've tried it. Jockey, I got so hungry on my trip through space that I stole the Little Bear's porridge—and boy, did he get sore! He called to the Big Bear and said, 'Papa, that naughty man's eaten my porridge! Slap him down when he goes by!' You see this scratch on my face? That's the kind of close call I had."

"Frank, do you mean to stand here and tell us you got that scratch from the Constellation Big Bear?"

"Well, I started from scratch and it's a good bear story, isn't it?"

"Yes—it's the bear story to end all bear stories. Now, Frank, we've had enough of your ridiculous, astronomical flights of fancy. Come down to earth and let us introduce you to a super being who's really been there."

Frank gave his best booming laugh. "Ho, ho, ho! You're such a kidder," he retorted, his eyes still following the script. "He's really *been* there?"

"Yes, Mr. Numar's come here from the planet Talamaya, a trillion miles away."

"A trillion miles!" said Frank. "Oh, yes—a mere trillion...the planet Talamaya...I passed it on my way home."

Numar had remained motionless before the microphone during this banter. He seemed vastly amused. "Mr. Morgan," he said, "it would be interesting to know in what sort of a space vehicle you traveled?"

Morgan stared at his script. He began searching his pages. "I don't see that line," he said, finally. "Where is it?"

Danny Dingle came running up. "Please, Mr. Numar—say what you're supposed to say. Look! Here it is, right here." He put Numar's script back in his hands and pointed to the lines.

Numar disregarded it. "I don't like it," he said, simply.

"You don't like it?" raged Danny, not caring whether the radio

audience heard it or not. "We're paying a gag writer five hundred dollars a week to write those lines!"

"All right," consented Numar. "I'll read the closing words he's written for me. Well, folks—I'm glad to have been here, and as Mae West would say, "Come up and see me some time.""

This was the straw that broke the camel's back, including Danny's. He gave Numar a push and tried to pull the microphone from him at the same time.

There was a blinding flash. Danny did a backward somersault. The audience screamed. There was a short circuit and the radio went dead. Engineers in the control room worked frantically. A quick switch was made to another studio.

"Ladies and gentlemen," an announcer said over the air. "Due to technical difficulties beyond our control, we have been compelled to leave the Sackswell Coffee House program which will be with you at the same time, same station, next week. Remember—Sackswell Coffee is good to the last drip—and we do mean—drip."

CHAPTER NINE

IT WASN'T a long hop to Hollywood for hopping mad Harry Hopper. The Flight Lieutenant had entertained himself by turning his radio on commercial programs. By coincidence, he had tuned in on the Sackswell Coffee House broadcast.

"That's the man I'm after," he said, when he had heard Numar introduced. The program itself may have been funny but it left Betty's boy friend considerably confused. "I can't make the guy out," he said. "He must be a screwball all right."

This is about the opinion that the entire country had of Numar. His unpredictable conduct during the Sackswell Coffee broadcast had everyone guessing. But whatever people thought about him, he had most definitely caught the public fancy and was a lead topic of discussion.

"I don't blame Numar for acting like he did," some people said. "If he really came from another planet, it's disgraceful for us to be treating him like we are."

"Numar's clever all right but it's all a put up job," said the out-and-out skeptics. "He can't fool us! As for that broadcast, the show was written that way."

So the pro and con comments went, everywhere building up more interest in Numar. Who was this Green Man, anyway? And what was he? How could anybody tell—and how could it ever be proved that he'd come from another planet? Regardless of all this, what was the mysterious Green Man going to do next?

In response to the widespread interest, newspapers kept Numar's name and activities in the front page headlines, and photographers still kept on trying to get his picture.

Clifton Fadiman, in New York, after listening to Numar on the Sackswell Coffee program, professed no concern. When queried by news reporters about Numar's coming appearance on *Information, Please*, he said: "Our program is made to order for Mr. Numar, since it is free and unrehearsed. Everyone knows we let our guests say what they choose at all times. Mr. Numar should, therefore, have no difficulty answering our questions in his own words."

In Chicago, Big Hank Morrison, publicity director of the University of Chicago, was tickled.

"Anything Numar does that gets him more publicity is all to the good with us," he said. "It's like a football. You can do more with it when it's inflated. We hope Numar is the sensation of the age when he reaches Chicago. Incidentally—if any of you folks would like to get in Soldiers' Field to see him this coming Saturday, you'd better buy your tickets now. Everything points to a sellout."

LT. HARRY HOPPER decided to set his plane down at the Los Angeles Municipal Airport. It was his intention to grab a cab and make a beeline for Professor Bailey's home in La Canada. He had everything memorized that he planned to say and do.

"I'm going to save her from herself," he said. "No girl can do what she is doing and be in her right mind. She's almost made me lose mine."

Harry came shooting through the pass between the mountains that marked the approach to the airport. He circled the field and looked down. There was a big crowd gathered around an American airliner that was about to take off. Harry could see little figures boarding the plane.

"Most likely some movie star," he thought. "Beats all how their fans will follow them anywhere."

There were no tall chimneys in the vicinity and Harry had nothing to tempt him on the way down. On getting his signal to "come in" he landed at a far end of the airport and turned his plane over to mechanics.

"Just in for a couple days," he said.

"Bed this baby down for the night and give her some oats. I'll be seeing you!"

He ran across the field toward the air depot. As he passed the crowd surrounding the American Airlines plane, his curiosity got the better of him. He couldn't get close to the plane so he stood on tiptoe and craned his neck. He saw a dazzling blonde, standing on the steps leading up to the door of the airliner. She was apparently posing for pictures.

"Who is she?" he asked of those nearby. "I can't make out from here."

"Who is who?" asked a woman. "Who are you talking about?"

"That girl!" pointed Harry. "She looks like Betty Grable!"

"Oh, *her*," said the woman. "I don't know who she is. But that man in the white robes is Numar."

Lieutenant Hopper let out a wild yell and tried to burrow through the crowd. He was repulsed with angry shoves and comments. Looking about, Harry saw an empty baggage truck. He clambered on top of it and began to shout and wave his arms.

"All right, Miss Bracken," said talent scout Alex. "That's all the picture-taking. Hurry up and get aboard. We're the last ones in."

"Oh, wait just a minute!" said Betty. "Who is that nice-looking aviator out there? He seems to be calling to me."

"Get in the plane," said Mr. Alex, "It's already late leaving."

"Oh—but he's waving to me!" said Betty. She lifted her arm and fluttered a handkerchief at the frenzied figure on the truck. "I suppose it's all right to wave back. One has to be nice to the boys in the service."

"Get in that plane before I bop you one!" said Mr. Alex, slightly impatient.

He gave her a push and she got in the plane. Mr. Alex jumped in after her and the door slammed shut.

A porter began pulling the baggage truck upon which an almost deranged flying officer was shouting curses into the air.

"Get off there, boss! I gotta use this right away!" said the porter.

He began trundling the truck in one direction as the plane went the other. It taxied down the runway to its takeoff point. Harry still remained on the moving truck so he could keep the plane in sight. He saw the face of the dazzling blonde pressed against one of the plane windows. Harry shook his fist.

"You can't do this to me!" he shouted. Then, to the porter, "Where's that plane going?"

"New York," said the porter.

Harry made a flying leap off the truck and started running. The mechanics were just wheeling his plane into a hangar.

"Hold everything!" cried Harry. "Gas her up. I'm taking off."

MRS. BAILEY was delighted with the interior of the huge transport plane.

"Why, it's just like a home on wheels," she said. "And what roomy compartments. Do you mean to tell me, Mr. Schwartz, that they turn these into beds when we get up into the air?"

"They sure do," said Warner Brothers' representative. "But if I were you, Mrs. Bailey, I'd fasten that belt around my waist."

"My goodness," said Mrs. Bailey. "What a noise those engines are making! Can't they do something about that?"

"They're tuning them up before taking off," said Mr. Schwartz. "Here, let me help you with your belt."

Professor Bailey sat in the compartment just ahead with Numar. Betty was located across the aisle in the company of talent scout Alex.

"I just love flying," she said. "Oh, Auntie…just wait until you get up in the air! I'm going to try to point out your house to you."

Mrs. Bailey shut her eyes and grasped hold of the seat.

"Don't you suggest such a thing!" she said.

The American Airliner had swung about and the pilot was giving her the gun. The big plane roared down the runway.

"You can open your eyes now," said Mr. Schwartz. "We're off the ground."

"Oh!" said Mrs. Bailey. "You don't mean it—" She ventured a look and shut her eyes again.

"Auntie!" cried Betty, pointing out the window. "There it is…I believe that's your house. No, it must be that other one. Wait…this one looks like…oh, I guess that's not LaCanada at all."

Mrs. Bailey had her eyes half open but was looking straight ahead inside the plane. There was a slight tilting motion as it climbed for altitude. "How soon are we going to reach New York?" she asked.

"Not till tomorrow a.m.," said Mr. Schwartz.

"Oh, Auntie!" called Betty, "they serve the most wonderful dinners on this plane."

"Don't talk to me about food," said Mrs. Bailey. "I've other things on my mind just now."

Numar had been sitting quietly, studying the plane's operation and the changing scenery outside. Professor Bailey was also intensely interested in the flight, but suddenly a strange and troubled expression crossed his face.

"Mister Numar," he said. "I've just had a tremendous thought. In your spaceship, according to our concept of time, traveling at one hundred and eighty-six thousand miles a second—you would be in New York almost before you started! I feel like apologizing to you for our slow rate of travel."

Numar smiled. "In time and space all things are relative," he said. "You will attain greater speed as you find there's a need for it."

"Then you don't object to this snail's pace?" asked the Professor.

"Oh the contrary," said Numar, "I'm enjoying it."

THE American Airliner made two stops en route to New York, one at Dallas, Texas; the other at Nashville, Tennessee. All passengers were snugly in their berths when the big rubber-tired wheels crunched softly to earth at Dallas but a young and impatient flying officer from the United States Army was waiting. He approached the stewardess.

"How long are you stopping here?" he asked.

"Five minutes," she replied.

"Is anyone up in the plane?"

"Yes, sir."

"Is there a chance I could see one of the passengers? It's very urgent."

"Which one?" asked the stewardess.

"Miss Betty Bracken," said the flying officer. "I'm her fiancé."

"Oh yes," said the stewardess. "She's in lower berth four—right hand side. You haven't much time."

"That's okay," said the lieutenant. "I just want to give her a message."

"Right this way," said the stewardess. She led him inside the plane and down the darkened aisle. "Right here," she whispered, and reached inside to touch the sleeping form. "If you'll excuse me—I've got to pick up some supplies." The stewardess tiptoed back down the aisle and left the plane.

The passenger in lower number four had not stirred. Her caller knelt by the berth and then reached in and shook her gently by the shoulder.

"Betty..." he called, in a low voice. "Oh, Betty...this is Harry."

The blonde head turned on the pillow, but she did not waken.

Outside came the telltale sounds that the plane monkeys, the men who checked her over at each landing, were about to release her for further flight. Harry shook Betty more urgently.

"Sweetheart!" he said. "Wake up! It's me—Harry."

Betty came awake. She saw a hand through the curtain, touching her shoulder, and sat upright.

"Help!" she screamed. "Help, somebody! Help!"

"Shut up!" cried Harry. "For gosh sake, shut up!"

HEADS began to pop out of berths. Mr. Alex leaned out from his upper and konked the head of the man in uniform with his shoe.

"Ouch!" said Harry. As he stood up.

Mr. Schwartz, from the other side of the aisle, jabbed him in the face with his bare foot.

"Help!" Betty kept screaming.

Harry did not stop to deliver his message. He got out of the plane and cut across the field to his own ship.

"Betty!" called Mrs. Bailey, "what on earth...?"

"Oh, Auntie!" cried her niece, "I've just had a frightful experience."

"There was a man here to see you," said the returning stewardess.

"To see me?" asked Betty. "He almost scared me to death. Where did he go?"

"He left the plane. I'm sorry I let him disturb you. He said it was important."

"Why, the very idea. What did he look like?"

"He was an army pilot."

"He was?" said Betty. "Oh...well then maybe I know. Do you suppose? Yes, it must have been..."

"Must have been who?" asked talent scout Alex.

"That nice-looking soldier I waved at when we left Los Angeles," said Betty. "My goodness! It just goes to show you've got to be careful who you encourage these days."

"He said he was your fiancé," said the stewardess.

"Well, naturally," said Betty. "He'd say anything to get in the plane. My fiancé...now, who could that be?"

THE night flight was uneventful after the passengers had once settled down from this scare of Betty's. Professor Bailey stayed awake until the early dawn hours, lying in his berth and looking up at the entrancing patchwork of his beloved stars, many of which he knew by name. Every once in a while he would take hold of his flesh between his thumb and forefinger and pinch it hard.

"I suppose I'll be black and blue in the morning," he said to himself. "But it still seems incredible to me that I could be going through an experience like this. My, this plane must be making over two hundred miles an hour! That seems awfully fast to me. It's wonderful to be up here with the feeling you get that you're so near the sky. I can only imagine the sensation Numar feels as he whizzes through space! When he passes a planet, it would seem to be standing still, although we know our sun is rushing through space, taking our whole solar system with it, at the rate of seven hundred miles a minute! I wonder where all these universes are going—and why?"

Professor Bailey reminded himself that it was questions like these he wished to ask Numar when and if they could find some quiet place of solitude on earth.

Mrs. Bailey had overcome some of her early misgivings about being up in a plane and, since the night was clear and the air smooth, she had enjoyed a good sleep.

"Where are we now?" she asked Mr. Schwartz, when she had risen in the morning, astonished to find an appetite for breakfast.

"About an hour out of New York," said Warner Brothers' representative. "Why? Are you thinking of getting out?"

"My, no," said Mrs. Bailey. "I'm only sorry this trip's so near an end. Why, I felt more comfortable in that berth than in my bed at home...that is, except for that time in the night when we took that awful drop."

"You mean—when we hit that air pocket?" asked Mr. Schwartz.

"Oh, is that what you call it?" said Mrs. Bailey. "Well, why doesn't the pilot watch out for those places in the air and go around them like a bump in the road?"

Mr. Schwartz smothered a smile. "That's an idea," he said. "Why don't you suggest it to him?"

"I'll do it," said Mrs. Bailey, "the very first chance I get..."

IT WAS Betty who saw the other plane first. It had the insignia of the United States Army upon it. The airliner was passing through clusters of fleecy clouds that seemed to blow away in the breeze of the propellers. This little plane kept bobbing up and down, coming closer and closer. Betty watched it with increasing fascination.

"Oh, look!" she exclaimed. "I do believe the pilot's waving at me!"

The plane had an open cockpit so the figure of the pilot could be plainly seen behind the cowling.

"Now, Betty," said Mrs. Bailey, "do control yourself. You have much too vivid an imagination."

"No, Auntie! I'm not imagining things!" cried Betty, excitedly. "The pilot is waving! Oh, Auntie, get out your field glasses and let me have a good look at him."

"For gracious sake!" said Mrs. Bailey, fumbling inside her bag. "Here they are, child."

Betty took the glasses and adjusted them. She had now attracted the attention of everyone on the plane and passengers on the other side were standing in the aisle, staring out.

As the army plane came close and stayed alongside for a moment, Betty let out a shriek. "Why, Auntie...it's Harry...well, what do you know. Why, of course…why didn't I think of him before? Look at him wave. Oh! Did you see his plane wobble? Harry, be careful!" Betty waved against the windowpane. "He sees me, too! Oh…that's wonderful. Auntie, isn't this romantic?"

The army plane swerved as both planes hit an air pocket and almost came together. The copilot of the airliner came down the aisle.

"Who is that fool out there?" he demanded. "What's he think he's doing?"

"He's signaling to me," said Betty. "It's sign language we learned when we were going together in New York." She had her eyes fixed on the figure in the army plane, trying to make out his semaphore movements. "Sorry, Harry. You'll have to do it over," she said, shaking her head and gesturing. "I didn't get it."

THE figure in the other plane took his hands off the controls and began the motions again, just as they went into a cloud.

"Oh, that's too bad," said Betty, and turned to the copilot. "Can't you please keep this plane out of the clouds for a few minutes? I can't see what he's saying."

"Young lady," said the copilot. "This isn't any time or place for wig-wagging. You come away from that window before that dizzy Romeo runs into us or goes into a tailspin! He'll get demoted for this."

"Demoted?" asked Betty. "A man who can fly like that? Just a minute now. I'm getting it. Don't move the plane…hold it still…keep close to him…a little closer…he's spelling it out for me…here it is… *w-a-i-t- t-i-l-l I g-e-t y-o-u a-l-o-n-e.*"

"If that's a threat, I'm in favor of it," said the copilot.

Betty made an answering gesture. "I can't imagine what he means but I've signaled to him 'message received', anyway. Oh…look at that…"

The army pilot had pulled up in a sharp climb and was looping the loop. He was soon lost to sight.

"Now, Betty," said Mrs. Bailey, "perhaps you can take time to tell me who this man Harry is…"

"Oh, Auntie," said Betty. "I feel so humiliated! He must have been the one who called on me in the plane last night. The poor boy…to think I treated him like I did…"

"I should have hit him harder with my shoe," said Mr. Alex.

"I almost broke a toe on him," said Mr. Schwartz. "But I wish I'd laid him out. The sky isn't safe with a guy like that on the loose."

"Oh, Nellie!" called Professor Bailey, excitedly. "Look…look out your window! There's New York down there!"

LA GUARDIA Airport was agog with excitement. As the terminal for scores of incoming and outgoing celebrities, it had always attracted crowds of sightseers. But this morning a city of twenty-five thousand population had transported itself to the airport by subway, automobile and bus line. These citizens from every walk and run of life were not there to welcome Eleanor Roosevelt or Mahatma Gandhi. They were there to see and to greet the mysterious Green Man who had temporarily displaced war, politics, domestic troubles and the weather as subjects of discussion. Several hundred of New York's finest had been rushed to the airport to protect the runways from invasion and the bulging crowd had been, temporarily at least, successfully roped off.

A welcoming committee was anxiously waiting. Prominent among the welcomers was, of course, the distinguished intellectual, Clifton Fadiman, of *Information, Please* fame. Standing beside him and looking wistfully up at him was the man after whom this great airport had been named—His Honor, Mayor Fiorella "Little Flower" LaGuardia.

"Isn't it a fine morning?" he said, squinting at the sky.

"I don't answer questions," said Mr. Fadiman. "I *ask* them."

Behind these two solid citizens was arrayed the greatest battery of hard-boiled reporters and photographers ever assembled for any event anywhere. To say that they were "loaded for bear" would be a gross understatement. The photographers had been ordered to get a picture of Numar on their film negatives—or else. The reporters, feature writers, columnists and other members of the writing profession too ornery to classify, had been instructed to get under Numar's green skin and get the everlasting low-down on him.

All the world's best fakirs had headed for New York sooner or later. They might be able to fool the natives out in Oshkosh, Podunk or even Los Angeles, but when a pretender ran up against the sophistication of New York City, he was soon as unveiled as Gypsy Rose Lee.

A few of the Big Town's smartest literati stood off from the pack and put their intellects together. In this group was Walter Winchell, dean of all newspaper pundits, who knew what everyone was going to do before they did it. Then there was the venerable H. V. Kaltenborn, dean of every American foreign correspondent since the Civil War.

"I tell you, Walter," said Mr. Kaltenborn, clipping each word as though he were chipping a diamond, "we must treat this situation with the utmost sagacity. It is not for us to turn back now. We must not permit ourselves to be out-flanked by a sly maneuver on the part of this green invader. We should hem him in on all sides and demand to know how he stands on our foreign policy."

DOROTHY THOMPSON, dean of all she surveys, which was considerable, edged herself into the conversation.

"It is the moral aspect that concerns me," she said. "If Numar is an imposter, and if he is not speedily exposed, the ethical repercussions of this monstrous fraud are apt to reach down to the very roots of our civilization. I think, therefore, that Mr. Numar should be called upon to state unequivocally his position in this matter and to furnish unassailable proof as to his identification and purposes on this planet."

"If he doesn't, I will," said Winchell. "I just had a tip that his name's really Izzy Zwankenstein of Brooklyn, and that he fell in a vat of green dye at a chemical works. My informants state that he was taught a few tricks by a broken-down magician who has joined forces with him in an attempt to gain fame and fortune. I hope to have more information on this case before I go to press tonight, but—first—I'm giving Mr. Numar a chance to come clean with the inside story, himself. If he doesn't, I'll turn him over to the FBI."

There was a sudden shout from the crowd and thousands of faces turned upward as the American Airliner was seen circling the field. High above it was an army pursuit plane, which seemed to hover protectingly. As the airliner came down on the runway and started taxiing to the unloading platform, this army plane dipped low over the field and then landed on an outside runway.

"Looks like the army's after Numar," said Winchell. "I'll have to make a note of that. Maybe he's a draft evader."

Inside the airliner, all was a flurry of excitement.

"My, but we took a dip coming in," said Mrs. Bailey. "William, is my hat on straight?"

"I can't tell you, Nellie," said the Professor. "I'm still dizzy myself."

THE two talent scouts nudged one another.

"Jeez," said Sid, glancing out a window. "Just look at that crowd—it's a publicity man's dream."

"Have you talked business with Numar yet?" asked Sam.

"How could I?" said Sid, "with you watching me all the time?"

"I dropped to sleep for five minutes last night," said Sam. "What were you doing then?"

"That must have been the same time I fell asleep," said Sid. "What were you doing?"

Betty was primping like mad, if not madder. She emerged from the ladies lounge, dressed for her public. Talent scout Alex caught the first glimpse of her.

"Good God!" he said, grabbing Sam's arm. "Do you see what I see?"

Sam ventured a look. "I don't think Numar's going to like that," he said.

Betty was wearing a gay little green hat over one ear and half of one eye. She was attired in a gray suit that had been closely riveted to her curves. Her shoes were green and her pocketbook was green. But the eye-stopping thing about her was her makeup. Each cheek was delicately highlighted in green and she winked at her two flabbergasted observers from beneath drooping green eyelashes. Then she puckered up her green lips and blew them a kiss with expressive green-lacquered fingertips.

"Mrs. Bailey," said Mr. Alex, swallowing his gum. "Will you please take a look at your niece?"

Mrs. Bailey, who had been waiting for the line of passengers in front of her to move out of the plane so she could catch her first terra firma glimpse of New York, turned about.

"Hello, Auntie," said Betty, and flashed a green Mona Lisa smile.

Mrs. Bailey took one look and slumped in a half-faint in the aisle.

"Why, Auntie," said Betty, "what's the matter? Don't you like it? I think it's very appropriate for the occasion."

PROFESSOR BAILEY glanced worriedly at Numar, who was last in line and who had been quietly observing Betty's fearful yet wonderful composition.

"I don't know who ever gave her that idea," said the Professor. "I hope you don't mind too much. I think, myself, it's far too theatric. It may give the people a wrong impression of you."

Numar shook his head. "You do not need to be concerned about me," he said. "I would say she has quite a dramatic sense."

The passengers had begun to move out of the plane and it was time for Numar's party to make its exit.

"Don't you think if I came out last, it would be more effective?" suggested Betty.

"She's stealing scenes already," said Sam, "and she hasn't even been in pictures yet. That's a sure sign she's going to be a star."

"Yeah," said Sid, dryly. "Only trouble is, we'll have to be shooting her in Technicolor." Then, to Betty, he said, "You can't get top billing on this tour, Baby. You're lucky to be along for the ride. So, you be a good girl and listen to your Uncle Sid. Stick with me and you're certain to wear phony diamonds."

Mrs. Bailey was the first out. Sight of the tremendous throng behind the ropes almost brought on another near-fainting spell. She leaned on the arm of Mr. Schwartz for support. At least fifty cameramen had their lenses aimed at her. Off to one side, newsreel men were assembled in a semi-circle. In front of them was the welcoming committee. Mayor LaGuardia was moistening his lips and getting ready for action. Clifton Fadiman straightened his tie, removed an imaginary hair from his coat lapel, and said, "ahem" several times. Both men looked toward the plane, expectantly.

Next to appear in the plane's doorway was something entirely unannounced. Those within eye-view gasped in unbelieving astonishment.

"Who's that?" said a man, "Numar's wife?"

The feminine bundle in green smiled and took a bow. Flashlight bulbs exploded. Mayor LaGuardia and Mr. Fadiman looked questioningly at one another.

"Is this one of Numar's party?" asked Mr. Fadiman.

"You'd better ask someone on *Information, Please*," said the mayor. "I don't answer questions for a living."

Talent scout Alex gave Betty a shove from behind. "Get moving, Baby," he said. "Don't wear out your welcome!"

"Oh!" said Betty, pointing. "Are those the official greeters over there?"

"That's them," Mr. Alex.

Betty started forward, face beaming. "Oh, Mr. Mayor…how do you do? I've read lots about you. You look just like your pictures—maybe just a pound or two heavier."

There was no escape for the Mayor. She had seized his hand and was pumping it. "You look like somebody," he said. "Who are you?"

"Why, Mr. Mayor!" exclaimed Betty. "Hasn't anyone told you? I'm Professor Bailey's niece and he's the man Mr. Numar's staying with—and I'm under contract to MGM."

Betty had given the crowd something to look at and it was looking. Even blase New York had never seen a golden-haired blonde with glistening lips and fingernails of green.

SHE turned to an uncomfortable Clifton Fadiman. "Oh, aren't you the man who writes the Encyclopedia Britannica?" she asked, extending her hand. "I just love brainy men—they're so intelligent."

"This is an unexpected pleasure," said Mr. Fadiman. "Very unexpected."

His eyes went from Betty to the plane entrance where a figure who was really green was stepping out. Numar was an impressive sight in the morning sun as he stood in his simple white robes and turban, a friendly smile on his green countenance. Betty lost her limelight at that moment.

Cameramen made a rush for Numar and began shooting at him from all angles. Professor Bailey, exiting somewhat shyly from the plane, kept to the background and crept around to stand beside his wife, where they watched proceedings.

"What are we going to do with Betty?" he whispered in her ear.

"Don't ask me!" said Mrs. Bailey. "I can't even bear to look at her."

Police were having their difficulties with the crowd as men and women pulled and shoved, trying to get a better glimpse of the mysterious green man. Numar now was being directed toward the welcoming committee. He motioned to Professor Bailey to join him.

"Might I suggest," ventured the Professor, in a low voice. "Your electric power...have you turned it off?"

"Oh, yes," said Numar. "Thank you for reminding me."

Mayor LaGuardia advanced with hand outstretched. As the two shook hands, the newsreel cameras went into action to record what might prove to be an historic event.

"Mr. Numar," said the Little Flower, in a voice that trembled with emotion. "As Mayor of this great City of New York, which contains more Italians than Rome, more Irish than Dublin, more Germans than Bremen, and one-fifth of all the Jews in the world, I take pleasure in welcoming you, the first foreigner to visit us from another planet..."

Before the interplanetary visitor could make answer, Clifton Fadiman stepped forward.

"Mr. Numar," he said, in a voice rich with culture. "We, my sponsors—the Fifty-Seven Varieties—and the thinking people of this country, including myself, deeply appreciate your having come a *trillion* miles to appear on the *Information, Please* program."

NUMAR bowed in acknowledgment but said nothing, as the cameras kept on grinding. Mr. Fadiman then turned and shook hands with Professor Bailey. He was followed by the Mayor.

In the next instant, Numar was surrounded by a fearsome mob of highly trained inquisitors, the reporters. Their tongues and pencils had been sharpened for the encounter and questions flew at the Green Man from all sides with the bewildering ferocity of a robot bombing attack. They didn't care where they hit him or how often. If Numar's elaborate and clever defenses could be broken and he could be put to rout, they were going to do it. It was an all out assault, which had never failed to make any previous artful deceiver break and run for cover.

But, after an intensive half-hour barrage, the Green Man was still standing, unmoved, despite all charges and thrusts. His answers were direct and to the point. They were unable to shake his story. He was on a tour through the universe and had stopped off on Earth to deliver a message. No, he would give no inkling of what that message was to be. They would have to wait until his address between halves of the football game in Chicago. Where was he going from here? To another planet which was in about the same state of undevelopment. Beyond that, he would not go. There was no evidence of any attempt at evasiveness but the statements Numar made could, unfortunately, not be judged by any human standards or verified.

Finally Walter Winchell, the greatest runner-downer of higher-uppers, stepped to the front. "We're not getting anywhere this way," he said. "Will you boys and girls let me go to work on him?"

"Go to it!" chorused a baffled newspaper fraternity.

"All right, Mr. Numar," said Winchell. "You've had us all up in the ethereal regions. Let's get down on earth where we all live. What do you know about Brooklyn?"

"Brooklyn?" questioned Numar. "What is that?"

"That's the home of the Brooklyn Dodgers," said Winchell. "Also the home of Izzy Zwankenstein. Do you remember him?"

Numar shook his head. Winchell consulted his notes.

"Were you ever employed in a chemical works?"

Again Numar shook his head.

"All right, now. Think hard on this one. Did you ever fall into a vat of green dye?"

For the first time since Professor Bailey had been in Numar's company, the Green Man laughed out loud.

"You human creatures are very amusing," he said.

Winchell tore up his notes and threw them on the ground.

"Just a minute; Walter," called Mr. O'Neill, science editor of the Herald-Tribune. "Ask Mr. Numar if he'll give us a demonstration of his electrical powers."

THE Mirror's little boy, Walter, gave Numar a dubious look. "Well, Mr. Zwankenstein, what do you say to that?"

"Select one of your number," invited Numar, agreeably. "I shall be glad to cooperate."

"Good heavens!" said Professor Bailey. "Here it comes again."

"I was kissed by him once," said Betty, who was standing beside the Mayor. "It was a great experience."

"It must have been," said the Mayor, eyeing her.

"I can't quite make him out," said Mr. Fadiman.

"Oh, you needn't feel badly about that," said Betty. "Neither can anybody else."

New York's smartest literati had gone into a huddle. H. V. Kaltenborn was speaking.

"No, Walter. I really must decline. I think this honor should go to you. Your Hooper rating is higher than mine."

Mrs. Winchell's bad little boy, Walter, was not so easily swayed. "Why not observe the good old American custom of women first?" he proposed, "and let Dorothy touch him."

"How long since women have been first in this country?" said Miss Thompson. "No, Walter, dear, you're the Number One Investigator of the newspaper profession. You're elected."

Spectators, who could get a view of what was going on, passed the news along to others who could not see. Numar was standing in an open area and was actually visible to quite a number. The reporters, however, now pressed forward to more closely observe the experiment.

"I suggest," said Numar, "that the rest of you stand back..."

WINCHELL'S collar had suddenly become too tight. He loosened his tie. There was perspiration on his forehead.

"My hands are rather moist," he said. "Will that make any difference?"

"It should help," said Numar.

Winchell dried his hands on his handkerchief.

"Now what shall I do?" he asked.

"Suppose you shake hands with me," directed Numar.

"What can I lose?" said Winchell, and held out his hand.

There was a flash, but it wasn't the kind Walter Winchell usually gave to the world. He was getting this flash exclusively from Numar.

"Looks like he's jitterbugging," said the Mayor.

It only lasted a few seconds and the country's leading *scoopolumnist* was picking himself up off the ground.

"Would anyone else like to...?" suggested Numar, pleasantly.

"No, we'll take Walter's word for it," said a cautious scribe from New York Times.

"You will?" said Winchell, dusting himself off. "What a change in policy." Then, turning to all assembled and raising his voice, he declared:

"I haven't any word for it, except to say that I'm reporting this man to J. Edgar Hoover for carrying concealed weapons."

This broke up the newspaper interview and Winchell was now surrounded by his curious fellow writers who sought to get from him just how it had felt to touch the Green Man.

"Touch him, yourselves, and find out," said Winchell. "Or else read about it tomorrow morning in the *Daily Mirror*."

Mr. Fadiman and the Mayor now approached Numar but stood at a respectful distance.

"The Mayor and I have arranged," said the interrogator of *Information, Please*, "to show you some of the sights of New York."

Numar smiled. "I shall be glad to accompany you," he said.

The Mayor looked around at the other members of Numar's party, including Mr. Alex and Mr. Schwartz.

"I'm sorry," he apologized. "I have only one city car here. Had I known there were to be so many of you…"

"Oh, that's" perfectly all right," said Betty, helpfully. "These two gentlemen here," indicating Mr. Alex and Mr. Schwartz, are just picture people. They won't mind taking the subway."

"Not at all," said Mr. Alex, glancing about at the crowd. "Especially when this mob starts getting out of here."

"You said it," chimed Mr. Schwartz. "They claim it's the longest ride in the world for a nickel. Brother, they're sure right."

"Well, then," said Betty, airily, "you can get a taxi—that is, if you can find one." Then she turned to the Mayor as she counted each one off on her fingers. "Now, that just leaves you and Mr. Britannica…and Mr. Numar…and Mr. and Mrs. Bailey—and myself. That makes six. How big is your car?"

"It holds five," said the Mayor.

"Why, that's just right," said Betty. "There'll be plenty of room. I'll sit on your lap!"

THE Mayor gave an uneasy sidewise glance at the photographers. "I'm afraid you won't be very comfortable."

"Oh, don't you mind about me," said Betty. "You just think of yourself."

The Mayor looked like a candidate who was being defeated for office.

It was a block's walk to his chauffeured car and it was while covering this distance that most of the tremendous crowd tried to get a look at Numar personally. They broke through the police lines and surged about. Various cries went up.

"Say, he's green all right. Look at that dame with him. Boy…is she a sight! Officer, let me through. I'm an astrologer. I've got to talk to Numar…please, my leetle boy, he's seek. I want for Numar just to touch…"

Despite all entreaties, the police fought back the crowd and delivered the Green Man and his party to the Mayor's car, untrampled and untouched. But, far on the outskirts of the throng, making frenzied efforts to get through, was a young flying officer. Finally he appealed to one of New York's finest.

"I'm in a terrible jam," he said.

"Who isn't?" said the big Irish copper, holding back at least a hundred squirming arms and legs.

"I don't mean the crowd, I mean my girl!" said Harry.

"Domestic trouble, eh? Well, I can't settle that. You'd better see the judge."

"You don't understand," cried Harry, in desperation. "She's getting away from me!"

"If she's in this crowd," said the copper, "she can't get away from anybody."

"But she's with that guy Numar!" yelled Harry. "And I've got to get through to her."

"Well, why didn't you say so?" said the copper. "Crawl under this rope. You'll have to hurry. She's just about leavin' in the Mayor's car now."

MR. ALEX and Mr. Schwartz stood forlornly and wistfully by as the rest of Numar's party climbed into the Mayor's open limousine.

"I'm not used to this kind of treatment," said Mr. Alex. "If I don't land Numar, it won't be worth it."

"The same goes for me," said Sam. "But that bird Numar—he gets bigger every minute. He's got New York City right where he wants it."

Betty, last in the car, had waited for the Mayor to seat himself. She now noticed an extra space beside the chauffeur in front. Her face brightened with a new idea.

"Yoo hoo! Oh, Mr. Alex…Mr. Schwartz…I've found a place for you after all. Do you mind sitting up front with the driver?"

"I'd ride on the roof to get out of this crowd," said talent scout Alex.

"I'd even sit on the chauffeur's lap," said Sam.

The two men lost no time in following Betty's suggestion.

"You know," Sid confided to Sam, "she may be slightly screwy, but she's not such a bad sort after all."

"I don't know which is worse," said Sam. "That Mrs. Bailey would talk an arm off the Venus de Milo."

Betty, still standing in the back of the car, looked about her to see if anything else needed supervising.

"Better get moving," urged a police captain. "We can't hold this crowd back much longer."

Just at that moment, the handsome but somewhat ruffled form of a young flight lieutenant burst through the wall of spectators. In front of him was a circle of photographers, aiming their cameras at the car as it started to pull away.

"Betty!" he cried. "Wait for me...Betty!"

"Are you comfy, Mr. Mayor?" asked Betty. "Here I come." She plopped herself down upon his lap.

"Betty!" cried an anguished voice, and then, for the first time, Harry Hopper got a full front view of the girl of his dreams. His eyes almost left their sockets. "Good gosh almighty!" he said.

In that instant, Betty saw and recognized him.

"Harry!" she screamed, and stood up again. "Oh, Harry! Quick—catch on the back here! Come on! There's room for one more..."

But the car was now picking up speed and the crowd broke ranks behind it, swallowing Harry up in its midst.

Betty sank back down upon the Mayor's knee.

"Was that someone you knew?" he asked.

"Well, yes, slightly," said Betty. "He was my fiancé."

CHAPTER TEN

IT WAS natural and proper that the world's first interplanetary visitor should be taken to one of the Earth's finest hotels. The Waldorf-Astoria, at Fiftieth and Park Avenue, New York, had long been so recognized. It had swank in the quiet but expensive manner. Those desirous of making the right impression on business acquaintances, friends or poor relations always carried away silverware bearing the famous Waldorf monogram. Today, there is an increasing number who, having completed sets for themselves, are working on sets for their grandchildren. No greater proof of a hotel's distinction may be cited than this. And, no celebrity from any land would think of stopping anywhere else than at the Waldorf, or at least making sure that he or she was seen there.

When the whine of police motorcycle sirens announced the arrival of the Mayor's car at the main entrance of the Waldorf, the noon luncheon crowds stopped to gape and wonder. Who was the green gold blonde on the Mayor's lap? There was the Green Man—well what do you know. And there was Mr. Fadiman, famed conductor of *Information, Please.* That must be Professor Bailey and his wife. And those two men, in the front seat with the chauffeur, must be detectives attached to the Mayor's strong-arm squad. A load of real big shots—what a break to see them this way.

In no time at all, the car was surrounded. Once more it was a job for police to clear the way as Numar and his party entered the hotel. News had reached the manager that these distinguished guests were in the lobby and he met them at the head of the stairs to escort them personally to his private office, where he brought out a special registry for celebrities.

"Will you honor us by signing this?" he requested of Numar, "I think I may safely say," he continued, proudly, "that this guest book contains the signatures of all of the world's great, dating well back before the turn of the century." He dipped his pen in the ink and handed it to Numar, then thought better of it and took it back. "Just a moment," he said. "You shouldn't sign it this way. I want your signature in green ink…" He reached in a drawer of his desk and produced a bottle, then wiped off the pen point and dipped it in. "Now, Mr. Numar, if you will, please."

NUMAR smiled, and with all in the party watching, inscribed his name in flowing, graceful style. He hesitated momentarily, and then wrote after his name:

"Resident, Planet Talamaya

Of the Constellation Universa…"

"So that's your address," said Betty, looking over his shoulder. "My, if you ever jumped a hotel bill, they'd have a hard time reaching you."

"I could not pay even now," said Numar, "since we have no currency on my planet you would recognize here."

"Oh, well," said Betty, "I'm sure that Mr. Britannica or the Mayor or somebody…"

"Of course," said Mr. Fadiman. "Mr. Numar understands he is the guest of *Information, Please.*" Then, directing his remarks to the manager, he added, "We will need some extra accommodations for this young lady and Professor Bailey's wife."

"Oh no you won't," said Mr. Alex, stepping forward. "MGM is taking care of Miss Bracken."

"And Warner Brothers are taking care of Mrs. Bailey," said Mr. Schwartz. "Just charge it to our companies."

Mr. Fadiman looked relieved. "Well, if you gentlemen insist," he said.

"I'll show you to your suites," offered the manager. "But, first, Mr. Numar—it's our publicity director's suggestion—would you mind posing for a picture with Oscar, our chef? We'd like to get a photograph of you holding our bill of fare and giving him your order. Then we'll publish it with the caption: 'Oscar of the Waldorf, serving Numar, man from another planet, the best meal on earth.'"

Numar smiled. "It's an interesting idea," he said, "but it so happens that I eat no food."

"He has no stomach," said Professor Bailey, helpfully.

"No stomach!" said the manager, startled.

"He lives on distilled water," said the Professor.

"Oh," said the manager, quite dazed and crestfallen, "I'm sorry to hear that. No stomach eh? Well, well. I've heard of those operations. But how in heaven's name do you live on distilled water?"

"It's the way he's made," said the Professor. "He had no operation."

A frightened look came over the manager's face. "I'll get the keys to your suites," he said. "Thank you just the same, Mr. Numar. Thank you very much." He started backing away, then he whispered to himself, "No stomach. Wait till I tell Oscar."

PROFESSOR BAILEY, as Numar's host, was assigned to the same suite with the Green Man while Mrs. Bailey, traveling under the delusion she was Betty's chaperone, paired with her. The two suites were situated across the hall from one another on a top floor. They were the first and last word in elegance, so there remained nothing for Mrs. Bailey to say about them. All she could do was gasp her amazement and go around, exclaiming, "Well, I never!" to Mr. Schwartz, however, she did remark: "This must be costing your company a pretty penny." His reply had not reassured her. "Don't worry—before we're through with you, we'll get it back some way."

The Professor, Mrs. Bailey and Betty were guests of the Mayor and Mr. Fadiman for lunch in the Green Room of the Waldorf, but the Green Man remained in his suite and sipped his distilled water. His appearance in a public eating place, stomach or no stomach, would have upset too many digestive tracts and disrupted the dining service.

"I can see right now," said the Mayor, "that it's going to be a problem showing Mr. Numar the city."

"Quite," said Mr. Fadiman, in a masterpiece of understatement.

The representatives of MGM and Warner Brothers had taken a suite for themselves on the same floor so that they might watch each other more easily.

"We've both got a stake in this thing," Sid said, "so why should we cut each other's throats—until we have to?"

"Sure," said Sam. "We might as well work together till one of us gets Numar. But if he won't let himself be photographed, he's not going to be much good for pictures."

"Not unless they shoot him as the invisible man," said Sid. "I've already listed that title with the Will Hays Office, so you can't beat me there."

The two men had arranged to have all telephone calls routed into their suite since neither Numar nor Professor Bailey were interested in anything but the primary purpose for which they had come to New York.

"If we can line up enough big offers between us," said Sam, "we ought to break this Numar down somehow. He's got the world by the tail now. I can't figure what else he wants."

"Well—you know these performers," said Sid. "Their egos are always bigger than their bankroll. I'll bet that guy never dreamed, when he started out with this stunt, that he'd be a sensation like this."

"Maybe he's gone so far he's afraid to stop," said Sam. "Or else he's begun to believe he's from another planet himself."

"I don't know," said Sid. "All I know is—he's terrific box office."

THE telephone began to ring and both men jumped for it.

"It's my turn," said Sid.

"I hope it's a wrong number," said Sam.

Sid shifted his cigar to a far corner of his mouth and answered the phone.

"Begin the conversation," he said. He waited a moment, listening intently, as Sam watched him with a hawk-like expression. "Is that so?" said Sid, into the phone. "Is that so? *Is that so?*"

"Is *what* so?" demanded Sam.

Sid motioned for silence and covered the mouthpiece with his hand. "There's a soldier in the lobby who says he's engaged to Miss Bracken. He sounds…to me…like he's tight. He says he's got to see her right away or he's going to tear down the hotel."

"Is that so?" said Sam. "Well, what are you going to tell him?" Miss Bracken is *your* department."

"I'm gonna invite him up," said Sid. Then, into the phone, "Miss Bracken isn't here just now but I'm her representative. Would you like to see *me?*"

There was a sudden sharp click on the phone.

"He would, very much!" said Sid.

"Do you suppose it's that crazy guy who's been following us from Hollywood?" said Sam.

"I don't know," said Sid, "but I'm sure as hell going to find out."

There was a rap on the door that almost split the panels.

"Two to one, it's him," said Sam, getting up and retreating toward an inner room. "Well, goodbye. I'll be seeing you."

"You stick around," urged Sid. "It sounds like I'll be needing you."

He went to the door, slipped the lock, and pulled it open. The husky form of a fiery-eyed flight lieutenant strode in.

"What have you done with her? Where is she?" he demanded. "Who are you?"

"I," said Sid, "am Mr. Alex of MGM Pictures."

"And who is he?" said the irate figure, pointing at Sam.

"That's Mr. Schwartz of Warner Brothers," said Sid, "an old pal of mine."

Sam glared.

"And now," said Sid, his voice dripping with syrup, "Who might you be?"

"I," said the caller, "am Harry Hopper. I've come here to bust this guy Numar in the nose and take Miss Bracken back with me."

"Is that so?" said Sid, giving a sidewise glance at Sam.

"That's very interesting," said Sam. "Do you have an option on her?"

"OPTION!" raged Harry. "Why, I'm going to marry her!"

"Now, sit down, my good fellow," said Sid. "Have a cigar. Take the weight off your heels. I believe we've met before."

"Never saw you before in my life," said Harry.

"But I've seen you," said Sid. "I saw you first when you so touchingly waved farewell to Miss Bracken in Hollywood. I saw you a second time and helped 'shoo' you out of the plane at Dallas. I saw you next when you damned near wrecked the plane I was on. I saw you again when you bucked the crowd at LaGuardia Airport and almost made a touchdown! And I'm seeing you now!"

"All right, all right!" broke in Harry. "So, you've seen me. But what I want is to see Betty."

"Sorry, my friend," said Sid. "She's all booked up."

"Now, listen!" Harry's attitude became pugnacious. "I haven't flown across this country for nothing. My girl's making a damn fool of herself and I'm going to put a stop to it."

"Not while she's under contract to MGM," said Sid.

"We'll see about that," said Harry. "I've got *some* rights around here. And another thing—who's responsible for that green getup of hers?"

"Not me," said Sid.

"Are you sure?" demanded Harry, eyeing him, suspiciously.

Sid backed away. "Positive. That was her own idea."

"If it was," said Harry, "it just goes to show what you've done to her. You picture guys are a bad influence." He looked wildly about the room. "Don't tell me," he said, "that Miss Bracken is staying here *with* you?"

The two men registered instant horror and denial.

"Calm yourself, my dear lieutenant," said Sid. "You know Will Hays wouldn't permit that. She has a nice suite on this floor with a chaperone."

"Her own dear auntie is with her," supplied Sam. "You don't have anything to worry about."

"Oh, no!" said Harry. "I know what goes on in your racket. I've been an actor, myself."

"Why, of course," pacified Sid. "I can tell…I was just going to ask…"

"No, Sid, let me ask him," interposed Sam. "Has anyone ever told you that you bear a striking resemblance to Clark Gable?"

Harry was momentarily stopped. "Why…yes…I believe they have," he said. "You don't mean Betty hasn't been talking about me?"

"Not to me, she hasn't" said Sam. "So she thinks you're the Gable type, too, eh? What a coincidence."

"Wait a moment, Sam," said Sid. "Gable belongs to MGM. I saw this man first. If there's going to be any deal…"

"No, you don't!" said Harry. "I'm off pictures—don't like 'em. And I'm taking Betty out of pictures, too. I can see right now I'm not going to get any help from you guys. I'm going to wait right out here in the hall till Betty comes back." Harry marched to the door. "And don't try any funny business, either. If you do, I'll come back and crack your heads together!"

Harry went out and banged the door.

The two talent scouts could hear him treading up and down the hall.

"How are we going to get rid of him?" said Sam.

"Listen and you'll find out," said Sid, taking up the telephone receiver. "Hello," he said. "Give me the house detective… Hello, this is Mr. Alex of MGM. I'm up here in suite 28-B. There's a man who just left my room—says his name's Harry Hopper. He's an actor out of work who's wearing a uniform. That's right—he'll be impersonating an army officer. Yeah, it seems that he's gotten a crush on Miss Bracken and he's been threatening me… You'll take care of him? Thanks very much." Sid hung up the receiver and turned to Sam. "That disposes of Mr. Hopper," he said.

THE Mayor had to give the City of New York a little of his time that afternoon. He regretted very much, and was secretly glad, that he could not accompany Numar and his party on their sightseeing tour of New York. He was already worried about how his picture was going to look in the papers, with this Miss Bracken person sitting on his lap. The great J. P. Morgan had once been photographed with an attractive little midget perched on his knee, and had survived the public reaction. However, this sort of thing could certainly not be called dignified.

In addition, Numar, the alleged visitor from another planet, was still a question mark. As mayor of the world's greatest city, he could hardly afford not to have welcomed Numar—in the event he should prove beyond all doubt to be genuine. If he should later be exposed as a fraud, the Mayor felt reasonably assured that he had not gone out on a limb by himself. Too many important personages had now seen the Green Man and had been equally baffled. There was the case, some years ago, of the famous Count Romanoff, an engaging impostor from the Flatbush regions of Brooklyn. He had fooled the blue bloods of society and made them like it, ending up in pictures and as proprietor of a nightclub. If Numar were a charlatan, his fate could not conceivably be worse than this.

On the agenda of Clifton Fadiman for the afternoon entertainment of Numar and party, was a visit to the top of the Empire State building, a journey by boat to the Statue of Liberty, and a trip in The Times Square subway at rush hour. These three points of interest were thought best designed to give any visitor to New York a vivid impression of the city from above, on the surface, and below. It perhaps did not represent Mr. Fadiman's personal choice. He would, no doubt, have preferred to escort Numar on a tour of the New York Public Library, pointing out to him his own Book-of-the-Month Club selections. But Mr. Fadiman was generously deferring to popular taste on this occasion, and submerging his own finer instincts.

The Empire State Building, so the guidebooks say, towers 102 stories above the street. You can see fifty miles in every direction, perhaps a hundred, on a clear day. This afternoon chanced to be one of those days.

Fortunately, Numar's trip to the observation tower had not been publicized in advance. Even so, he was followed by a small army of reporters and photographers who jammed the top floor cupola.

AL SMITH, head of the Empire State Corporation and one of New York State's former governors, had joined the party personally to point out spots of interest. He was wearing his familiar cigar and brown derby hat.

"You see down there!" he was saying in his choice East Side drawl, "that's the fish market section where I was born. Mr. Numar, I was brought up on the sidewalks of old New York. I have breathed the atmosphere of this great city from the Bowery to the Bronx. I have risen to this present height from a poor boy—and this demonstrates what any man can accomplish who joins the right party and pursues the democratic way of life…"

Numar seemed deeply impressed but said nothing.

Mrs. Bailey was impressed also, but mostly by the height of which Al Smith had been talking. "My goodness!" she said, clutching Professor Bailey and Mr. Schwartz at the same time. "Were we ever this high up in the plane? Somehow I don't feel so safe when I have my feet on the ground."

Betty now had Mr. Fadiman by the arm and had edged herself in to a position beside former Governor Smith.

"I think it's just wonderful what you've done with your life," she said, "and you wrote a big hit song, too, didn't you? I used to sing it and I even remember the title. Now, let's see—what was it…? Something about sidewalks and Rosie O'Grady…oh, yes…'East Side, West Side'!"

"I didn't write the song," said Al Smith. "But it sort of became identified with me."

"I should say it did," said Betty. "Why, I heard you sing it yourself once—at Madison Square Garden. Oh, Mr. Numar—you should hear Mr. Smith sing."

Al Smith rolled his cigar back and forth in his mouth.

"That's a good idea!" took up the newsmen and photographers. "How about it, Al? Give Mr. Numar an idea of how it goes. Give him the real spirit of New York! You start—and we'll join in."

Al Smith grinned, amiably. "Well," he said, "if you can stand it, I can." He cleared his throat and cut loose, in his best barber shop manner.

"East Side, West Side, all around the town…"

Numar was listening with great interest. A chorus of voices joined in. The song was sung with gusto and brought to a rousing finish.

"…Boys and girls together…me and Mamie O'Rourke…we tripped the light fantastic on the sidewalks of New York."

There was applause and laughter at the finish as Al Smith did a dance step and took a bow.

"In all my travels, I have never heard anything like this," said Numar.

THE little Statue of Liberty boat was thronged to the gunwales. The members of Numar's party were pressed against the rail on the side overlooking New York's skyline, and the rest of the passengers were pressed against them.

"Oh, Auntie," said Betty, "I just had a terrible thought."

"I don't see how you can think in a crowd like this," said Mrs. Bailey.

"But that's just what *made* me think," said Betty. "Poor Harry. Do you suppose he ever got out of that other crowd alive? I haven't seen or heard of him since."

Mr. Alex and Mr. Schwartz nudged one another.

"Say, Sid," said Sam, pointing to the Statue of Liberty, "wouldn't you think that dame would get tired holding up that torch all the time?"

The boat was now docking at the little island but the crowd was much more interested in Numar, the man from another planet, than in the Goddess of Liberty. They pushed and jammed around him as he and his party went ashore.

"I suppose you are acquainted with American history," said Mr. Fadiman to Numar as they entered the base of the Statue of Liberty, "You know we won our independence in 1776?"

"You had to *win* your independence?" asked Numar.

"Oh, yes," said Mr. Fadiman, "every race has had to fight for its liberty on this earth. This Statue, given us by the country of France, is symbolic of our fight for freedom."

"I see," said Numar, quietly.

They went by elevator and winding stairway, arriving finally in the crown of the Goddess. They looked out upon her uplifted right arm, which held high above them, a huge glass torch.

"This monument cost the people of France a quarter of a million dollars," said Mr. Fadiman," and the Americans contributed an additional three hundred fifty thousand for the pedestal and base upon which to erect the statue."

"Its monetary value is then its greatest significance?" asked Numar.

Mr. Fadiman's face colored. "No, but we people here usually like to know how much things cost."

"Apparently," said Numar, "you have been paying an extremely high price for everything worthwhile."

"Isn't it funny?" said Betty. "I've lived in New York for years, and this is the first time I've ever been out to the Statue of Liberty. It just goes to show that the transients, like Mr. Numar, see more of New York than we do."

"It says here, on this tablet," observed Mrs. Bailey, "that this monument we're in is three hundred and one feet, three inches high."

"It also says," observed Numar, "Liberty Enlightening the World."

117

"Oh, yes," said Mrs. Bailey, "I knew that before."

TIMES Square at rush hour is a daily spectacle unequaled at any other place beneath the earth's surface. Into this stone and concrete cavern, lined with tile, is poured, pushed, packed and jammed every nationality in the world, regardless of age, race, color or creed. Here, visitor and citizen alike may observe genuine democracy at work. Here, the principle that "all men are created free and equal" is seen in operation. Here, there is no discrimination or class difference. Here, Democrats, Republicans, Socialists and Communists fight for their very lives and a seat on the subway, without favor or prejudice. Here, the great industrialist, the Wall Street broker, the white-collar man and the laborer is each just as apt to have his feet stepped upon and lose half the buttons on his pants. Here, human dignity is sacrificed that the rights of all may triumph. Here, the women members of a proud human race, whether they belong to high society, the league of housewives, or the working girl fraternity, may reduce themselves to the same common denominator by re-enacting a rush on a bargain counter.

It was into such a caldron of human flesh and spirit that Numar and his party were led by their guide and educator, Mr. Clifton H. Fadiman. The reporters and the photographers had been taking considerable punishment on this tour. They had often become separated from the principals and had been compelled to get their stories and pictures as best they could.

"This'll be a great story if we live to turn it in," said one of their number, as he entered the mad stream of humans pouring through the clicking turnstiles and was swept onward, not toward the sea, but toward the subway trains below.

"You'd better hang onto me, Auntie," said Betty. "I'm used to this. We want to be sure we all get on the same train."

"Good gracious!" gasped Mrs. Bailey. "What people! That man bumped into me and he never stopped to apologize!"

"Hang onto your pocketbook," warned Betty. "I got out of here once with another woman's purse and a man's umbrella. I don't know how it happened...I wonder where Harry is now?"

"Never mind about Harry," said Mrs. Bailey. "I'm being crushed! Why don't the police do something? I don't see an officer anywhere."

"Of course not," said Betty, as they were pushed and poked along. "They're not needed. You're supposed to take care of yourself."

"Well, how can I?" said Mrs. Bailey. "When I'm just one person against a million."

NUMAR, Professor Bailey and Mr. Fadiman were being swept along just behind. A greatly distressed Mr. Alex and Mr. Schwartz brought up the rear.

"This is earning your living the hard way," said Sid as he removed someone's elbow from his eye.

"That's why I moved to California," said Sam, "to get me in the wide open spaces. Imagine paying a nickel for this."

They were all now on the platform itself and a train had just pulled in.

"We'll get on this express, if we can," said Mr. Fadiman, "and ride up to Ninety-Sixth Street. If any of us should get separated, I'll see you tonight on the *Information, Please* program."

"Follow me, Auntie," said Betty, "and I'll show you how to get in." She put her head down and began to burrow.

"I can't breathe!" said Mrs. Bailey.

"Then hold your breath till we get on, said Betty. "Keep pushing, Auntie. We're almost there!" She called to the subway guard who stood on the edge of the platform. "Hold the door, please!"

The guard took a look at her and whistled.

"All right, Greenie," he said. "Come ahead."

"I've got my Aunt with me," said Betty, "and four other gentlemen."

The guard looked around. "That green man one of 'em?" he asked.

"Yes! He's from another planet," said Betty. "He's never been on a subway before."

The guard grinned. "Okay, Swami...come on...I'll put you in here somewhere... Is this gent with you?" He caught Professor Bailey by the arm and gave him a push. "Step lively, brother..."

The entrance to the car was jam-packed. It looked totally impossible to insert another human being but Betty identified all the members of her party and the guard herded them together.

"Get in there, lady," he said, and leaned his weight against Mrs. Bailey's back. She pushed a fat woman in front of her, who was holding a large package above her head. There was a crunching sound and the woman cried out: "There goes my new hat!"

"Move right up in the car!" shouted the guard. "Make room here! All right, you." He grabbed hold of Numar. "Where you playing this week, Swami? Coney Island?"

Mr. Fadiman, Mr. Alex and Mr. Schwarz were still on the platform. The Professor, Mrs. Bailey and Betty were in the vestibule of the train.

"I don't know, Sister," called the guard, "whether I can get your friends all on or not."

"We can wait for the next train," proposed Numar.

"Your friends can wait," said the guard. "But I'll get you on. Here's a place right here."

THERE was a bare foothold beyond the open door of the train. He gave Numar a sudden shove and pressed him hard against the fat woman and Mrs. Bailey. There was no electric shock received from Numar—yet. No one gave way. It required a blasting operation.

"Come on, Swami...push! Give me a little help," said the guard. "I can't do it alone!" He put his shoulder against Numar's back and gave a mighty shove. The crowd inside the vestibule shifted and bulged but Numar's white robed form would not quite permit the door to be pulled shut against it.

"You're almost in!" yelled the guard. "One more good push. Move up, you people! Move up in there!"

The guard drew back and threw himself against Numar. He rebounded as though he were shot. Passengers in the vestibule moved forward into the car, with astonishing alacrity bowling all before them. It was as though they had been propelled by an invisible force. Numar was left standing with ample space around him. The shock was felt by all in the car who had an unbroken contact with those packed in the vestibule against the Green Man.

Mr. Fadiman, Mr. Alex and Mr. Schwartz boarded the train with ease.

"Mr. Numar," said Sid, "you're a wonder!"

"You're what this subway system needs," said Sam.

"I'm sorry," said Numar, "I didn't mean for this to happen."

Another guard came pushing through, grabbed the car door and pulled it shut. The train started moving from the station. A new crowd surged around the platform. Photographers had been busy taking pictures.

"What's the matter with you, Joe?" said Guard Number Two. "Don'tcha' know we gotta keep these trains movin'?"

Joe leaned dazedly against the iron railing.

"Man," he said, "Something must have gone wrong at the powerhouse. What a short circuit. It knocked me stiff!"

NEW YORK'S afternoon papers went overboard on Numar. Not since Lindbergh's unbelievable flight to Paris had so much front-page space and photographs been devoted to a single individual. The World-Telegram even had its all-important weather report crowded off Page 1. Its editor, Roy Howard, broke another precedent with a boxed in, black-faced editorial, which read:

WELCOME TO THIS PLANET

The Scripps-Howard papers, in keeping with their custom and reputation of always being first in the field, now again take the lead in officially welcoming Numar, this distinguished visitor from another planet.

While much mystery still surrounds his arrival here and his personal manifestations, the one unassailable fact remains that he has come, we have seen him, and—so far—all of us have been conquered by him.

The human brain can barely conceive of any creature traveling a trillion miles through space. Numar's arrival here comes at a time when we have been excitedly looking forward to commercial air travel at the possible rate of 500 miles an hour, placing Los Angeles within 5 to 6 hours of New York and London not much longer away.

How amusing this must be to a being who annihilates time by traveling at the speed of light.

We hope to learn much from Numar during his stay here. If we are later proved to have been premature in extending such a welcome, we will still feel that we have been justified in keeping with our forward-looking policy.

H. I. Phillips, writing for the New York Sun, had this to say in his famous Sun Dial column:

It's an old adage that "there's nothing new under the sun," but this Sun reporter wished to declare that Numar is as new as Adam must have been when he first came to earth.

If Numar should take one of his ribs and make himself an Eve, he might start a new green race on this planet.

The question then is, would he eat a green apple and start the downfall of man all over again?

Bugs Baer, in the Journal-American, exploded in this manner:

Well, folks, you've always wanted the Baer facts so here they are.

I've seen everything now—pink elephants and green men. So help me, I don't know which is the most real! Super Man's grand pappy has arrived from space looking as fresh and green as though he'd been shipped here in a hermetically sealed bottle.

Incidentally, most of the boys who met him at LaGuardia Airport have taken to the bottle. All the cameramen can see, in their delirium, is "the little green man who wasn't there." This guy from another planet doesn't photograph.

The Eastman Kodak Company has their laboratory staffs working overtime trying to develop a new emulsion that will bring Numar's image out on the film.

Meanwhile, the photographers have gone crazy and are trading their cameras in for straitjackets.

THE New York Evening Post considered Numar's arrival of such astronomic importance that its editor assigned their astrology writer to cover the story. His item contained this lead:

In answer to a flood of questions, let me first assure our thousands of betting patrons and those who live by our daily horoscope that none of our astrological computations have been upset by Numar's arrival.

It should be pointed out that he comes from a section of the universe beyond our sphere of influence. Other suns, unknown to us, and other planets concerned with his local system, control and direct his destiny.

It is not true, as some have suggested, that discovery of new planets destroys the entire theory of Astrology. You may still rely upon the prognostications as given each day in the Post—if, of course, you interpret and apply them correctly.

The papers, in their regular news stories, gave a full account and chronological report of Numar's activities from the time of his arrival at LaGuardia Airport. They featured the photographs that had been attempted of Numar at the time of his welcoming by the Mayor and Mr. Fadiman. Numar, as Los Angeles photographers had already discovered, was nowhere to be seen. This made all celebrities who had posed for pictures with him look slightly, if not hilariously, ridiculous.

As the Mayor had surmised, the photograph of His Honor, holding a "pretty baby" on his lap, was too good not to be used. One of the captions over this little scene read as follows:

THIS IS HOW OUR MAYOR ATTENDS TO OFFICIAL BUSINESS.

A comment in smaller type, underneath the picture, had this to say:

This should have been a color photograph! The charming young lady, who preferred the Mayor's lap to a seat in the subway, is the actress-niece of the eminent astronomer, Professor Bailey. She, herself, is a follower of the stars—all those fixed in the Hollywood firmament. She was doing some starring of her own when this picture was taken. Her ruby lips were a rich green, as were her eyebrows and eyelashes. Her complexion was a lighter shade of the same pastureland color. Her fingernails bore the same tint as her lips. All in all, she made quite a delectable dish of greens. And you can see by the expression on the Mayor's face that he is pleased to no end.

HAD the Mayor not been a man of stout heart, inured to the barbs of satire, ridicule and criticism, he no doubt would have ground his teeth into a pulp. As it was, he only wadded the paper up into a ball and jumped on it.

The honorable Clifton Fadiman, getting in a plug for his *Information, Please* program, and also his Book-of-the-Month Club connection, let himself be quoted in all the papers as follows:

"Speaking, not only as conductor of *Information, Please*, but also as editor of the Book-of-the-Month Club, I am frank to say—Numar is the greatest mystery story I've ever reviewed."

With this as a send-off, is it any wonder that human tongues were set wagging and human ears flapping? This advance publicity had assured *Information, Please* a bigger listening audience for tonight than Bob Hope or Jack Benny.

Back in their suites at the Waldorf-Astoria, the Professor and Mrs. Bailey gently collapsed on their beds. Betty, a little the worse for wear, was in need of a new green makeup.

Mr. Alex and Mr. Schwartz were sitting beside one another on the edge of their bathtub, soaking their dogs in hot water.

"Ye gods, what a day," said Sid.

"The army never did this to me," Sam replied.

"It's a good thing we're leaving for Washington tonight," said Sid.

"Yes," said Sam, "And climb the Washington monument tomorrow. How did I ever get mixed up in this?"

"Why did that Green Man have to land on this planet?" moaned Sid.

Numar, himself, was unfatigued. He stood by the open window in his suite with Professor Bailey stretched out on the bed, drawing in deep breaths of fresh air and sipping his distilled water.

"A most interesting day," he said.

MRS. BAILEY, while flat on her back in her suite, still had enough energy left to take Betty to task.

"Your conduct today would do credit to a Jezebel!" she said. "Just look at these papers. Can you think of anything more disgraceful than your riding on the Mayor's lap?"

"Yes," said Betty, "but I won't mention it."

"Sometimes I can't believe that you're any relation of mine," said Mrs. Bailey. "Will you please go in the bath room and take off all that green ornamentation? I declare to goodness, with your yellow hair, it makes you look like a dandelion!"

Betty sat down hard on a chair. "Now, Auntie," she said, "you've touched me to the quick. I'm wounded immortally. I don't think I'll ever feel the same!"

"Well, it's about time you came to your senses," said Mrs. Bailey. "You can't be a freak like Mr. Numar, no matter how hard you try!"

Tears began to gather and flutter on Betty's green eyelashes. "The papers are making fun of me," she said.

"You're lucky you weren't run out of town," said Mrs. Bailey. "I just can't imagine what those nice picture men must be thinking of you."

Betty got up and headed toward the bathroom.

"All right, Auntie," she said. "I guess the world doesn't appreciate pioneers. I'll go back to being old fashioned and I'll probably die an old maid." Her eyes suddenly widened and a look of great concern came into them. "Speaking of old maids," she said, "Where's Harry? Oh, I hope nothing terrible's happened to him. I hope he hasn't forgotten me!"

"You can expect anything," said Mrs. Bailey, mercilessly. "After the way you've looked today."

Betty fled to the bathroom and went to work.

"Of course, I'm who I say I am," insisted the man in uniform for the umpteenth time. "You've seen my identification. Now, for pete's sake, let me out of here!"

"Now, now, not so fast," said the Sergeant. "You could have picked this identification up along with your flying outfit. We're checkin' on you in Texas and that takes time."

"But I've got important business. My girl's apt to be leaving town. You don't know what you're doing to me."

"Just keep your shirt on," said the Sergeant. "If we get a wire back sayin' you're okay, you'll walk out of here a free man."

"But it's almost time for the *Information, Please* program," said the soldier, "and I've got to be there."

The Sergeant laughed and gave a wave of his hand.

"Aw, you haven't a chance. They've got the riot squad up at Radio City right now. There's about fifty thousand people in the streets. That studio's so packed you couldn't squeeze another person in with a shoehorn. Tell you what I'll do, if we don't get back a report on you before broadcast time, I'll bring my portable in your cell and we'll listen to the Green Man together."

"Green Man!" raved the incarcerated victim. "I don't give a damn about the Green Man. What I want is my girl!"

The Sergeant looked at his prisoner and shook his head. "Maybe we've got you in here for the wrong thing," he said. "Looks like the place for you is the nut house."

CHAPTER ELEVEN

IT is perhaps a poor and abbreviated pun on words to suggest that radio's question and answer fad may have begun with Mr. Fadiman and the *Information, Please* program. Certain it is, that the kilocycles have almost killed listeners with the awful cycle of quiz programs which have followed in its wake. That *Information, Please* has still retained its position as the number one intellectual entertainment on the air, has been attributed largely to the unorthodox and super educated humans comprising its board of experts.

They were seated now, each behind a table microphone, facing out toward an audience which packed the largest National Broadcasting Company studio and overflowed onto the stage. At the head of the table sat the guest of honor, the mysterious visitor, Numar. At the other end of the table sat his host and sponsor, Professor Bailey. At a separate and smaller table sat the one and only Clifton Fadiman, an expectant look on his face, as he waited for the red light to flash and the program to begin.

"Errr eh Errr eh Errrrrrr!" crowed the rooster.

"Wake up, America—it's time to stump the experts," said the announcer. "Fifty-Seven varieties presents America's favorite program, *Information, Please*. And now," he continued, after devoting exactly fifty-five and one-half seconds to the gentle art of selling, "we turn this program over to the master of ceremonies, the man who asks the questions and tries to break the brain trust—Clifton Fadiman!"

THE country's leading intellectual bowed to the studio audience and waited patiently for the applause to die down.

"Tonight," he said, in tones of repressed excitement, *Information, Please* holds the rare and unparalleled distinction of having as its guest a man from another planet. Mr. Numar, of the planet Talamaya, a trillion miles away from us—as the crow flies—has been on earth little more than seventy-two hours, yet—in that short space of time, he has managed to baffle fifty-seven different varieties of experts.

"This evening, he encounters our own special brand of experts on *Information, Please*. These learned gentlemen, Mr. F. P. Adams, Mr. John Kieran and Mr. Oscar Levant have come here tonight in their finest possible mental fettle.

"I think you listeners would be interested in knowing that Mr. Adams has been studying the stars like mad since he learned Mr. Numar was to be on this program. Mr. Kieran has prepared himself by reviewing the entire works of Jules Verne and re-reading H. G. Wells' story of the Martian Invasion. As for Oscar Levant, he cancelled a concert tour and came in off the road to be with us tonight.

"In that connection, Mr. Levant wishes me to apologize for him to the good people of Altoona, Pennsylvania, who will hear his fine rendition of George Gershwin's *Rhapsody in Blue* at a later date. There, Oscar—I hope that relieves your mind...?"

"Not quite," said Oscar, "you forget to mention—tickets three bucks, including tax."

M. C. Fadiman smiled for the studio audience and chuckled for the radio audience.

"It seems like we're having to do a lot of explaining tonight," he said, "but this is no ordinary occasion. Our other guest tonight is the noted astronomer, Professor William Bailey of Mount Wilson Observatory. We hope, Professor, if Mr. Numar leaves our experts too speechless, you will come to their rescue.

"Now, as you all know, this *Information, Please* program is completely informal and unrehearsed. I am the only one who knows the questions and answers for I have them right in front of me, written on little cards. The first expert or guest who raises his hand after the question is read, gets the privilege of answering it.

"One final word regarding the questions. Our sponsors, the makers of Fifty-Seven Varieties, deemed it only right and fitting that our questions tonight should be submitted by the more prominent intellects of our time. Acting upon this suggestion, we have solicited their weighty contributions. If your name is not among those used, we hope you will not feel too slighted.

"And now, gentlemen and Mr. Numar, with these necessary preliminaries out of the way, we proceed to the first question which is from Mr. Fred Allen..."

THERE was a titter of laughter from the studio audience.

"Mr. Allen states," he continued, "You came to the right brain cell when you invited me to present a question on your cosmic broadcast. I've lived in a world of stars all my life. Now, here's my fifty-seven dollar question..." Mr. Fadiman consulted his card. "You'll have to get all five of these right. Mr. Allen wants you to name five different types of heavenly bodies."

"I know that one," said Oscar. "Hedy Lamar, Betty Grable, Dorothy Lamour, Anne Sheridan—and my wife! Boy am I glad I thought of her."

"That's very interesting, Mr. Levant—and very educational," said Mr. Fadiman, "but none of those names are on the list I have here."

"Well, they should be," said Oscar. "You're missing something."

The studio audience roared.

"Let's keep our discussion academic, Mr. Levant," said Mr. Fadiman. Then, turning to the guest of honor, "Mr. Numar, will you please enlighten our impetuous young man?"

Numar leaned forward in his chair, with his green countenance close to the microphone. His tone was clear and even as he spoke, with a dignity which was at once compelling.

"Do you wish me to list only the types of heavenly bodies that you humans know about?"

The conductor of *Information, Please* coughed and looked sheepishly at the answer card in his hand. "I guess you'd better," he said, "or we won't have any means of checking."

The studio audience was all eyes and open mouths.

"The five heavenly bodies requested by Mr. Allen and perhaps most familiar to you," said Numar, "are comets, meteors, stars, planets and asteroids."

The answer drew applause and Numar smiled as though amused.

"Very good," commended Mr. Fadiman. "This agrees perfectly with my own information." The cash register tinkled. "Unfortunately, however, Mr. Levant gave his answer first which has just cost us fifty dollars and a set of the Encyclope—"

"You'll get the Encyclopedia back," said Oscar, "Fred won't know what to do with it."

Mr. Fadiman gave Mr. Levant what passed for a look of reproof. It would have been good for television.

"Our next question," he said, "comes from our good friend, Eleanor Roosevelt. She has written a little note in which she says…This news about Mr. Numar fascinates me. I am especially interested in anyone who travels. I feel that there is something definitely broadening in going about from place to place. That's why I always keep on the move. But, when I consider how Mr. Numar gets about, I must confess to feeling quite like a novice. Now, here is my question…"

MR. FADIMAN looked up at his board of experts. "I think you gentlemen should get all of this…Mrs. Roosevelt asks…If I were to fly through space, what three constellations might I use as a means of transportation? All right, may I have a show of hands?" Mr. Fadiman drummed the table with his fingers. "Come, come, gentlemen. Don't tell me that Mrs. Roosevelt has stumped you all."

John Kieran half raised his arm.

"All right, Mr. Kieran—you tell us."

"Well," said John, feeling his way. "If Mrs. Roosevelt wanted to fly through the heavens, she could probably travel on the Swan—that's what the constellation *Cygnus* means...or, I suppose she could take a ride on the winged horse, *Pegasus.* Then, of course, there's the Eagle, which is known as *Aquila.* I presume, for sentimental reasons, she'd take the eagle."

The studio audience burst into applause.

"Excellent, Mr. Kieran, excellent!" praised Fadiman. "You have restored my confidence in the human race." He eyed Mr. Levant who promptly made a face at him.

"This question is from Edna St. Vincent Millay," continued the master of ceremonies. Then, as an informative aside to the guest of honor, "Miss Millay is perhaps our greatest living poetess."

"A really great poet is rare throughout the universe," said Numar.

"Well, well," said Mr. Fadiman, "That's interesting to know. Congratulations, Miss Millay—if you're listening in." Then he looked down at the card. "Her question is...boys, I think you should get all three of these...name three songs or poems in which the word 'star' is used."

There was a show of hands.

"Well, Mr. Adams, it's about time we were hearing from you this evening. Where have you been?" beamed Fadiman.

"I've been lost in the Milky Way," said Mr. Adams, clasping his hands in front of him and rolling his eyes.

"Dear, dear—what a place to be!" twitted Mr. Fadiman. "You'd better stay out of Mr. Numar's backyard."

THE gentleman known as F. P. A. pursed his lips and looked skyward. "Twinkle, twinkle, little star," he said.

Numar eyed him strangely.

"Very good!" cheered Mr. Fadiman. "Can you go on?"

Mr. Adams knit his brow in two places. He tapped it with the tips of his fingers.

"Yes—I—believe I can," he said. "How I wonder what you are...up above the earth so high..."

"...Like a diamond in the sky," finished Oscar Levant.

Mr. Adams put his head down and looked deeply wounded.

"Mr. Levant!" rebuked Mr. Fadiman, "you're most impolite tonight.

You know you're supposed to raise your hand before you speak."

"I was afraid he wouldn't get it," said Oscar. "Shall I sing it for you? It goes something like this…" He began to beat time in the air, humming to himself, then broke into snatches of song: "though I dream in vain…in my heart…la dee da…will remain…a stardust melody…the melody of love's refrain… Or something like that."

"Mr. Adams, you knew that last line, didn't you?" queried Mr. Fadiman.

"Indubitably," said Mr. Adams.

The studio audience laughed and broke into applause.

"You see, Mr. Levant, your assistance was entirely unnecessary," said Mr. Fadiman. "That makes one right. Now, who else? Professor Bailey, do I see your hand?"

Professor Bailey started. "Why, yes, I guess you do," he said, a bit sheepishly. "I didn't know it was up."

"Do you have an answer?" asked Mr. Fadiman.

"'I've told every little star, just how sweet I think you are," said the Professor, timidly.

"Why, that's very nice of you," said Mr. Fadiman. "Do you suppose you could sing that for us?"

The Professor blushed. "Well…I don't know about that…"

There was a ripple of encouraging applause.

THE Professor started out in a voice that quavered at first but gathered strength as he went along. He knew the words and, as he finished, he had fixed his eyes on Mrs. Bailey who was seated in the front row.

"I've told every little star, just how sweet I think you are—why haven't I told you?" he sang, ending on a little note of triumph.

The studio reverberated with applause and Mrs. Bailey dabbed tears from her eyes.

"Of course that's an exaggeration," she whispered to Betty. "There's too many stars to tell everyone of them—but that was sweet. I haven't heard him sing in years."

"Well, Mr. Adams," Fadiman was saying, "You have a real rival at last. You have an excellent voice, Professor. You're not only a great astronomer, but…well…you know we're uncovering new talents on our *Information, Please* show every week. We need one more answer on this question. Who has it?"

"When you wish upon a star…" sang Mr. Adams, in a cracked voice.

"That's enough," said Mr. Fadiman. "After Professor Bailey, that's sacrilege. All right, gentlemen, we've gotten safely past that question. Here's the next one. It's from Secretary of the Treasury Morgenthau. He's had us thinking in astronomical figures for years. There's one man, Mr. Numar, who can comprehend a *trillion* miles. Mr. Morgenthau wants to know how far is the moon from the earth? How far is the sun from the earth? And, how far is the most distant planet in our solar system from us? We should be able to get two out of three on this."

"That's a cinch!" chirped Mr. Levant. "But the first part of that question isn't clear. Does Mr. Morgenthau want the distance of the earth from the moon when the moon is full or just half full?"

"He wants the answer, whether *you're* full or half full," said Mr. Fadiman.

"Oh," said Oscar, subsiding, "That's different."

"Then you don't want to answer the question?" asked Mr. Fadiman.

"No," said Oscar, pouting. "I've been insulted."

Mr. Kieran raised his hand. "On a dark night," he said, looking quizzically at Mr. Levant, "the mean distance of the moon from the earth is exactly 238,855 miles."

"Is that correct, Professor Bailey?" asked Mr. Fadiman.

"All but the last digit," said the Professor. "It should have been a '7'."

"So he was off two miles," piped Oscar. "Who cares?"

"You forget, Mr. Levant," reminded Mr. Fadiman, "Astronomy is an exact science. Now, who knows how far the earth is from the sun?"

"On a cold or a hot day?" asked Mr. Levant.

"You are splitting infinitesimal hairs," said Mr. Fadiman.

"Well, that might alter my estimate by a couple of miles," said Oscar.

"Let's stop all this quibbling," said Mr. Adams. "Even a school boy knows the sun is ninety-three million miles from the earth."

"But I'm not a school boy," said Mr. Levant.

"He never went to school," said Mr. Kieran.

"That's right," said Oscar. "I'm a self-made man. You guys have to get your knowledge from books. I get mine out of my own head."

NUMAR'S face spread into a broad smile.

"Do you think I'm kidding?" Oscar added.

"He's not kidding," said Mr. Fadiman, "he's *bragging*. But let's get back to this program. I can't imagine what our guest of honor must be thinking of this puerile display of intelligence."

"This is very interesting," said Numar. "Humor is enjoyed throughout the universe."

"You see," said Oscar, "I'm not so dumb after all."

"Enough of your life history," said Mr. Fadiman. "Let's get the last part of this question. I know Mr. Morgenthau must be waiting patiently, somewhere, for it."

"What was the question?" asked Oscar.

"If you'd keep quiet for a moment and pay attention," said Mr. Fadiman, "you might know."

"Who's talking?" said Oscar.

The conductor of *Information, Please* tried a path of utter indifference. "What is the planet most distant from this earth?" he asked.

The experts registered a complete set of blank expressions.

"Mr. Numar," addressed the impeccable interrogator of *Information, Please*, "perhaps you can enlighten us?"

Numar bowed and bent toward the microphone. "The answer, according to your card, is Pluto," he said. "And its distance from the Earth is three billion miles—but Pluto is by no means the most distant planet. There are planets so far away from your earth that it would take an eternity of time to reach them."

"Think of *that*," said Mr. Fadiman.

"I can't," said Oscar. "It hurts my brain."

"He's bragging again," said F. P. A.

Mr. Fadiman tapped on the table for order. He shuffled the cards before him. "My, we have so many profound questions here tonight, it's difficult to choose. Here's one from that great Shakespearean actor, Walter Hampden. He wants you gentlemen to give five quotations from Shakespeare in which reference is made to 'heaven.'"

Mr. Kieran's hand shot up.

"'My hopes in heaven do dwell,'" he said.

"What an honest confession," said Mr. Adams.

"That's from Henry, the Eighth, Act Three, Scene Two..."

"What page?" asked Oscar.

MR. KIERAN looked up at the ceiling and rubbed a finger alongside his nose.

"In my edition—page...four hundred and...fifty-nine," he said.

He received a tremendous ovation.

"Now, Mr. Levant, will you be good?" said Mr. Fadiman. "That's truly remarkable, Mr. Kieran. I don't have that information on my card but I accept your word for it."

Mr. Kieran lowered his eyebrows to permit a modest blush to pass.

"All right...who has another Shakespearean quotation with the word 'heaven' in it?"

"I shall see you in the next world," popped Oscar. "World means heaven...doesn't it? Who wrote that?"

"Not me," said Mr. Adams, "or Shakespeare for that matter."

Mr. Kieran raised his head, a look of recognition in his eyes.

"Apud orcum te videbo," he recited.

"What's that mean?" asked Oscar.

"What you just said."

"It doesn't sound like it."

"Of course not," said Mr. Adams. "That was *Latin.*"

"Oh..." replied Oscar, "Kieran Latin in Manhattan! Why don't you tell a guy before you switch languages on him?"

"Your quotation was by Plautus, from his writing, *Asinaria,*" informed Mr. Kieran.

"It was?" asked Oscar, pleasantly surprised. "How do you know these things?"

"He studies, Mr. Levant," said Mr. Fadiman. "He applies himself. He has an orderly mind."

"Then how come I know these things?" demanded Oscar.

"I suspect because your mind is like a sponge," said Mr. Fadiman. "Now, please stop interrupting. Mr. Kieran, do you have another answer?"

"I'll follow thee and make a heaven of hell," recited Mr. Kieran. "To die upon the hand I love so well... That's from *A Midsummer Night's Dream*, Act Two, Scene One..."

"What *page?*" challenged Oscar.

"I forget," said Mr. Kieran.

Oscar beamed. "You're slipping," he said.

"Mr. Numar," said Mr. Fadiman, looking in the direction of the green alien. "Is your hand up?"

Numar nodded as all banter ceased and the experts turned his way.

"Shakespeare's most familiar quotation containing the word 'heaven' has not yet been mentioned," he said.

"Which one is that?" asked Mr. Fadiman, with raised brows.

" 'There are more things in heaven and earth than are dreamt of in your philosophy'," said Numar, quietly.

"Gosh," said Oscar. "How's Mr. Numar know that? Is Shakespeare on his planet now?"

"It was in Mr. Kieran's mind," smiled Numar, "waiting to be expressed."

"That's very good," laughed Mr. Kieran. "I was just going to raise my hand."

"So Numar's a second Dunninger," cracked Oscar. "Boy, have I got to watch my thinking."

A murmur of wondering comment passed through the audience.

"That's not fair," complained Mr. Adams. "If Mr. Numar read our minds, then he's getting his knowledge from us. That's against the Queensbury rules."

Mr. Fadiman looked a trifle upset.

"You don't really read minds, do you, Mr. Numar?" he asked.

Numar smiled and nodded. "That is one of our regular means of communication," he said. "You will acquire this faculty in time."

"What's my wife doing now?" chirped Oscar.

"Stop it!" commanded Mr. Fadiman. "This is a radio program, not a seance. We must get on to the next question. It is asked by the famous physicist, Dr. Arthur Compton. He wants to know when did the human race originate on this earth?"

Mr. Kieran's hand was first up.

"It's only a guess. Science doesn't really know. Between five hundred thousand and a million years ago."

"My ancestors don't go back that far," said Oscar.

"Not any further than the Bronx zoo," quipped F. P. A.

"Gentlemen!" scolded Mr. Fadiman in a good-humored manner. "Please keep your relatives out of this. I think I can accept your answer, Mr. Kieran...that is...unless...Mr. Numar, did you wish to say something?"

The Green Man had taken hold of his microphone.

"Yes," he said. "I was slightly over a million years old at the time and I recall the exact moment human life originated on your planet, since I was assigned to study events here."

The wise men of *Information, Please* stared at the guest of honor. Mr. Fadiman dropped the card he was holding to the floor.

"Did I hear you correctly?" he asked in unbelieving tones.

"You did," assured Numar. "Our scientists, with their highly developed instruments, had been keeping a record of all important evolutionary developments on your planet as well as many others. We had been watching with great interest the pre-human life stages on your earth. We were waiting to see what forms of life would finally come together to originate a creature of higher intelligence here."

"And you actually saw or heard or in some way knew of the time and occasion when our human species came into being?" exclaimed the giver-away of Encyclopedias.

"I remember it as though it were yesterday," said Numar. "What you call 'Man' came into existence on this planet—computing these figures on the basis of the present moment—exactly nine hundred eighty-seven thousand, five hundred twenty-three years, four months, eight days, thirteen hours and—according to that clock on the wall—fifty-seven minutes ago."

Mr. Fadiman had to find his voice and when he did, he said: "That's remarkable, Mr. Numar. But, according to that same studio clock, our program time's about up. I'm sorry we couldn't hear more from you but it seems that our Mr. Levant thought he was the star of the show. But we would have enjoyed hearing more from you. Do you have any comment now you would like to make?" *

Numar leaned toward the microphone, as though he had anticipated this moment. The audience, which had come largely to hear and see him, sat on the edge of its chairs.

"Yes," said the man from another planet, as each listener hung on his every word, "I would like to announce that this Saturday, between halves of the Chicago-Notre Dame football game, I will have something of great importance to say to the world."

The suave interrogator of *Information, Please* made a mighty effort to recover his savoir-faire. "Thank you, Mr. Numar and Professor Bailey for being with us tonight," he said. "Your presence here was very enlightening…"

The demands of the closing commercial cut Mr. Fadiman off the air.

"Jeez!" said Sam, as he stood with Sid against the back wall of the studio auditorium, with everyone buzzing around him. "That Numar's no dumbbell. What a plug he got in for his talk on Saturday."

"Yeah," said Sid, "and, brother, it had better be good!"

"I'D LIKE some information, please," requested a young flying officer of the girl at the information booth at Radio City.

He had literally fought his way through a crowd that still jammed the streets outside and packed the lower level of the National Broadcasting Company building. In the hubbub around her, the girl had not quite heard this young man correctly.

"I'm sorry, sir," she said. "*Information, Please* is just over. You couldn't get in to see it anyway. That's what all this crowd's about."

"I know that," said the young flight lieutenant, impatiently. "I said I'd like some information, please!"

"Oh," said the girl, "what is it? I'd be glad to help you."

"Well, my name's Lieutenant Harry Hopper. I must reach Mr. Numar and his party. Will they be coming this way?"

The girl eyed the soldier, warily. "I really couldn't say, sir," she said.

"I've got to know," said Harry. "Isn't there someone here who can tell me?"

"You might see the head usher over there," said the girl.

"Thanks," said Harry.

The head usher was a handsome looking 4-F, six feet, six inches tall. He could really see what was going on and, this evening, he hadn't liked the view at all. It had been the maddest night in Radio City history. None of the outstanding radio stars, either with giveaways or, box tops, had ever pulled such a crowd. This was one of those unexplainable phantasms of an unpredictable business. You could never tell what was going to take the public by the ears.

"Yes, sir, what can I do for you?" said the head usher.

The young flying officer tried the approach of the long green. He held out a dollar bill. "You can slip me in an elevator and get me up to Mr. Numar and his party," he said.

The head usher pushed back the money. "Sorry, Bud, it's no go," he said. "I could have made a hundred bucks that way tonight. I've got strict orders. That studio's jammed and the crowd's just starting to break now. Please step out of the way. When these elevators open, you'll get run over."

A look of wild frustration came into the face of the flight lieutenant. "You don't understand," he said. "I'm engaged to be married and my girl…"

---

*Scientists have been trying to estimate the date of Man's appearance on this planet for many years with little success. They have devised many "clocks" such as the uranium method of determining the age of rocks; but in the final analysis, the various branches of science, because they have been "specializing," have failed to agree. For instance, a geologist will tell you that the age of certain rock strata in which artifacts are found are so many thousands of years old, and then point to other strata presumed to be a hundred million years old, containing human or semi-human remains. Archeologists place the oldest man on earth at between 25,000 years and 75,000 years. On the strength of existing ruined cities, dwellings, caves, others will go back only some six thousand years. Astronomy gives other dates. Perhaps BEST evidence lies in legends. So far, only a book named *Oahspe* has successfully correlated all legends into a reasonable continuity. It would be well for more investigation to be made into these legends. —Ed.

The head usher pushed him to one side. "If she's upstairs, you'll have to take your chances on finding her as she comes out. Get back in that line, sir."

Harry Hopper had always been a resourceful young man. He had known his way about New York but never, in all his life, had he received such a pushing around as he had been getting recently. An astrologer would have said that he must be operating under a bad sign. Something must be wrong with his planets. But Harry, himself, knew what was wrong. It was this guy from another planet who had caused him all this trouble.

"When I get to Numar," he vowed, "it'll be murder in the first degree…"

FOR three-quarters of an hour, Harry permitted himself to be stepped on, jostled and pushed as he watched desperately for some glimpse of the girl of his dreams—and Numar. Those waiting in the lobby and on the street for a sight of the Green Man, were apparently just as disappointed as Harry. But no ordinary human would have risked life and limb in such a mob and broadcasting officials were seeing to it that Numar, himself, was protected. He and his party had been spirited out a secret exit and hurried back to the Waldorf-Astoria.

When Harry realized that he had missed Betty, he made a dash for the street and started running along Fiftieth toward Park Avenue. Arriving at the hotel, he asked to be connected with the Numar suite.

"Hello," said Mr. Alex.

"Is Miss Betty Bracken there?"

The two talent scouts were packed, ready to leave for the night train to Washington. Sid put his hand over the mouthpiece and said to Sam, "It's *him* again!"

"That's not very considerate," said Sam. "He might at least have given us a chance to get out of the hotel."

"The guy sounds like he's slightly upset," said Sid. "You don't suppose he'd have it in for us for getting him arrested, do you?"

"It's possible," said Sam. "Anyway, it was your idea. I'll go out and round up the rest of our party and take 'em to the train. You stay here and see what the guy wants."

"Nothing doing," said Sid. "This is a two-man job. This bird can cause us plenty of trouble. I've got an idea but I need your help." He turned back to the phone. "You say you want to see Miss Bracken?"

"Yes," said the voice. "Right away."

"Fine," said Sid. "Come up to 28-B…"

Sam looked at Sid. "What're you going to do this time?"

"Never mind, you just do what I tell you," said Sid. "I didn't work on all those horror pictures for nothing."

He jerked the telephone cords loose from the wall, disrupting all service in the suite.

"Put that key in the bedroom door," he directed.

Sam did as instructed. "What part do I play in this great drama?" he asked.

"When I get him in the bedroom, you pull the door shut and lock it," said Sid.

"That's simple," said Sam.

There was a racket at the door. Sid grabbed up their bags and tiptoed across the room, setting them down near the door, which he opened.

"Well, hello!" he greeted. "Miss Bracken's been waiting for you. Where have you been?"

"You know damned well where I've been!" said the lieutenant, striding in. "I'll attend to you guys later. Where is she?"

"Right in there," said Sid, gesturing to the bedroom.

"So, it's just as I thought!" raged Harry.

He rushed into the bedroom.

This was Sam's cue and he took it. The door was shut and locked.

"Here's your bag," said Sid. "I think we'd better be going."

There was a hammering on the bedroom door and what sounded like someone yelling for help.

"These drunks sure make an awful lot of noise," said Sam.

They closed and locked the outer door.

"So far, so good," said Sid. "This should keep him amused for some time."

IT required two taxis to take Numar and his party to the Pennsylvania Station where they were to board a sleeper for the nation's capitol. Mr. Alex and Mr. Schwartz, old hands at handling train accommodations and traveling problems, had arranged everything. On a flip of the coin, Sid took charge of Numar and the Professor, while Sam shepherded the women out of the hotel to the waiting cabs.

As they reached the sidewalk, they found a curious crowd, standing at a respectful distance, looking up at a window on the twenty-eighth floor. From the window, everything that was apparently movable in the room was flying. Sid and Sam looked up just in time to see a chair come sailing down. It bounced off the roof of the nearest taxi and ricocheted into the street.

Shielding their heads, everyone in Numar's party made a dash for it. A wall mirror landed right behind them. Safely entrenched in the cabs, Sid and Sam stuck their heads out the windows.

"Imagine this happening at the Waldorf," said Sam.

"It's disgraceful," said Sid, "I'm glad I'm leaving the place."

The cabs started to pull away from the curb. Sam looked upward.

"Good gawd!" he said. "Look, Sid…he's pushing out the bed!"

CHAPTER TWELVE

SENATOR ALFRED B. HOOLIHAN, in a morning suit and spats, with a white carnation in his button hole, looking more like an undertaker than a politician, paced importantly up and down in Washington's Union Station.

It was time for the night train from New York to arrive, bearing the now terrifically sensational Numar and his party. The Senator was a big man, at least physically, and spent his waiting moments jubilantly trying to pat himself on the back. Washington reporters and cameramen were present, although the public had not been advised as to the time of Numar's arrival.

"I think I played a good hunch when I invited Numar to Washington as my guest," the former isolationist Senator said to himself. "There'll be no bills passed in the Senate and House today. All anyone can think about is this Green Man's appearance before both houses of Congress. The President, himself, can hardly wait to meet him. I mean no disrespect to Eleanor when I say that this is certainly 'My Day'."

The Senator had a copy of New York's Daily Mirror in his hand. He stopped now to re-read Waiter Winchell's column. This is what he saw:

WALTER WINCHELL

Numar, the Green Man-About-Space, yesterday became New York's leading man-about-town. The whole country, Numarically speaking, is this 'n' that way about him.

Make no mistake—this Numar is a shocking individual. He has the skin you love not to touch. Your reporter offered himself as a guinea pig yesterday morning and was nicely roasted on all sides. In fact, he is still being roasted.

This Numar appears to be quite a Nu-miracle. We don't know whether he came from another planet or not but we could not pin Izzy Zwankenstein of Brooklyn on him. According to Numar, Zwatzkenstein and Brooklyn must have been "two other fellows."

Your little boy, Walter, admits that this Green Man's got him guessing. It's been suggested that he may be a reincarnation of the two Harrys—Thurston and Houdini. Whatever he is, his style of magic has never been seen on earth.

Numar's got the camera clickers talking in their sleep. He didn't show up in any of their pictures and the same goes for the newsreels. Consequently, he's been chosen by the picture snappers as "the subject they would most like not to photograph."

Speaking of photographs, Dorothy Lamour lost her sarong the other morning, while making a re-take of the picture, "Revelation." Those who saw her said she was a sin-spiration...

"When Walter Winchell goes overboard for anyone like this," said Senator Hoolihan, "that means something. Look how he's jumped on Martin Dies and Nye—and *me!* I guess, after today, he'll change his tune."

THE night train from New York was now backing into the station. Reporters and cameramen rushed down the platform ahead of the Senator. They had welcomed every kind of celebrity on earth with a calloused indifference but, this morning, there was an air of genuine interest and excitement. Here was something totally new and refreshing.

"I much prefer traveling by plane," Mrs. Bailey was saying as she moved down the aisle with Betty and Mr. Schwartz. "You don't have any wheels pounding under you all night. They might at least have greased them. One of them squealed frightfully every time we turned a corner!"

"You mean—took a curve," said Sam.

"Well, whatever it was," said Mrs. Bailey, "It was very disturbing." Then, turning to Betty, "I must say you look like a new girl this morning. That red dress is very becoming. Of course, I think your lips and your fingernails are too bright but since they're not green, I won't object."

"Do you think the President will like this?" asked Betty.

"Land sakes, child! You're not going to sue the President! He's only interested in seeing Mr. Numar."

"I'll bet you I see the President," said Betty. "Want to bet, Mr. Schwartz?"

"I bet on horses, not dames," said Sam. "You can tell what a horse is going to do—at least part of the time."

Numar, Professor Bailey and Mr. Alex were in the aisle ahead of them, slowly moving toward the vestibule. The passengers, before and after them, were naturally all eyes and slowing up their progress.

"This should be a big day," said Mr. Alex, addressing Numar. "By the time you get through speaking to Congress and seeing the President, you can have anything you want in this country!"

"I desire nothing," said Numar.

"Just the same," said Sid, lowering his voice and giving a backward glance at Sam. "When you get through pulling your camera trick, and want to appear in pictures, don't forget MGM."

Numar looked at Mr. Alex. "What makes you think my not photographing is a trick?" he asked.

Mr. Alex stared, uncertainly. "Well—it's got to be, hasn't it? Things like that just don't happen here."

They had now reached the car steps and were descending to the platform. The usual light bulbs were exploding.

"It's no use, boys," said Mr. Alex, waving his hand. "You're wasting your film."

But they only laughed and kept on snapping.

Reporters with paper and pencil in hand pressed around the Green Man.

"Well, Mr. Numar," said one of them. "You certainly turned New York upside down."

"New York was very kind to me," said Numar.

"I heard you on *Information, Please* last night," said a second reporter. "You didn't have much to say. Somebody should shoot that Oscar Levant."

"I thought Mr. Levant very amusing," said Numar.

"But Mr. Fadiman was right—the public wanted to hear from *you.*"

"The public is going to hear from me," said Numar, "Tomorrow afternoon, between halves of the football game at Chicago."

Pencils scribbled furiously.

"What are you going to talk about tomorrow?" asked a man from the Post. "Mrs. Patterson wants to know."

"Tell Mrs. Patterson to listen in on her radio," said Numar, pleasantly.

"But can't you give us a tip as to what you're going to say?" persisted the newsman.

"I'm sorry," said Numar, "that is not permitted."

"Not permitted!" exclaimed a reporter. "Not permitted—by whom?"

"By the ones who sent me here," said Numar.

The newspapermen looked at one another dazedly and did some more scribbling.

"The guy talks in circles," said one.

"He doesn't make sense," said another.

SENATOR ALFRED B. HOOLIHAN had been having difficulty getting through to Numar and his little group, who were hemmed in by the crowd of passengers as well as the newspaper people.

Betty spied him first. "Oh, Uncle! Mr. Numar! I believe that's the Senator you're waiting for...yes, I'm sure it is. Won't you people please stand aside and let the Senator through?"

"Hello," said a reporter, eyeing her. "Who's little red riding hood?"

"That must be the gal in green who's traveling with Numar," guessed a fellow reporter. "Only she's changed colors on us."

The crowd had made a lane for the Senator in answer to Betty's request.

"Thank you, my dear young lady," said Senator Hoolihan, removing his high top hat and bowing. "This is indeed a great honor to be meeting all you good people. I presume this is Mrs. Bailey and Professor Bailey...and, of course—Mr. Numar."

He shook hands with the Professor and extended his hand to the man he had invited to Washington. Numar took it, graciously, and smiled.

"Well, I suppose you'd all like to get to the hotel as quickly as possible and freshen up," said the Senator. "I always hate these sleeper jumps from New York. They bounce you around a great deal."

"They certainly do," said Mrs. Bailey. "And there's a wheel on this train they ought to have fixed!"

The voice of a Western Union boy could now be heard.

"Telegram for Miss Betty Bracken!" he was calling. "Miss Betty Bracken...is Miss Betty Bracken...?"

"Why...that's me!" said Betty, surprised. "Right here, boy. Yoo hoo!"

The boy stopped, looked her direction and whistled. He came on the run.

"Hmmm..." said Betty, "I can't imagine who'd be wiring me. Maybe it's a stage offer." She tore open the yellow envelope and then looked up. "Oh, Senator—I haven't any change. Will you tip the boy for me, please?"

Senator Hoolihan jingled some coins in his pocket, brought them out in his palm, pawed a half-dollar and a quarter aside, and took out a dime. As he handed it to the messenger he saw the reporters were watching.

"I've got to be careful with the taxpayers' money," he said.

The reporters laughed and recorded his comment. Senator Hoolihan was mightily pleased with himself. This was good public relations. It was high time for economy in government and this quotation of his might sweep the country. It had been so long since any politician had shown any concern over the taxpayers' money that this simple statement should get the headlines. It might even run Numar a close second.

Betty was now reading the wire. "Why, it's from Harry!" she cried as she read it. "I don't understand this at all. Listen to what he says: *Was locked in your hotel bedroom by men who claim they represent you. Am flying to Washington. Please leave message for me with Western Union, your city, advising where you are stopping, so I can find you on arrival. Love, Harry.*"

Betty looked up. Mrs. Bailey and Schwartz were standing beside her. "This is the strangest thing," she said. Then, catching Senator Hoolihan by the coat sleeve, she turned him about. The Senator had been posing for pictures with Numar and Professor Bailey.

"Excuse me a minute," said Betty. "But can you tell me where we are stopping?"

The Senator was a trifle annoyed as politicians usually are when anyone interrupts them at such important moments.

"I have reservations at the Mayflower," he said, and turned his back on her again. "That's no good," said Sam, helpfully. "You won't be there much of the time. Better just wire your boy friend that you're stopping at the White House."

"Yes," said Betty, brightly. "I guess that would be safer. Will you take care of this for me?"

"Glad to," said Sam. "Leave everything to me. What's your fella's name?"

"It's Lieutenant Harry Hopper," said Betty.

Sam turned to the messenger who was still standing by.

"Boy," he said, "take this wire..."

The messenger held his pad in readiness. "Shoot," he said.

"To Lieutenant Harry Hopper, Care of Western Union, Washington, D. C. Here's the message..." Sam turned sidewise so that Betty, who was trying to edge into the pictures, would not hear. " Am stopping at White House," he dictated. "Get in touch with me through the President. And sign it, oodles of love and kisses, Betty."

"That'll be thirty cents, plus tax," said Western Union.

"Send it collect," said Sam. "Mr. Hopper will pay for it when he picks it up. And here, boy—here's half a buck for yourself."

The messenger boy had one bad eye that revolved in its socket. "Thank you, Mr. Morgenthau," he said.

"Sid will love me for this," said Sam to himself, as he looked after the departing messenger. "That wire ought to fix that guy—but good."

SENATOR HOOLIHAN had rented a large seven passenger limousine from Celebrities Taxi Service, Incorporated. Such a car was used only for state funerals and receptions. A liveried chauffeur came with it and all the trappings. The only thing lacking was the carpet that was usually laid from the station to the waiting conveyance on return trips of the President or upon visits of foreign potentates.

The Senator led the way, train passengers trooping along, carrying their bags and bundles. It had been an event for them to be on the same train with the Green Man, his first train trip incidentally, since he had been on earth. There was room in this spacious car for all of Numar's party, which was a trifle disappointing to Betty.

"If it's going to be too crowded, Senator," she said, "I wouldn't mind sitting on your lap."

Senator Hoolihan hastened to decline. "I think that honor," he said, "should be reserved alone for the Mayor of New York City."

"Oh, that's so nice of you to say," said Betty. "But I wouldn't want anyone to think I'm being partisan. My, Senator...I just love that carnation in your button hole." She plumped herself down between the Senator and Numar in the back seat, linking her arm with his. Then she gazed about as the limousine started off, leaving a curious throng behind.

"Well, look at that!" she exclaimed. "What's that big building over there with the dome?"

"That's the United States Capitol," said Senator Hoolihan.

"Oh," said Betty, "Of course! You'll have to excuse me, Senator. This is the first time I've ever been to Washington."

The Senator looked at her oddly.

"My husband and I haven't been here, either," said Mrs. Bailey. "Do you suppose we could see Lincoln's Memorial?"

"If she mentions the Washington Monument, I'll kill her," whispered Sid to Sam.

"Well," said Senator Hoolihan. "Mr. Numar doesn't have to speak to Congress until two o'clock this afternoon. His appointment with the President is at three. After you people have checked in at the hotel, we might have a few hours for sight-seeing."

"Here it comes," said Sam.

"Oh, Senator..." said Betty, putting her blonde head against his shoulder. Her hair tickled his chin—but he liked it. "That's wonderful! To think of you being our guide..."

"She's got him," muttered Sam. "We're in for it now..."

ONE of the great sublime—and slightly ridiculous—traditions of the United States of America is that every boy born in this country has a chance to be President. Moreover, since the advent of woman suffrage, theoretically at least, every girl born in this country has a chance to be President.

But, if you are a boy or a girl, don't count on it. Get your family to settle for a visit to Washington rather than the Presidency. Most fathers and mothers plan such a trip at some time in their lives, for themselves and their children, anyway. Many of them feel it is a duty they owe their offspring, as though the journey to their nation's capital would, in itself, inspire them to become better American citizens. In truth and in fact, it should, particularly if youngsters are taken to Washington during what their parents choose to call their "impressionable years."

Professor and Mrs. Bailey had no offspring to bring to this national shrine. But—they had Betty! She was somebody's offspring so it amounted to one and the same thing. However, Betty was slightly past the so-called "impressionable age" and had arrived at the time in her life when she was more interested in impressing others. The historic significance of Washington was largely lost upon her. She remembered that George had once cut down a cherry tree and that Honest Abe Lincoln had once walked an interminable distance to pay back six cents in change. These were great traits of character in our Presidents, which should be revered for all time, but Betty had no ambition to be President. She did, however, have her heart set upon being seen and photographed with the people in Washington who counted, including the President.

The Professor and Mrs. Bailey were like two kids themselves. It had been a life-long desire of them both to see the Capitol of their country, these picturesque and historic spots of which they had read so much, and actually to meet some of the great minds, such as Senator Alfred B. Hoolihan, who were integral parts of the government. To find themselves really embarking on a personally superintended sightseeing tour with the Senator, in company, of course, with Numar and the other members of their party, was a life's dream come true.

"If I just live through today," Mrs. Bailey managed to say aside to her husband, "I can die happy."

"Nellie," said the Professor. "Sometimes your stamina astounds me."

Senator Hoolihan, who had Betty by his side, was talking: "I think, Mr. Numar, one of the first places you might be interested in seeing is the Bureau of Engraving and Printing. That's where our paper money, government bonds, postage and revenue stamps are printed."

"Oh, yes," said Numar.

"My," said Betty, "I'd like to see that. Is it true, Senator, with all the billions it takes to run this government, that you can print money faster than we can spend it?"

"We have been able to...so far," said the Senator.

"My goodness! If there ever came a time when you couldn't," said

Betty, "what would we do then?"

"I would stop running for office," said the Senator. "And run for the country."

THEIR car was now pulling up beside the buildings of the United States Mint. It was followed by three other cars filled with the ever-trailing reporters and photographers. As they went into the main entrance, one of the reporters came rushing up.

"Senator!" he called. "I want to get an exclusive for my paper! A picture of you pointing to a big pile of paper money, just off the press, and telling Mr. Numar about it. I want to title my picture: *Green Man Looks at Green Backs*. Is that okay?"

Senator Hoolihan turned to Numar. "It's all right with me. Mr. Numar, do you have any objection?"

"None at all," said Numar, quietly.

"That's swell," said the cameraman. Then, pleadingly: "But, listen, Mr. Numar—please don't pull that disappearing trick. My boss says if I don't come back with your mug on this piece of celluloid, that I'm a dead pigeon."

Numar smiled and shook his head. "I'm sorry about the dead pigeon," he said.

The other newsmen laughed.

Mr. Alex and Mr. Schwartz brought up the rear as the party filed into the Mint.

"I don't like to look at money that isn't mine," said Sid. "It makes me think of my income tax."

"I don't like to see money made," said Sam, "I'm afraid it might tempt me to become a counterfeiter."

Many of the departments were heavily caged in so that visitors could not get near the freshly printed stacks of paper money and government bonds. Numar and his party, led by Senator Hoolihan, walked over runways, looking down at the different processes in operation. In one department, a row of middle-aged women, white and colored, with rubber thimbles on their thumbs, were seated at long tables counting great piles of uncut paper money.

"You are gazing upon millions and millions of dollars," said the Senator.

"Fancy that," said Mrs. Bailey. "Gracious! I should think those women, after doing that all day, would get so sick of money they wouldn't want to touch it when they got home!"

"I'd like to try it once," said Sam.

Through arrangement with an official at the Mint, Numar and Senator Hoolihan were taken behind locked doors and photographed standing between great mounds of paper money.

"You know, of course," said the Senator to Numar, "that the United States is the richest country in the world?"

"Yes," said Numar, soberly. "I know that."

"This is a tribute to the great industry of our people," said the Senator, as he saw that the reporters were making notes.

"Your people," said Numar, "all work for money?"

"Why, yes," said the Senator, with a half laugh. "Naturally!"

"We have no money on our planet," said Numar.

Senator Hoolihan gave him a startled look. "No money?" he said. "Well, what incentive do your people have for living?"

Numar smiled. "Pursuit of the truth," he said.

"Your planet must be a strange place," said the Senator.

THE next important stop on this personally conducted tour of Washington was made at the Lincoln Memorial, which stands at the upper end of Potomac Park. There is perhaps no more beautiful structure in the world today, for—out of ordinarily cold and austere marble—Man has wrought a warm and living tribute to America's Great Emancipator.

You climb the steps to the Memorial and gaze up into the kindly, yet sorrowing stone face of this man, who sits in his chair and looks, with his deep-set, understanding eyes, into your very soul.

Here, all the cheap sounds of self-seeking politicians are swallowed up into the nothingness that they are. Here, even the most shallow American can be turned from a heart of stone. Here, beside the still banks of the silent Potomac, the waters of American life run deep. Here, you bring as your offering to lie at the feet of Abraham Lincoln, what you really are. And here, on this bright morning in the Washington, D. C. of today, Senator Alfred B. Hoolihan brought this visitor from another planet, and his party.

Professor Bailey put fumbling fingers to his head and removed his hat. There was a mist across his eyes. Mrs. Bailey reached out her hand and placed it within his. They stood like two small school children at the base of the great monument and looked up into Lincoln's face.

Standing somewhat apart from them was Senator Hoolihan, his high top hat in hand. On one side of him was Betty and on the other, Numar. Behind them were Mr. Alex and Mr. Schwartz, foremost in a fringe of other sightseers and the inevitable reporters and cameramen.

"Jeez," said Sam, respectfully. "This kind of gets you, don't it?"

"Yeah," said Sid. "I've been in Washington half a dozen times on picture business, but I've never run out here. This is real competition for the movies."

"I guess Lincoln was a greater man than I thought he was," said Betty.

"He was one of the great souls born on your planet," said Numar.

"I'm glad to hear you say that," said Senator Hoolihan, a gleam of pride in his eyes. "He was our first Republican President."

Numar's dark eyes searched the Senator. "In your opinion, did that make him a great soul?" he asked.

"N—no," said Senator Hoolihan, defensively. "But I dare say—it helped."

The moment of reverence was broken by the reporters and cameramen who must carry to their insatiable public the smallest thought and action of every person in the news.

Senator Hoolihan was quite conscious of the possible political significance of his pilgrimage to the Lincoln Memorial with Numar. This gave him a chance to pledge anew his loyalty to the lofty ideals set down by this greatest of all Republicans. Whenever any earnest Senator or Congressman or high government official felt the need of spiritual replenishing, it was always good Emily Post for him to visit some such national shrine and there consecrate himself, once more, to the principles of true freedom. The memory of the great American public, thank God, was short. You could promise it something one week and take it back the next, and it would forget and forgive you. Great political machines had been founded upon this vulnerable quirk in human nature.

"Would you care to make a statement, Senator?" asked one of the reporters.

Senator Hoolihan cleared his throat and looked up at Lincoln. "I'd like to say," he began, "that I consider this one of the most auspicious moments of my life. To be here, present, with a distinguished visitor, not from another land but from another planet, paying homage to the memory of a man whom Mr. Numar, himself," with a patronizing gesture toward the green-visaged figure at his side, "has declared to be one of the greatest souls ever born upon this earth."

Senator Hoolihan bowed his head, reverently.

The camera shutters clicked and pencils flew.

"Now, Mr. Numar, would you like to say something?" asked the newsmen.

"Senator Hoolihan has spoken for me," said Numar.

Professor and Mrs. Bailey had wandered off to read some of Lincoln's great and historic utterances cut eternally into the marble walls. They spoke them, under their breaths, in chorus.

"This has been worth the entire trip," said the Professor. "I guess, Nellie, I've been looking out, for too many years, upon the stars. It is good to come back to earth and to find what is contained in the soil of our own country."

The Professor felt the light touch of a hand upon his shoulder. Numar had disengaged himself from the press and the publicity seekers.

"Perhaps, Professor," he said, in a quiet voice. "You can understand now, why I chose you as my host on this planet."

IT WAS not a long journey by motor to Mount Vernon. This trip had been made scores of times by Senator Hoolihan in company of various visiting notables and important people from his home state who had to be shown the sights. A politician must always keep on good terms with his constituents. Any real or fancied slight could easily cost him the election. But a Senator was always safe in taking his guests to the tombs of the nation's great, because dead men do not talk. And, since George Washington never was known to have told a lie, it was always good to associate one's self with his name.

The small family vault containing his mortal remains was located on a hillside at Mount Vernon, overlooking the Potomac River. The view from this spot must have been enjoyed by Washington in life as it was now enjoyed by all fellow Americans who visited this hallowed place and were moved by its serenity. Again, there was a peace and simplicity not found in the streets and byways of this now rushing and confused world.

"This man was the first President of the United States and the Father of his country," said Senator Hoolihan. "He didn't believe in foreign alliances."

As a former isolationist, Senator Hoolihan hoped that this comment would be heard by the reporters who would realize that he had not been the originator of this policy, only a temporary advocate.

"Of course," he continued, "had Washington been living today," and here he put words in the great man's mouth, "I have no doubt that he would have recognized the economic and spiritual necessity of a union, not only of states, but of nations."

"Can we quote you on that?" asked a reporter.

"By all means," said the Senator.

Professor and Mrs. Bailey were again off by themselves.

"You know, Nellie," he said, simply. "I'd like to be buried in a place like this."

"Ssssh!" said Mrs. Bailey, looking about self-consciously. "William,

148

don't be sacrilegious!"

Betty was standing, looking through the ironwork at the crypts.

"Lincoln got all the best of it," she said.

Numar had made no comment but now he was prodded by newsmen. "Do you have something to say?" they queried.

"I should like to ask the Senator a question," said Numar.

Senator Hoolihan beamed and bowed. "I should consider it an honor," he said.

"Could you tell me," requested Numar, "Do you humans revere any of your living men and erect monuments to them?"

Senator Hoolihan drew in his breath. "Why—why, no," he said. "Why should we? It's too risky. They're apt to do something, any day, to undo what they've done."

"I see," said Numar. "Then it is possibly just as well that Washington died before his glory was dimmed and Lincoln was assassinated?"

Senator Hoolihan laughed, uncomfortably. "I guess we've seen all there is to see here," he said.

THE Congress of the United States is a mighty body of important little men. The people of the forty-eight states have elected these men to represent their sacred rights and liberties in the government in Washington. In principle, if not always in fact, these elected representatives are known as public servants. Since so few Americans have ever read the Constitution of the United States or its Bill of Rights, it is just possible that an equally small number know how many Senators and Representatives there are in the halls of Congress. For the record then, let it be said there are ninety-six members in the Senate and a total of four hundred and thirty-five Representatives in the House.

On rare occasions, when the President of the United States wishes to address both houses at the same time, on some matter of great national urgency, or when some foreign visitor of sufficient political import should be paid tribute, these two bodies foregather in the House and pretend that they are fraternizing with each other. Actually, as every child should know, the Senate and the House are supposed to provide a legislative checkmate, one upon the other. What one body originates in the way of a bill, the other body either alters, tables or annihilates. This is Democracy in action.

But, this afternoon at two p.m. all regular business was being suspended. The Representatives, because they belonged to the biggest chamber, were once again playing host to the Senators. Not only that, but almost every notable in Washington, especially those on good terms with the administration, had crowded into the House to see and to hear this new man of the hour, this Green Man from outer space, this being from another planet, this stealer of all newspaper headlines—Numar!

Five choice seats had been reserved on the aisle steps in the gallery for the Professor, Mrs. Bailey, Betty, Mr. Alex and Mr. Schwartz. The atmosphere was electric with excitement. Numar and the man who was to present him, Senator Alfred B. Hoolihan, had not yet appeared on the floor. Comments could be heard on all sides.

"It's utterly fantastic, taking up our time with a session like this…"

"Yes, that throws my state relief bill over till tomorrow—and I wanted to get away for a week's vacation."

"I hate Senator Hoolihan's guts, anyway! He's not fooling anybody. He's feathering his own nest by making this tie-up."

"Well, if this Numar's really from another planet, since he won't let himself be photographed, I'd like to see what he looks like."

"One thing sure—he can't be running for office or he'd let them take his picture."

"This Green Man's certainly getting a terrific press. There *must* be something to him."

"I'm an amateur astronomer myself. If Professor Bailey says he's genuine, that's good enough for me."

Being within earshot of these diverse commentaries, Mrs. Bailey nudged her husband. "Did you hear that last remark?" she asked. "William, your opinion *does* count for something in this country."

"Apparently," said the Professor, in pleased surprise.

"I'd like to have the concessions license in a place like this," said Sam. "Can you imagine the soft drinks and crackerjack you could sell?"

"Don't forget the hotdogs," said Sid.

"I hope they begin on time," said Betty, fidgeting. "So we won't be late for our appointment with the President."

"Betty!" scolded Mrs. Bailey. "Not so loud. You don't know whether you're going to see the President or not."

Betty looked wise but said nothing.

IN the anteroom behind the rostrum on which was the Speaker's chair and desk, were a group of noted government officials. In addition to the Speaker of the House, himself, there was the Vice-President of the United States. These two gentlemen, in company with Senator Alfred B. Hoolihan, were having a brief discourse with Numar.

"You say you have no democracy on your planet?" the Vice-President was asking.

"Not what you would call a democracy," Numar answered. "Our people are individually self-governing."

"I see," said the Speaker of the House, with a blank look on his face.

"That sounds rather advanced," said the Vice-President.

"It is," admitted Numar. "We have only enjoyed this state of development for the past ten million years."

Senator Hoolihan poked a jocular finger at the Vice-President. "I guess there'd be no place for us on his planet," he said.

Numar smiled. "Probably not," he said. "Our people are their own representatives."

The Speaker of the House looked at the clock on the wall.

"Well," he said, "it's time we were entering the Chamber." Then, a bit uneasily, "I hope, Mr. Numar, what you are going to say will not be too radical for this body. It should be obvious to you that any such individual government as you have on your Planet would bring chaos and anarchy here."

"That I well know," said Numar.

A hush came over all members and visitors in the House as the Speaker and Vice-President entered with Senator Hoolihan and the man from another planet, following. Everyone stood as though by common consent, and began applauding. Thanks to the press of the country and his two radio broadcasts, Numar was already well known to his audience.

The Vice-President seated himself in a chair to the left of the Speaker's desk, while Numar sat on his right. Senator Hoolihan remained standing beside the Speaker who raised his hand for silence. There was the usual shuffling and shifting of feet and chairs as everyone sat down.

The Green Man, of course, was the cynosure of all eyes. He remained perfectly composed and looked quietly about at the waving sea of faces.

"Members of the Senate and of the House of Representatives," began the Speaker. "We have come together today, in joint body assembled, for the purpose of welcoming to this country, yes—even to our planet, this distinguished visitor from a remote region in space. It is my considered pleasure to present the illustrious Senator Alfred B. Hoolihan, who will introduce to you our guest of honor." He turned and nodded. "Senator Hoolihan."

NUMAR'S Washington host stepped to the front of the rostrum as photographers again went to work. He was greeted with polite applause, with most eyes still fixed upon the Green Man.

"Never before," commenced Senator Hoolihan, in tones of stentorian grandeur, which he felt befitting the occasion, "in the long, tortuous history of life on this planet, has there ever occurred a phenomenon of this magnitude. Never before, has mankind been given such cause to pause and consider the immensity of space and the possible fact that our earth is not alone the only inhabited sphere in this great and grand universe. Never before, either in the time of Washington or of Lincoln, have the people of this country and of the world been at such a critical turning of the ways.

"It's no idle figure of speech to say to you, my fellow colleagues in the Senate and in the House, that we are at the crossroads. Just as we now are compelled by the presence of a man from another planet, to look at the stars—so, we are also compelled to look beyond our shores to the peoples of other lands. Yes, my friends—to realize, in the changing tides of men, that isolationism is a thing of the past—that the Brotherhood of Nations is at hand—and, in the not too distant future, God willing, the Brotherhood of Planets."

This was the point that Senator Hoolihan had depended upon for applause and he got it. The Senators and Representatives looked a bit bewildered but they knew when to take a cue. They knew, also, that Senator Hoolihan was putting on an exhibition of acrobatics and, insofar as his former isolationist attitude was concerned, he was doing a backward somersault. This occasioned a burst of cheers that grew into a small ovation.

"He reminds me slightly of William Jennings Bryan," said Professor Bailey to his wife. "His oratory, I mean."

"And now," Senator Hoolihan was saying, in a voice which trembled and shook with emotion. "It is my unbounded pleasure, and honor, and privilege to present to you, for the first time on this earth, a man who has come from his home planet Talamaya, through interstellar space, for the express purpose of visiting us here. As you all know, I have taken it upon myself, as a Senator from that greatest of all states...I need not mention it by name...to invite Mr. Numar to Washington that he may address this august body...and later meet our noble Commander-in-Chief and President..."

At mention of the President, there was resounding applause. This was another point in his introductory speech that Senator Hoolihan had marked in advance for the taking of a deep breath.

"And so," he said, his voice reaching a crescendo of volume and feeling. "And so," he repeated for emphasis, "without further ado, I now give to you the most unusual personage who has ever set foot inside this United States Capitol building since the day it was erected. Members of the House, Senate, Friends, Visitors and Guests—I present to you the honorable, the most austere, and the most mysterious, Mr. Numar."

Senator Hoolihan had done himself proud. As Numar stood up and advanced to the front of the rostrum, the walls of the House all but came down. Everyone was on his feet, cheering and hand-clapping. Not even Winston Churchill or Madame Chiang Kai-Shek had received such a greeting. Senator Hoolihan shook Numar's hand and held it until the photographers had finished shooting.

"I've never heard anything like this," he said, in Numar's ear. "Go to it...the floor is yours."

The Senator then tiptoed extravagantly back to his seat beside the Vice-President.

The shouts and the plaudits died away like the sound of a pounding sea which had been instantly hushed. The white-robed figure of the Green Man, Numar, now, seemed to fill the Chamber. He stood, unspeaking, looking smilingly out upon his now breathless observers. Half a minute must have passed and the tension was as taut as a violin string about to snap.

"Why doesn't he say something?" whispered Sam. "I can't stand this much longer"

"Maybe he's forgotten how to speak English," said Sid.

The figure of Numar moved—and took a step forward.

"I bring you greetings," said Numar, "not only from the beings on my planet but from the various types of creatures on at least a thousand inhabited planets between my world, Talamaya, and your own."

There were gasps of surprise throughout the House which, breaking through the silence, came like pistol shots.

"You human creatures, here," Numar continued, "have probably been so concerned with your own affairs, that you have given little or no serious thought to the possibility of any other planet being inhabited. Would it interest you to know that the Universe is filled with *millions* of inhabited planets?"

There were more gasps, many of them on the borderline of incredulity.

"No," smiled Numar, "not planets necessarily populated with Democrats or Republicans, such as yourselves, nor even by human creatures—but forms of higher intelligence entirely unfamiliar to you here..." He was speaking easily and with a quiet conviction and charm that was captivating. "Many of these planets have existed billions of years longer than your earth. Partially because of this, the creatures on them have been enabled to reach a much higher state of evolution. They have developed instruments far beyond the capacity of your telescopes and radio which have made it possible for them to view your struggles here and to benefit, in their way, from your experiences. That is how I, myself, first became acquainted with you peoples of earth.

"May I say to you, now, that we are all caught up in a great cosmic destiny together and, as your own Abraham Lincoln has said—if I may choose to apply some of his words in the universal sense—all creatures on all planets, must proceed with malice toward none, with charity for all, with firmness in the right as God gives us to see the right. Let us strive on to finish the work we are in...to do all which may achieve and cherish a just and lasting peace among ourselves, and—in the great far distant ultimate, between the creatures on all planets, throughout this mighty universe..."

There was a moment of tremendous silence following Numar's unusual paraphrasing of Lincoln's immortal words. It was as though he had softly pounded the brain mass within each cranial cavity. His observers looked at one another with expressions of awe, disbelief and faint glimmerings of recognition. The impact of his remarks was due to be felt for days by many present, if not for a lifetime.

"I'll never be the same again," one Representative was heard to whisper.

"I don't get it," said another.

But silence must give way to sound, and whether his words had been comprehended or not, the earnestness and poise and sincerity of Numar could not be doubted. A stunned audience gave him sober and respectful applause as he left the Chamber followed by an obviously dazed Vice-President who sheepishly shrugged his shoulders at the gallery, as much as to say, "You and me both...I don't get it, either..."

CHAPTER THIRTEEN

AT about the time when Numar was delivering his "message" to Congress, a young flight lieutenant was picking up his message from Betty.

"Good gosh!" he exclaimed, as he read it. "The White House! The President! How does she do it?"

Lieutenant Hopper rushed out of the Western Union office and hailed a taxi. At last he was getting somewhere. Maybe there was some method in Betty's madness after all. After all, any girl who could be staying at the White House! "Guess maybe I'd better go a little slow about jumping on her," Harry decided. He sauntered through the door of the White House with the air of a man who has an appointment. He was stopped inside by a kindly, white-haired gentleman with badge and bulging muscles.

"Whom did you want to see?" inquired the man.

"Well, according to this wire," said Harry, "I've got to check with the President."

He showed the telegram to the official way layer of all unofficial business.

"Am stopping at White House," read the man. "Get in touch with me through the President." The official looked questioningly at Harry. "Who is this Betty person?"

"Her name's Miss Betty Bracken. The President will know," said Harry.

"The President is very busy now," said the official. "Maybe I can locate Miss Bracken for you. Does she work here?"

"No, she's visiting here," said Harry. "Just a moment," said the official. He disappeared and Harry paced about in the reception room of the White House.

The official was gone about ten minutes and returned.

"There's no Miss Bracken here," he reported.

"But why would she wire me like this if she's *not* here?" demanded Harry.

"I can't answer that," said the official, "I've checked with the President's secretary. She's never even heard her name, and it's not in the President's personal appointment book."

Harry was momentarily floored. "That's funny," he said. "If you don't mind, I'll just stick around here for awhile. Maybe she'll turn up."

"Sure," said the official, agreeably. "Why don't you get yourself a visitor's pass and go through the White House while you're waiting?"

"That's a good idea," said Harry. "I think I will."

FOLLOWING Numar's address to Congress, Professor and Mrs. Bailey, with Betty, Mr. Alex and Mr. Schwartz met the Senator and Numar by pre-arrangement, at a side entrance to the floor of the House. It was the Senator's intention to drop them off in his car at the Mayflower Hotel while he continued on to the White House with his interplanetary visitor for the appointment with the President. But they had no more than reached the door of the limousine, with reporters, photographers and an excited crowd following them, when Betty began her button holing campaign.

"Oh, Senator!" she exclaimed. "That was the most magnificent speech I ever heard. I was never so thrilled in my life. I don't think I'll ever be that thrilled when you introduce me to the President!"

Senator Hoolihan had helped Mrs. Bailey into the car and was waiting for Betty to follow, but she was holding up the procession. Numar, for his protection, had been slipped in the limousine first.

"I'm sorry, Miss Bracken," he said, "but the President..."

"It's too bad your speech wasn't broadcast," said Betty. "I'm sure he'd have loved it."

"We must hurry or we'll be late to our appointment," said the Senator, trying to push her in the car.

"Oh, Senator!" cried Betty. "When I think of your introducing me to the President, I could just hug you."

She suited the action to the word and a cameraman nearby shouted, "Hey...that's a pip! Do that again, will ya, babe? Give the Senator a smacker on the cheek."

Betty was only too willing to take direction. She couldn't have responded better had she had a movie director.

"My God, how that girl can act," said Sid. "I'm beginning to think I've got something there."

"What's Mrs. Bailey good for?" moaned Sam. "She kisses somebody and nobody cares..."

The Senator had never encountered this sort of a campaign before. With cameras being aimed at him and with his remembrance of Mayor LaGuardia's experience with this impetuous young thing, he had to do something and do it quick.

"All right!" he hissed in her ear. "You're meeting the President. Now, behave yourself. I can't afford to be kissed in public."

"Oh, Senator Hoolihan!" exclaimed Betty, shaking her finger at him as she got in the car, "What you just *said*..."

The Senator said even worse things under his breath.

For some strange reason, the Senator's hired limousine never stopped at the Mayflower Hotel at all. It proceeded directly to the White House with all on board, to keep Numar's and Senator Hoolihan's appointment with the President.

LIEUTENANT HOPPER had become so interested in viewing the President's trophy room, in company with other gaping-mouthed sightseers, that he had momentarily forgotten his cross-country quest of Betty. As he emerged into the hall, with some elderly schoolteachers from Minnesota who had attached themselves lovingly to him, he saw what at first glance appeared to be another sightseeing group, hurrying past. However, this small party was possessed of an escort of White House police who had brought them in a special entrance. There was a white-robed figure in their midst and it was the elderly school teachers who first observed: "Why, for mercy's sake...there's the Green Man!"

By this time Harry had caught sight of a blonde in red, clinging to the arm of a tall, pompous-appearing man, who carried a high stiff hat.

"Betty!" Harry shouted, and left his school teacher acquaintances without an adieu.

They looked after him in blank amazement.

"Well, I suppose that's what we've got to expect at our age," one of them said to the other.

Numar and his party were already turning the corridor as Harry gave chase. Betty, hearing her name called, glanced backward, saw Harry, and waved.

"Hello, Harry!" she called. "I can't see you now. I'm going to see the President."

A White House guard blocked Harry's mad dash after her.

"Where do you think you're going?" he said.

"I belong to that party," said Harry. "Let me go!"

"I don't think you do," said the guard. "You'd better come with me."

"I'll prove it to you," said Harry, and produced a crumpled telegram. "Read this..."

The guard looked at it. "Who's Betty?" he asked.

"That girl I was calling to," Harry explained.

"That may be," said the guard, skeptically. "But that still doesn't mean you've got an appointment with the President. You come with me to the reception room while I check on this."

THERE was a momentary delay at the door of the President's private office as a somewhat flustered Senator Hoolihan offered apologies, explanations and entreaties to the President's secretary. Could he be allowed, as a special favor, to present all the members of Numar's party? The secretary stepped to the door and looked the group over. She did not act too impressed by the sight, even when Betty smiled and waved at her.

"I'll see what I can do," she said, and disappeared.

"Something tells me this is going to be the experience of my life," said Betty.

"I hope this doesn't ruin my political career," said the Senator, raising his eyebrows a little.

"Is my hair on straight?" asked Sam of Sid. "Thank God, I at least voted for the guy."

"What do you say to the President?" Sid wanted to know.

"Ask him if he's going to run for another term," said Sam.

Professor and Mrs. Bailey were very solemn and plainly nervous.

"Betty's got us this far," said the Professor, "but I still can't believe we're actually going to meet him."

The secretary reappeared at the door. She was smiling. "The President will see you now," she said.

As Numar's party entered the President's office, in the executive wing of the White House, a young flying officer was brought into the reception room by a guard. The guard caught the secretary's attention.

"You sit here," he said to the soldier, indicating a chair. "I'll find out about this." He crossed to the door and spoke to the secretary in a low tone. "That army pilot, there, claims he should have gone in with that party to see the President," said the guard. "Would you know anything about it?"

"No," said the secretary. "But there is an army pilot due to see the President this afternoon. I'll check up on his calendar as soon as this appointment is over. He's probably the one."

"Thanks," said the guard, and turned back to an expectant Harry. "Just sit tight," he advised. "We'll have you straightened out in just a few minutes."

"That's swell," said Harry, drawing a sigh of relief. "If you only knew what I've been through!"

"Yeah, it's tough trying to see the President these days," said the guard. "You've got to have influence."

SENATOR HOOLIHAN carried off the introductions of the different members of his party in his usual exemplary manner. Meeting and introducing people were two of the most important requisites to the making of a successful politician.

The President was seated at his desk, which in addition to state papers, contained an assorted collection of little dog figures in bronze.

"Oh, aren't these cute!" exclaimed Betty. She was standing with the party in front of the President's desk and impulsively picked up one of the bronze miniatures. "Why, Mr. President, I have this dog's very mate at home."

"Indeed," said the President, amused. "I wondered why that poor fellow had such a lonely look. Please take him with you."

"Why, Mr. President!" protested Betty, with the Professor stepping on one foot and Mrs. Bailey, the other. "I hope you don't think I—*ouch!*"

The President divined what was going on and laughed. "That dog appears to have bitten you," he said. Then, turning to his distinguished visitor, "Mr. Numar, I have been greatly interested in you since your reported arrival on the planet. I am sorry I was unable to hear you in your talk before Congress. Word has already reached me, however, that your remarks have caused quite a stir."

Numar was standing at the edge of the desk nearest the President, with Senator Hoolihan by his side.

"What I said today was relatively unimportant," he quietly declared. "I hope, Mr. President, that you will be able to hear me when I speak from Chicago tomorrow afternoon."

The President chuckled. "Do I have to listen to the first half of the Notre Dame-University of Chicago football game in order to hear you?" he asked. "I'm a busy man."

Numar smiled. "Perhaps not," he said, revealing his own sense of humor. "Even so, they seem to be the most popular teams in the country. I understand Soldiers Field is entirely sold out for this game—and they expect the biggest crowd in history..."

"All right," laughed the President. "You win...I'll be listening in."

"Out this way, please," said the President's secretary, with the interview over. She indicated a private exit through a side corridor away from the main reception room. Numar's party immediately filed out, as directed. It was met by four solid looking citizens, one of whom stopped Numar. He was a stout, dark-eyed, crinkly-haired man.

"My name's J. Edgar Hoover," he said. "Will you and your party come with me?"

Numar looked questioningly at Senator Hoolihan who seemed on the verge of an apoplectic stroke.

"Mr. Hoover," exclaimed the Senator. "Is something wrong? Have you got something on this man? Great heavens...don't tell me he's a *fake?*"

Mr. Hoover's face was a mask. "I want his fingerprints," he said.

Senator Hoolihan glanced apprehensively at Chief G-Man Hoover's strong-arm trio of plain-clothes men. "We'll go peacefully, of course," he said. "But if Mr. Numar's going to be exposed, for God's sake—don't involve me."

"Oh!" cried Betty. "What's the matter? We're not arrested, are we?"

Mrs. Bailey took her husband's arm, protectingly.

"Mr. Hoover," she said, in a voice which quavered. "I warned Professor Bailey at the very start but it seems like this man had him hypnotized. If he should turn out to be a crook, I hope things won't go too hard with my husband. He's really been an innocent, trusting victim."

"I'm in the clear," said Mr. Alex. "I'm just representing Miss Bracken here—for MGM."

"Me, too," said Mr. Schwartz: "I mean—I'm a Warner Brothers man. I haven't had anything to do with Mr. Numar."

The Green Man, under apparent indictment from members of his party, had eyed them each in turn. He was now looking at Professor Bailey.

"You can do what you want, Mr. Hoover," said the Professor, with spirit. "But I'll bet you Mr. Numar is exactly who he says he is, and furthermore, I'll bet you can't disprove it."

"Why, William!" said Mrs. Bailey.

"Come on," said Betty, taking a deflated Senator Hoolihan by the arm. "I've been wanting to see how the FBI works anyway."

The Senator emitted a groan that came from the very bottom of his spats.

"Mr. Hoover," he pleaded. "I have my car outside. May I save Mr. Numar and his party the public disgrace of going with you? I promise to deliver them all to your headquarters."

Chief Edgar Hoover nodded and gestured to his men.

"Very well," he said. "Let them go ahead, men. We'll follow."

A sober group of people, led by Senator Alfred B. Hoolihan, who now looked like the dead stick of a spent skyrocket, passed out the side door of the White House, drawing many curious glances and wondering comments.

ALL right, sir," said the President's secretary, motioning to the young flying officer who had been waiting impatiently in the reception room, "the President will see you now."

Harry leaped to his feet and hurried to the door. What he saw caused him to stop and stare. The Chief Executive was seated at his desk with several newsreel cameras pointed at him. There were a number of official looking gentlemen standing by.

"But where's Betty?" asked Harry. Impulsively, he looked around. "I don't understand...?"

"Please, hurry!" urged the secretary, "Don't keep the President waiting. He's half an hour late with his appointments now."

Harry advanced toward the President's desk, uncertainly. One of the men in front of him was a high-ranking officer in the army. He thought he had better salute, so he did. The salute was returned and the officer smiled and said: "At ease, Lieutenant. A man of your heroism shouldn't be nervous on an occasion like this."

"But, I—" Harry choked out. "There must be—"

"Mr. President," said the high ranking officer, "this is..."

"Of course," beamed the President, "the whole country knows him." He reached across the desk and extended his hand. "Charmed to meet you, Lieutenant."

Harry, eyes popping, clicked his heels together, saluted once more, and then shook hands with the President. The newsreel cameras began to grind.

"Step around here, beside the President," directed the military gentleman, placing a kindly hand on Harry's shoulder.

"But I came here," Harry started to say.

He was pushed in front of the President who was now standing, an official document of some sort in his hands...

"For heroic and undaunted service far beyond the call of duty," the Chief Executive was reading, "Lieutenant Peter Bauer..."

"But, Mr. President," broke in Harry, "*I'm* not—"

"Keep still," said the military officer, jabbing him in the back.

"...in the attack upon the Japanese island of Saipan," the President was continuing, "not only strafed heavily armed beaches at great risk of being shot down but blew up several large ammunition dumps in the operation. On preparing to leave the scene, while attempting to gain altitude, Lieutenant Bauer..."

Harry was wet with perspiration. "But Mr. President," he said again.

"Shut up!" hissed a voice in his ear.

"...was attacked," the President went on, "by six Japanese Zeros that had dived at him from above. By skillful and almost unbelievable maneuvering, the Lieutenant, although his plane was riddled with flak and bullets, managed to shoot down five out of six of his attackers and returned to his base, wounded himself, and with his tail surfaces shot away..."

THE President of the United States put down the document and took up a medal from his desk. The newsreel cameras were still grinding.

"Mr. President," said Harry, putting up his hand. "I can't accept this..."

The President turned upon the young flying officer his most reassuring smile. "Your modesty is most becoming," he said. "It is characteristic of our noble young men in the service."

Then, reaching out, the President began to pin the medal on Harry's chest.

"To Lieutenant Peter Bauer, I, the President of the United States, now present, as a token of his country's and his government's appreciation for valorous conduct under fire, this Distinguished Service Cross."

Harry's eyes looked wild as the President, once more, shook his hand. He was being patted on the back by the high-ranking officer, with other officials gathering around, showering him with congratulations.

The newsreel men started dismantling their equipment.

"Mr. President," said Harry. "I've been trying to tell you…"

"I know just how you feel, Lieutenant," said the President. "Goodbye, sir—and good luck."

Harry found himself being escorted to the door. He finally let out an inarticulate cry and rushed from the room. In the corridor he encountered the White House guard who had stopped him before.

"Well, did you get fixed up?" asked the guard. Then, on seeing the medal, he exclaimed, "I should say you *did.*"

"Listen!" cried Harry, grabbing the guard by the coat lapels. "My girl…Miss Bracken…she wasn't there!"

"That's right," said the guard. "She and her party just left here a few minutes ago."

"Oh my gosh," said Harry. "Where'd they go?"

"They went with J. Edgar Hoover," said the guard.

"So," said Harry. "The FBI's got her…what next?"

He dashed out of the White House. As he did so, another young flying officer entered the President's reception room.

"I'm sorry I'm late," he said, apologetically. "My taxi broke down. I'm Lieutenant Peter Bauer."

The secretary stared and gasped. "Oh," she said. "Just have a seat, Lieutenant. I—I'll tell the President."

ON THE ride to the Federal Bureau of Investigation in the Department of Justice Building, Betty suddenly thought of Harry. She turned to Mr. Schwartz.

"Oh," she said, "I just remembered. I saw Harry at the White House. He must have gotten that wire you sent for me. I wonder what became of him?"

"You're worrying about him and we're going to jail," said Sam.

Betty looked through the rear window of the limousine and saw Hoover's car following them.

"Senator," she said, "I'll bet you could get away from them, if you tried. Let's turn off here and go back to the White House. I've got to find Harry."

"Who in the name of Jumping Grasshoppers is Harry?" said the Senator, biting nails in two with his jaws.

"He's the most wonderful man in the world!" said Betty.

"An hour ago, I thought I was," said the Senator, dryly.

"But that was an hour ago," said Betty, "And Harry hadn't shown up then. He's been following me all across the country."

"I don't know why," said the Senator, "I should think he'd be running in the opposite direction."

"Why, Senator," said Betty, and patted his cheek. "You say the funniest things!"

She turned once more to Mr. Schwartz. "Oh, I've meant to ask you about that telegram Harry sent me. I never did understand it—about his being locked in my hotel bedroom."

"What's that?" said the Senator.

"Oh, it's all right," explained Betty. "I wasn't there at the time."

"I can't afford to have any scandal attached to my name," said the Senator. "If you're having men in your bedroom, I wish you'd have the decency not to mention it in public."

"Why, Senator. What are you talking about?" said Betty. "I'm as innocent as a new born babe."

"If you're innocent," said Senator Hoolihan, speaking with a loud snort, "then I'm a little girl with pig-tails!"

"Just the same, I've got to find Harry," said Betty. "He's my one and only."

Senator Hoolihan leaned back and resigned himself to the worst.

"Now, Mr. Schwartz," Betty persisted. "Where do you suppose Harry could have gone?"

"Search me," said Sam.

"Oh, don't be silly…" she laughed. "He's not on *you!*"

"I'm glad of that," said Sam. "That's what I've been afraid of."

"Me, too," said Sid.

"What are you two hinting at?" demanded Betty.

"You'll find out soon enough," said Sid.

The limousine had now pulled up in front of the government building containing the FBI offices. Senator Hoolihan restrained the members of his party while he looked up and down the street.

"Just a moment," he said. "I want to make sure that none of my…er…uh…political friends or…uh…enemies happen to be passing. Yes, the coast seems to be clear…everybody out…please." Then to Numar, "This is very distressing. It's something I didn't anticipate. I trust you are not too disturbed?"

"I am not disturbed at all," replied Numar.

THE aides of J. Edgar Hoover met Numar and his party inside the building and escorted them to their Chief's private office. They sat in this soberly impressive atmosphere, nervously awaiting head G-man Hoover's arrival.

Senator Hoolihan, most effected of all, paced about the room, clasping and unclasping his hands behind his back, head bowed. Betty, observing him, whispered to Mrs. Bailey.

"You know, Auntie—there's something about the Senator—the way he's acting now—he looks just like Washington at Valley Forge."

"I wouldn't know as to that," said Mrs. Bailey, her mind on other things.

"Or maybe Lincoln at Appomattox," dramatized Betty. "My, it's interesting to see a big man in a historic moment like this."

"Oh, God!" suddenly exclaimed the Senator, extending his arms imploringly toward the heavens.

"You see," said Betty. "I was right. He's at the turning point of his career—and he doesn't know where to turn."

J. Edgar Hoover's appearance brought an increase in the tension. He approached Numar and stood studying him for a moment.

"Walter Winchell has informed me about you," he said. "I've had other reports. Will you step down the hall, please? I want to get your fingerprints."

Numar stood up.

"The rest of you may come along, if you wish," said Mr. Hoover.

THE FBI Chief himself took Numar's right hand, pressed his thumb and fingers on an inkpad and then on a specially prepared sheet of paper. He examined the result, exclaimed in surprise, and turned back to Numar.

"Let's try that again," he said.

Numar smiled and extended his hand. Mr. Hoover repeated the process. The result was the same—five perfectly smooth, evenly colored black spots.

"Let's try your *left* hand," said Mr. Hoover.

Numar obliged and, again, the prints were examined.

All in Numar's party had been watching this development with growing interest and wonderment.

Without a word, the FBI Chief passed the prints he had made over to some of his associates for examination. They shook their heads. Mr. Hoover pressed a button and called more of his experts in. They also shook their heads. A new record of Numar's fingerprints were made. It came out the same. Mr. Hoover then called for a magnifying glass and he and his experts began a study of Numar's hands.

Senator Hoolihan was finding it not quite so hot in the room. He raised his brows significantly and nodded at Professor Bailey.

"We may be vindicated after all," he said, in a low voice.

"Mr. Numar," said J. Edgar Hoover, finally, "You have very remarkable hands. I suppose you are aware that they do not finger print. Your skin appears to have no lines at all—no arches, loops or whorls. Of course, if this is genuine, it isn't human."

"I am not human," said Numar, quietly.

"If he isn't," said the Senator to Professor Bailey, *"we're* all right."

The FBI Chief was still not satisfied. "We'd like to make some chemical tests on your skin," he proposed. "It's just possible..."

"There will be no chemical tests," said Numar, with authority.

Mr. Hoover went into a huddle with his staff of experts, which was being increased by the minute as word spread through FBI headquarters that the Green Man wouldn't fingerprint.

"Jeez," said Sam to Sid. "What an idea for a horror picture. A guy like the Green Man commits a perfect crime. He doesn't leave any fingerprints and he doesn't photograph."

"How do they catch him?" asked Sid.

"I should tell you," said Sam. "This is going to be a Warner Brothers picture."

Numar was sitting watching the conference being held about him. He seemed vastly amused. Betty came over to him.

"My, Mr. Numar—I think you're wonderful!" she said. "I've been so busy since we started this trip that I haven't had much chance to tell you—but I think you're the most wonderful whatever-you-call-yourself that I've ever met."

Numar smiled, reached out one of his hands and patted her cheek. "I think you're wonderful, too," he said.

Senator Hoolihan, surprised, caught his breath and let out a hearty guffaw.

Mr. Hoover came back to Numar. "I'm frank to say that you have us completely baffled. There have been no charges against you. But, you've been such a sensation in this country that we wished to check you for our own information. You are free to go now."

"Thank you," said Numar.

"Well, Mr. Hoover," said Professor Bailey, putting out his hand. "It's nice to have met you. I naturally feel quite relieved."

"I never really doubted this man's identity," said Senator Hoolihan. "But you know how people talk, Mr. Hoover, when you're called in on a case. A man in the public eye, like myself, has to be careful." He let out a healthy chuckle. "So you couldn't get Mr. Numar's fingerprints, eh? Well, well...that's going to be very interesting to the boys over on Capitol Hill." The Senator walked jauntily toward the door, motioning to his party to follow him. "You folks will have to be watching your time if you're catching that six o'clock train for Chicago."

"That reminds me," said Betty. "I've got to find Harry. Oh, Mr. Hoover, could you locate him for me? He's a young flying officer—and he looks like Clark Gable."

"That should be description enough," said the FBI Chief. "What's his name?"

"Lieutenant Harry Hopper," said Betty.

"He followed me to the White House and I..."

Mrs. Bailey took her niece firmly by the arm. "Come along," she said. "Mr. Hoover's got more important things to do. He's only interested in *criminals.*"

AS ONE elevator door closed on Numar and his party, the one adjoining opened to admit a young flying officer to the floor. He looked at the directory on the wall and headed, with all haste, to the office of J. Edgar Hoover.

"I must see Mr. Hoover, at once," he told the secretary.

"Whom shall I say is calling?"

"Lieutenant Harry Hopper," announced the flying officer.

"Just a moment, Lieutenant," said the secretary. She left the outer office and returned shortly. "Go right in," she said.

Harry burst in upon the FBI Chief

"Where is she?" he demanded.

"Where is who?" asked America's head G-man.

"Betty Bracken," said Harry. "I understand you picked her up?"

"Just how do you mean that?" asked Mr. Hoover.

"Well, I was at the White House..." Harry tried to explain.

Mr. Hoover picked up a slip of paper from his desk. "Yes, we've just had a report on you from the White House," he said. "It was nice of you to drop in. It saves us the trouble of going out and getting you."

"Getting *me!*" exploded Harry. "What have I done?"

"Apparently," said Mr. Hoover, rising and advancing toward Harry, "you've been impersonating a fellow officer." He pointed to the Distinguished Service Cross on Harry's chest.

"Oh, that," said Harry. "Well, I'll tell you, Mr. Hoover...you're right, it doesn't belong to me but..."

The FBI Chief reached over and unpinned the medal. "Then, I'll take it for safe-keeping," he said. "Or did you come to me to return it?"

"As a matter of fact," said Harry. "I'd forgotten I had it on. You see I'm so up in the air about Betty. Where is she?"

"You mean that young lady with Mr. Numar's party?" asked Mr. Hoover.

Harry nodded.

"She just left here," said Mr. Hoover.

Harry turned on his heel. "Where'd she go? I've got to reach her."

"Sit down, young man," ordered the FBI Chief. "I want to have a little talk with you."

Harry dropped on the edge of a chair, greatly agitated. "Listen, Mr. Hoover, please don't hold me up or she'll get away from me again. I've chased her from Los Angeles to New York and now to Washington. I've been having a hell of a time!"

"It sounds like it," observed Mr. Hoover, eyeing him, testily. "And, apparently, at the government's expense."

"Oh, I'm on a five day leave," said Harry. He fumbled in his pocket and produced the necessary papers. "Here. These will tell you who I am and everything..."

Mr. Hoover studied the different identifications and the pass signed by the Commandant of Kelly Field. "This pass appears to have been issued for you to fly your plane to California," he said. "I see nothing here which indicates you had permission to fly to New York or Washington."

"But, Mr. Hoover," protested Harry. "It was an emergency and I had to call upon my own resources and initiative."

"That's quite obvious," said Mr. Hoover. "And, for that reason, I'm compelled to call upon *my* resources and check up on this matter."

Harry sank back in his chair. "Oh my gosh!" he moaned. "How long will that take?"

"That depends," said Mr. Hoover. "But we have a place here where we can make you very comfortable."

"But, my girl," pleaded Harry. "What will I do about her? Mr. Hoover, have you ever been in—in love? And has your girl ever gone—nuts?"

"I'm sorry," said Mr. Hoover, "my romantic life is my own affair. I think your Commandant is going to be extremely interested to know that you have been burning up the army's high test gasoline and using your plane for private purposes."

"I can explain everything," said Harry.

"That's what they all say."

A groan of despair escaped Harry's lips that sounded like the wail of a dying cat.

"Betty!" he cried out, in anguished tones. "If you could only know what you're doing to me!"

CHAPTER FOURTEEN

SENATOR ALFRED B. HOOLIHAN entered the Senate chamber the following morning with an air of great self-satisfaction and importance. All was well with the world and all was well with him. He carried a bundle of Washington and New York newspapers as well as copies of the Life and Time magazines. All of these periodicals carried glowing accounts of Mr. Numar and his tour.

The morning papers had favorable things to say of the Senator, and while the photographs, as usual, did not reveal the presence of Numar, there were a number of excellent likenesses of the Senator. He looked somewhat foolish in a number of pictures, shaking hands with the "man who wasn't there," but this very fact was so sensational as to bring him into greater prominence. All in all, his audacious venture had placed him in just the limelight position he had desired and seemed bound to rebuild his political fences from Maine to California. Perhaps this might even place him in line for a Vice-Presidential consideration in the next national election.

The Senator walked to his desk on the Senate floor, bowing right and left to his colleagues, those who had already arrived and were not already asleep. The nightlife in Washington was really very strenuous and it was difficult for Senators or any government officials for that matter, to be awake and alert too early in the morning. Senator Hoolihan, however, could sense a rise in esteem toward him, which was radiated from certain of his fellow members who waved or called to him as he passed.

He seated himself at his desk and spread out the papers and magazines. Here was the New York Times whose slogan had long been: "All the news that's fit to print." And, here was Life Magazine, dedicated to the policy, "All the news that's fit to see." Both publications were devoting columns of space and pictures to the doings of Numar.

The Times, this morning, had a picture of the "Man from another planet" addressing Congress. It showed rapt attention on the faces of Senators and Representatives, their eyes fixed upon the rostrum, which was empty. In the place where Numar had actually stood, the Times had indicated: "X marks the spot."

"It's incredible," said Senator Hoolihan, as he viewed the picture.

"There I am, seated in the background, next to the Vice President. I can be plainly seen and yet there's no trace of Mr. Numar. No evidence that he was even there!"

The Senator thumbed through the ten pages of photographs taken by Life cameraman, of earlier episodes in Numar's short career on earth. One of them revealed Walter Winchell's gyrations in space at the time he was supposedly holding Numar's hand. The Life caption simply stated:

"Winchell Getting A Hot Tip."

TURNING from Life to Time Magazine, Senator Hoolihan sought out the summary of editorial comments concerning Numar. He read the following:

WHAT THE PRESS THINKS:

New York Times:
Mr. Numar impresses us as being of unusual democratic bearing and extraordinary poise. If he really comes from the distant and hitherto unheard of planet, Talamaya, as he quietly asserts, then his presence here is indeed remarkable. If he does not, he is unquestionably a remarkable fraud. We must await further verification of his most unusual claim.

New York Herald-Tribune:
Old time GOP and Conservative opinion is divided on the alleged arrival of a Green Man from some far-off planet in the Milky Way. We have met Mr. Numar and prefer to reserve judgment until other reactionaries, liberals and left wing elements have passed on him. At this writing, however, Mr. Numar appears to be holding his own.

The Daily Worker:
Labor views Mr. Numar as a threat to the peace and security of the American home and our way of life. Should it ever become possible for every human to derive nourishment from air and water, as he professes to do, then agriculture, the great meat industry, and all manufacturers of food-stuffs will be put out of business. It is obvious what such a development would do to the working man.

INDIVIDUAL OPINIONS:

Robert Ripley:
"I don't believe it!"

Bob Hope:
"The Green Man is Jerry Colonna in disguise."

Bing Crosby:
"Thank God, Numar is not another Sinatra."

W. C. Fields:
"What do I want with a Green Man? Just give me a bottle of Scotch."

Greta Garbo:
"I should think he'd want to go home and be alone."

Louella Parsons:
"He can't be real. He didn't let me report his arrival."

William Randolph Hearst:
"The yellow menace has turned green."

Henry J. Kaiser:
"No, we did not build the Green Man."

Eddie Rickenbacker:
"I doubt if he's genuine. I lived on air and water, myself, for three weeks in the South Pacific."

Walt Disney:
"The Green Man can't be photographed, so we're drawing him in a new cartoon series."

Clare Boothe Luce:
"Anything Dorothy Thompson says about him, I'm against!"

Eddie Cantor:
"He's just a minstrel in green face."

Ed Wynn:
"He's going to make a 'perfect fool' out of a lot of people."

Secretary of State Hull:
"I am not in the least disturbed."

Ethel Barrymore:
"The Corn looks mighty green from here."

Mary Pickford:
"I'm only interested in Buddy Rogers."

Harry Emerson Fosdick:
"This may change our whole concept of Religion."

William Green:
"I disclaim any relation to the Green Man."

Philip Murray:
"If he stays here, he'll have to join a union."

Man on the Street:
"What in hell is this all about?"

"Well," said Senator Hoolihan to himself, as he leaned back in his seat. "I certainly am in great company, at last. I'll probably be written up in Life and Time next week. No telling where this may lead to."

HE HAD been paying no attention to the business in the Senate that had been going on during his absorbed perusal of papers and magazines. He had voted automatically several times when the roll was called on different bills, but they didn't vitally concern him so why should he give them any consideration? But now, something was happening on the floor that brought him up with a start. Senator Bass, from his rival state, was on his feet, shaking his fist and demanding recognition from the chair.

"The chair recognizes Senator Bass," said the Vice-President, who was presiding.

"Fellow members," addressed the Senator, speaking from his desk position. "I would like to bring to the attention of this most responsible body in the framework of our American political structure, a matter of the most imminent and paramount importance." Here, he turned to shake an ominous finger at Senator Hoolihan. "It concerns," he continued, "the action taken by that Senator whose state adjoins mine on the West—I shall not speak his name—that action which brought before our two houses of Congress, this alleged creature from another planet…"

"Hear! Hear!" sounded from the Senate floor, with vocal support also

171

coming from spectators in the gallery.

Every Senator present immediately woke up or put aside what he was doing. Other members, who had been out in corridors or reception rooms, visiting with natives from their home state or listening to amateur or professional lobbyists, now began trickling back to their seats. Even grown men like to see fireworks.

Senator Hiram Ketcham Bass, having delivered himself, of this opening broadside, had worked up sufficient lather to shave the hide of Senator Hoolihan.

"I wonder," said Senator Bass, in tones of eloquent concern, "if my esteemed confederates have duly considered the possible implications of yesterday's unique and unparalleled joint session of Congress?"

"Yes...yes..." encouraged a friendly Senator on his right.

"What do we know," thundered Senator Bass, "about this man, Numar? What does *anybody* know? Then why, I ask you, should we, the Senate of the United States of America—and they, the House of Representatives of this same United States of America, have laid ourselves open to the possible criticism of our people for having harbored and abetted a most dangerous foreign character?"

"Mr. Chairman!" appealed Senator Hoolihan, leaping to his feet. "Will the Senator from my rival state yield?"

"I will not," said Senator Bass.

Senator Hoolihan remained standing and glaring.

"How do we know," charged Senator Bass, "that this Green Man, Numar, may not be a paid interplanetary spy? That he may be here as part of an insidious plot, using Senator Hoolihan as his unwitting tool? How do we know, I say, that this Green Man hasn't come to earth, to get the lay of the land, and that he will then return in force with an army of his native Talamayans, to take our earth people captive and convert us into a slave planet?"

There were cheers intermingled with roars of laughter.

"Don't laugh, gentlemen," continued Senator Bass. "We have slave nations today. Why not a slave planet? Your antecedents laughed at the advent of the telephone, the automobile, the X-ray and the radio...the world laughed at Columbus...but I say to you—this mysterious Numar may be the forerunner of a horde of such beings who will come shooting through space and over-run our earth."

HAVING divested himself of this robot bomb which he let fall where it would, Senator Bass sat down and surrendered the floor.

"Mr. Chairman!" Senator Hoolihan was shouting, so agitated that his coat lapels were flapping. "I should like to reply to the Senator whose state, unfortunately, borders mine on the east. He sounds very much to me like he's never recovered from that Orson Welles' radio program." Then, pointing a scornful finger, "He was perhaps one of those frightened citizens who listened to the Martians' broadcast and grabbed his ancestor's saber off the wall and rushed out into the street, prepared to give battle to the fiendish space invaders. I assure you, gentlemen, there is nothing you good Democrats and Republicans, with free consciences—if any there still be—need fear from the visit of Numar to this earth."

Having shot down Senator Bass' verbal robot bomb, Senator Hoolihan now awaited the next assault. This was not long forthcoming. The rotund Senator Bass was on his feet and pounding the desk.

"Mr. Chairman!" he bellowed. "I insist that this Green Man, Numar, should be compelled to state his purpose in coming here. No alien should be allowed to travel, at will, throughout this great country, without his intentions being known. I propose to introduce a bill regulating the entry into our stratosphere and arrival on this earth of beings from other planets. If Numar was able to get here, then we may expect an increasing number of visitors. Only God knows with what powers they will be endowed. This planet must be made safe from invasion from space, not only for ourselves, but for our children and our children's children!"

Senator Bass plumped himself in his seat amid applause. He looked defiantly about the Senate chamber. His heavy salvo had hit home. There was never-failing appeal behind that phrase of making something safe "not only for ourselves but for posterity." He had put through many bills upon this plea alone.

Senator Hoolihan once more had the floor.

"If my opponent, who always views things with alarm, is really serious," he said, "then I think he should be making these remarks in a psychopathic ward rather than this sober chamber of the United States Senate."

Senator Hoolihan had landed a direct hit. An explosion of laughter followed. The chairman almost broke his gavel rapping for order.

Senator Bass was furious. Jumping atop his desk, he shouted above the tumult: "As between your actions in this Senate and a psychopathic ward—what makes you think there's any difference?"

WHILE Numar and his party were making the sleeper jump to Chicago to be in attendance at the Chicago-Notre Dame football game in Soldiers' Field, a young flying officer, by the name of Harry Hopper had been compelled to remain in Washington, in custody of the FBI. He was the next thing to a wild man.

J. Edgar Hoover had been trying to reach the Commandant of Kelly Field, Texas, without success. It seems the Commandant was away on twenty-four hours leave and could not be contacted until eleven the following morning. At the designated time, the former temporary holder of the Distinguished Service Cross was brought to the head G-man's office.

"I am putting the call through to your Commandant right now," Mr. Hoover informed. "I want you in on this conversation. Pick up that extension, please."

Harry did so, just as the connection was made.

"Hello, Commandant? This is J. Edgar Hoover in Washington."

"Oh, yes, Mr. Hoover."

"I'm detaining a young flyer by the name of Lieutenant Harry Hopper."

"You *are*? What in hell is *he* doing in Washington?"

"He says he's following some girl."

"Great guns...is he still following her? I knew he'd gone on to New York but this is too much! How did you get hold of him?"

"He *didn't* get hold of me," broke in Harry, impulsively. "I came to see him, myself. I've had a hell of a time, Sir. I can explain everything."

"Get off the line! Where's that voice coming from? My wire must be tapped," the Commandant could be heard bellowing from Texas.

"It's all right, Commander," said Mr. Hoover. "I've had Lieutenant Hopper listening in. What do you want me to do with him?"

"Just let me talk to him a second," roared the Commandant. "Is he still on the line?"

Harry put his hand over the mouthpiece, apprehensively. "Mr. Hoover, you take the message for me," he said.

"Yes, he's still on the line," said the FBI Chief, motioning to Harry.

"Why, you low-down, no good son of a jackass! This is the last time I'll ever suspend the war to help a man straighten out his love affair."

"But, Sir," protested Harry. "It's not straightened out yet..."

The cry of rage almost melted the telephone wires. "I don't give a damn if it's never straightened out! You listen to me, Lieutenant Hopper...you put the seat of your pants in that army plane and you fly it back to Kelly Field like a bat out of hell! Understand?"

"Yes, sir!" Harry shot back. "But can't I stop over in Chicago? My girl..."

The long distance wire crackled and snapped.

"NO!" shrieked the Commandant. "Your leave is up...it's cancelled...you're under military orders! Get back here and get back here quick!"

"Yes, Sir!" said Harry. "But it wouldn't take much longer if I—I"

There was an inhuman cry and a sudden sharp sound in Harry's ear. He looked at J. Edgar Hoover.

"Why, I believe he's hung up," he said in a low innocent-sounding voice.

"And it sounds like you'll be hung up, when you get back," said Hoover.

CHAPTER FIFTEEN

ALL Chicago knew that Numar was coming. The Windy City was full of wind as everyone aired his views concerning the Green Man. His reputation had been growing every move he made and his day in Washington had capped a succession of climaxes.

The happiest man in Chicago was Big Hank Morrison, publicity director for the University of Chicago. He was at the station to meet Numar and his party with the grin that wouldn't come off. Mr. Morrison had some company. The station was jammed with a crowd of curious humans who were in the holiday spirit. Big Hank, with the acumen of a live-wire publicity man, had employed some college boys to parade with banners containing the words:

WELCOME, NUMAR
MAN FROM ANOTHER PLANET

There was another reason for the crowd. The University Band was there. No one could say that Chicago was going to be derelict in greeting such a rare and distinguished personage, especially since Numar had already wiped out all athletic financial deficits of the University, with all tickets to Soldiers Field sold, including more than ten thousand standing-room-onlys.

As the train began pulling in, Big Hank gave the band the signal. "All right, boys!" he called. "Give 'em *Hot Time in the Old Town Tonight.*"

It was a welcome that would have done any politician proud. As Numar and his party got off the train, he was met by the greatest bedlam of discordant sound ever let loose in Chicago's Union Terminal. He eyed the huge banners and smiled.

"That's very interesting," he said.

Betty was still wearing her red ensemble, having found it to be well received in Washington. She entered into the spirit of the occasion by waving and blowing kisses to the crowd. It responded in kind.

"I believe she's developing a public," said Sid. "When we get through with this tour, this little girl is going to be worth something in Hollywood."

"I wish Mrs. Bailey had more glamour," said Sam. "I guess I can't expect any salvage value out of her unless I'm able to land Numar for Warner Brothers."

"You can't get him," said Sid. "I know. I tried."

"Why, you louse!" said Sam. "I thought we agreed the other day that we'd both hit him together—and let the best man win."

"Well, I knew I was the best man," said Sid, "so I hit him alone. It's no go. He claims this no-photographing stunt is no trick."

"He's just holding out for bigger stakes," said Sam. "He's got something up his sleeve. I'll find some way to get him in pictures, even if we have to shoot him in *subtitles!*"

BIG HANK Morrison was pushing his close-to-three-hundred-pound-frame through the cheering crowd. He reached out an expansive hand to Numar.

"Greetings, Mr. Numar. Glad to see you. Certainly swell of you to be here. I appreciate it. President Hutchins appreciates it. The University appreciates it. The football team appreciates it—and the whole damn town…I mean, the whole city appreciates it."

This welcome came from the depths of Big Hank's heart as well as his pocketbook. He had played a hunch on a dark horse named "Green Man" and it had come home the winner, paying odds of a thousand to one. Nothing was too good for this horse now. It would get all the laurel wreaths, all the pats on the back, and all the oats of acclaim it could swallow. This was the biggest sporting day in the history of Chicago University. It no longer mattered whether its team showed up on the gridiron. In fact, it might be the better part of valor if it didn't. Notre Dame's Fighting Irish—being partial to green—were apt to put on a special field day for the Green Man, and murder the out-of-practice team entirely.

"I have reservations for all at the Palmer House," said Hank. "We'd better get going before we're mobbed in here."

He led the way up the stairs with the band members pushing through ahead of him and forming in the street. The boys with the banners lined up in front of the band. There were three waiting open cars. Hank Morrison was doing everything up in style.

"Just a little parade," he announced. "Down through the Loop to your hotel. Everyone wants to see you, Mr. Numar, since you don't photograph. Most of these people on the street are those who couldn't get game tickets. You know, we've got to keep in good with the public."

Numar nodded and looked down Jackson Boulevard, which was packed with people.

"Here, young lady, you get in this car with Professor and Mrs. Bailey;" directed Hank, "And you men," addressing Mr. Alex and Mr. Schwartz, "Ride in the car behind. I'll ride with Mr. Numar in this car up front."

Police had difficulty keeping men and women as well as youths from climbing over the cars. Requests were made for Numar's autograph. Newspapers, cards and pieces of paper of every description were pushed at him from all sides. He smilingly raised his hand and shook his head.

"You dopes!" yelled someone. "The Green Man can't write!"

"Sure he can!" shouted someone else. "Let him sign it in his own language."

The University of Chicago Band struck up a tune. It was *Boola! Boola!* that soon went into the *Beer Barrel Polka*. This was America. This was youth. No stiff collar welcome, no fancy dress, no pretense. Just good old midwestern hospitality of the sweet corn variety.

"I think it's wonderful," said Betty, popping up and down in her seat between the Professor and Mrs. Bailey, as she waved and called to the crowd. "My, it's great to be famous!"

"I think, Betty," said Mrs. Bailey, "You should be reminded that this parade is *not* for you."

"Maybe not," said Betty, joyously. "But I'm for *it!*"

Big Hank, seated with Numar in the lead car, after they had gone a block, made a suggestion.

"I guess you'd better stand, Mr. Numar. I'm so big, people on my side of the street can't see you. And, you are a curiosity you know."

Numar graciously arose and stood, balancing himself against the front seat. He quietly acknowledged the cheers, catcalls, whistles and wavings of the crowd. As the procession turned into State Street, a flood of torn paper, in confetti-like form, came floating down from the throngs in the windows, settling over those in the cars.

Someone, operating the loud speaker system, used by State Street merchants, bellowed out like a sideshow hawker: "Here he comes, ladies and gentlemen…here he comes! Here's the Green Man! Here's the visitor from that far-off planet! Stand back, folks! Give everyone a chance to see him. Hi there, Mr. Numar…welcome to Chicago."

Numar gazed up into the buildings, trying to locate the source of the sounds. He had a puzzled expression on his face.

"What a queer custom," he said.

The parade stopped in front of the Palmer House and police formed a line to help Numar and his party into the hotel. The train had been late and it was almost noon.

"The game begins at two o'clock," informed Hank. "This gives you people a chance to go to your rooms, get rested up and grab a bite to eat. I'll come back for you all at a quarter to two."

IF AMERICA has one love to whom it is always true, it is sport. It makes no difference whether that sport is tiddlywinks, ping-pong, bridge or post office, America loves sport. In fact, our educational system is based upon it. We give little thought to the curriculum of any school or college to which we are considering sending our children. Our first question is, "What kind of a football team does it have?" If the answer is "Not so hot," we usually pass up the institution and send our children somewhere else. The offspring must have something to cheer about and how can they get excited over Greek or Latin or Ancient History if they don't have a football star in their class?

The University of Chicago should have known better. President Hutchins made the mistake of believing that young people went to college to be educated. He and his institution had paid dearly for this mistake on the athletic side of the ledger. But, this afternoon, they were about to redeem themselves. The intellect as well as the brawn was to be handsomely served. A football game and a man from another planet on the same program! Here was an event unequaled in all sporting history and, moreover, what pleased President Hutchins most was the fact that the crowd was coming to see the man rather than the athletic contest.

"Perhaps, some hundreds of years from now, we can assemble a crowd like this to hear a debate on some important subject of national or international interest," he said, hopefully. "Of course, I shan't live to see it—but it's nice to contemplate."

PUBLICITY can create a new fashion, establish a new fad, make a star over night, ruin an individual's character quicker than that, change the course of thought, sell anybody anything—and even start a war. It is one of the greatest forces ever unloosed upon a seemingly always-unsuspecting public. No business or industry or ambitious individual can get along without it today. They must be known, either favorably or unfavorably, or the world will seek its mousetraps elsewhere.

But Numar had acquired, in four days time, a devastating barrage of publicity that had absolutely blanketed anything else concurrently taking place on earth. He arrived at Soldier Field, Chicago, to be met by a crowd of 130,000 people, by all odds the greatest assemblage of humans ever squeezed into this huge Lake Shore bowl. The presence of this enormous gathering was a tribute to the power of the radio and the press as well as to Numar, himself. He was already the great question mark of the Twentieth Century. Could Soldier Field have held every man, woman and child in Chicago, it still would have been too small. But those who could not get in were making sure that they were near a radio to hear, if not to see, this man from another planet.

Five minutes before game time, Big Hank Morrison, with police escort, led Numar and his party to box seats at midfield on the University of Chicago side. There, the party was met by President Hutchins and members of his staff. While Numar was being presented to them, the customary news reel cameramen and photographers were at work. The mammoth crowd looked on, taking its attention entirely off the Notre Dame and University of Chicago teams, which were warming up, on the field. The football players themselves were so interested that they broke formation and stared.

"I suppose, Mr. Numar," said President Hutchins, "that you've never been in such a crowd as this in your life."

"Oh, yes," smiled Numar, "I've been in large gatherings on other planets."

"Other planets," repeated President Hutchins, eyeing him doubtfully, "you mean there are turn-outs for you like this on other planets?"

"Curiosity is the same everywhere," said Numar.

"We certainly appreciate your doing this for the University," said President Hutchins, feeling his way.

Numar smiled. "I appreciate your doing this for me," he said.

"I suppose you've never seen a game of football," speculated President Hutchins.

"No, I have not," said Numar.

"I'll be glad to explain it to him," said Betty. "I know all about it." She had wormed herself in beside President Hutchins, to whom she had been introduced.

"You may have to do a great deal of explaining," said the U. of C. president, "I'm not so sure we're going to see a game of football this afternoon."

Mr. Alex and Mr. Schwartz were sitting, looking over the crowd. Mr. Schwartz's lips were moving and he was pointing to different rows.

"What are you doing?" asked Sid.

"I'm counting the house," said Sam. "Jeez, but this is tough on the picture business…"

"It sure is," agreed Sid. "We'll have to get Numar in pictures or he'll ruin us. I'll bet *Gone with the Wind* couldn't draw better at the box."

Mrs. Bailey was seated beside her husband. He had acted of late as though all these activities had him in a daze, which, in fact; they had. "You know, our little home was so peaceful before this all happened," she said.

"That's just what I was thinking," said the Professor. "Here I've never cared for crowds; I've always tried to avoid them, and now I can't seem to get away from them. But, maybe, after today…" He left the thought unfinished and looked toward Numar.

"What do you think he's going to say?" asked Mrs. Bailey.

"My dear Nellie," said the Professor. "I haven't the remotest idea. But this Mr. Numar has super-human self-assurance. Just look at him. He's sitting there as composed as a boy on a back fence—and yet he knows the whole world is going to be listening to him in a little over half on hour. I'd be so nervous I'd probably pass out."

"I'm nervous, anyway," said Mrs. Bailey, "I'll be glad when this is over. How can any person, no matter who they are, live up to this advance notice?"

"That's the question, my dear," said the Professor, "that only time— and Numar—can answer."

PRESIDENT Hutchins' misgivings as to whether or not a game of football would be played on this particular afternoon were quite justified. Sports writers, with only two minutes remaining of the first half, were calling the game a track meet and giving all points to Notre Dame. The score was Notre Dame, 55; University of Chicago, 0.

"I can't explain any more," said Betty, to a strangely silent Numar. "I'm all out of breath!"

The great crowd was fidgeting in its seats and watching the time clock. It wouldn't be long now until the extra-added attraction which had caused them to buy tickets to this football massacre, would be at hand. They would soon see and hear the Green Man.

"I hope he's worth the price of admission," said a spectator. "This game certainly isn't."

At this moment, there came the sudden roar of an airplane motor. It was a low flying plane, tearing in from the east. It passed quickly over Soldiers Field, then circled and came back. The pilot dived, then banked and spun around over the heads of the 130,000, as though looking for someone.

"It's an army plane," said Sid.

"Yeah," said Sam. "Seems like I've seen it before, somewhere."

"They all look alike," said Sid.

But Betty, who had been watching with two hearts in her throat, suddenly jumped to her feet and began shrieking, "It's Harry! It's Harry! Look! He just waved to me!"

"Betty, behave yourself!" exclaimed Mrs. Bailey. "How can he see you in a crowd like this?"

"It's my red dress!" said Betty. "Just look at him go. Oh! He almost hit that flagpole. Harry...be careful!"

The crowd was getting an unexpected thrill, almost too close for comfort. This army pursuit plane had roared around the top of Soldiers Field, almost like a motorcycle on a vertical track. But, suddenly, the engine began to sputter and cough. A trail of black smoke shot out from it. The pilot was seen to be having trouble. His plane dipped and rocketed out toward the Lake.

"Goodbye, Harry," said Sid.

Sam held hands over his ears. "Tell me when he crashes," he said.

The great crowd was in an uproar. Top row spectators on the stadium east side, stood up to follow the course of the plane. There was a moment of great suspense...and then a man with powerful field glasses cried out, "Well what do you know...he's landed on that carrier in the Lake. Boy...what a close call!" The word was quickly passed around to the relieved crowd and the unknown daredevil pilot was the subject of excited speculative discussion.

"I'm so glad he's safe!" said Betty. "I know he did that just for me."

"He didn't do it for the army, that's sure," said Sam.

"He's got a nice persistent quality," said Sid. "He's apt to get there some day."

"Get where?" said Sam.

"Well, that's the point," said Sid.

A whistle was blowing which no one had been paying any attention to. In the excitement of the moment, the Chicago University right end had grabbed the ball away from a Notre Dame player and run the length of the field for his team's first touchdown of the year.

Those in the crowd who had been ashamed to admit they were Chicago alumni, now gave vent to an entire season's pent-up emotions. The first half ended with the score: Notre Dame 55; U. of C. 6. The shock had been too great. They couldn't kick the point after touchdown.

IT HAD been a quiet Saturday afternoon on board the Naval Training

Aircraft Carrier, laying at anchor on Lake Michigan, with most of its officers and crew on shore leave, when this unidentified army pursuit plane had come hurtling out of the sky for a forced landing on its deck.

"Whew!" said the young flying officer, as he climbed out of the plane, one wheel of which was dangling over the side. "My motor went dead! Dang! I saw this ship just in time. I'm sure glad it was down here. That water looked pretty grim."

"Where are you from?" asked the officer in charge.

"I'm just in from Washington," announced the pilot. "Are you the commander of this ship?"

"No, he's at Soldiers Field," said the officer in charge.

"Soldiers Field!" exclaimed the pilot. "What's the quickest way to get there?"

"Well, we can take you ashore by launch and the rest of the way by motorcycle sidecar."

"Then, what are we waiting for?" said Harry. "Let's go!"

He got action in the traditional Navy style.

BACK at Soldiers Field an unusual spectacle was taking place. By special arrangement, the University of Chicago and Notre Dame bands had combined and were marching in formation. They were putting on a show, not in honor of each other, but for the exclusive edification and entertainment of the Man from Another Planet.

Numar had now been brought down, in company with President Hutchins, to a portable platform, with battery of microphones, which had been set up near mid-center field. Everything was in readiness for the most unique broadcast in all earth history. But, first, a tribute was being paid to Numar.

The two bands formed an enormous letter "T," emblematic of the planet Talamaya, from whence the Green Man had come. This fact was pointed out to Numar by President Hutchins, just as the combined bands, standing at attention, in the form of the "T" struck up the tune, "Home, Sweet Home."

"Our publicity director thought this might be appropriate," explained President Hutchins, "for a man a trillion miles from home."

"It's what the newspapers like," said big Hank Morrison, a bit uncomfortably. "You understand?"

Numar nodded and smiled.

The cheerleaders suddenly went into action. They ran up and down the sidelines holding up large cards on which directions were written. The crowd quickly caught on and over one hundred thousand voices burst forth in a typical college yell.

*"Rick! Stack! Frizzle-back! Kutchu! Kutchu! Boom-a-lack! Sis! Boom!
Bah! NUMAR! NUMAR!*
Rah! Rah! Rah!"

This was followed by tremendous laughter and great applause. The voice of the radio announcer now filled the loudspeaker:

"Ladies and gentlemen. For this special broadcast, all national and international networks have joined together that the entire world, from pole to pole and hemisphere to hemisphere, may hear the message of Numar, the Green Man from the Planet Talamaya. I give you now, President Robert Hutchins of the University of Chicago, who will introduce this distinguished personage to you...President Hutchins..."

A hush fell over the vast stadium and when 130,000 people are silent, that silence can be felt.

Professor and Mrs. Bailey had taken hold of hands. Both of them were trembling and almost afraid. Even Betty was still. Mr. Alex and Mr. Schwartz were all but holding each other's breath.

"May I address you, my great visible and invisible audience," spoke President Hutchins, "as fellow human creatures everywhere. I feel that this occasion calls for such a form of address because, if Mr. Numar is who we believe him to be, then he, himself, is not a human creature like us, but a different and higher type of being from another planet. That he should have come here, as he claims, a trillion miles through space, to deliver to us creatures of earth a sober message of great importance is sufficient reason for us to stop all worldly thought and action and to listen to what he has to say in a most respectful and reverent spirit.

"As you who are acquainted with my ideals of education must know, I highly favor the advancement of the mind and spirit in man. I do not decry the exercise of physical energy on the athletic field. I only decry its over-emphasis. Let us hope that what Mr. Numar has to say to us may lead to a higher advancement of our life on this earth. It is my pleasure now to present to you this visitor to our earth from the planet Talamaya...Mr. Numar!"

CHAPTER SIXTEEN

THE white-robed figure of the Green Man came forward to take his position before the microphones and face his great visible audience. A vast shadow of silence passed over the face of the earth. The ear of the world was pressed against the radio. People of every race, color and creed who could speak or understand English; millions of others who would hear the voice of this man from another planet and have his words translated for them, almost as he spoke; the high brow, the low brow; the rich, the poor; the sick in mind or body; the devout, the profane—something in the unbelievable story of Numar had caught and held their attention. Man had always feared the unknown, was intrigued by the mysterious, and in awe of the Infinite. Numar represented all of this to the mind on the street and the intellect in high places.

"I, Numar, the Awakener, am here," said the voice. "I have been sent here to speak a prophecy to you.

"A great light is soon to appear in the heavens. Its brilliance will startle all mankind. It will cast an illumination over the entire earth. It will mark the beginning of the great change to take place on this planet. It will awaken all humans to the realization that there is a power far greater than themselves."

There had scarcely been a physical movement among the 130,000 people massed in Soldiers Field. The figure of the Green Man and what he was saying had so magnetized the throng that it was unconscious of the passage of time. His resonant voice had an easy, majestic, compelling flow. Each word not only entered the human ear, but the mind as well.

"Scientists, looking through earth telescopes," the voice continued, "will describe this light as a far distant universe being destroyed, the light rays of which have just reached you in this present day. The presence of this great phenomenon, in the heavens, will cause the greatest spiritual revival known to man. All grades of intelligence will be caused to think now, not in global terms, but in cosmic terms…"

A bright shaft of light from the setting sun outlined the white-robed figure of the Green Man, giving him a transcendent unearthly appearance.

"This great light," the voice went on, "will deal the forces of darkness the greatest blow since the appearance of Christ on this earth. Awe-struck millions will search their souls as never before. There will arrive, at this time, a host of higher beings assigned to work with the new spiritual leaders who will take their places among their fellow humans. The floodgates of revelation will be opened up in Science and man will commence to grope from threatened chaos toward a new harmony of being with all things. The time is not foreordained. It is to be synchronous with developments on your planet. The first evidence of this great light will be detected in the east. When this comes to pass, you will know that I, Numar, the Awakener, have spoken."

THE shadow of silence rushed back over the earth, giving way to a tidal wave of comment. On Soldiers Field, a referee's whistle was blowing. Time for the second half of the football game to begin. While, over the radio, as the worldwide network was broken, an announcer's voice was heard to be saying:

"Green's Vitamin-Plus Spinach has been glad to relinquish its time between halves of this game, that this special broadcast might take place…"

And, at one of the main gates of the stadium, a Navy chief petty officer, in company with an army pilot, was speaking to the head usher.

"Here's the Commander's seat location. We've got to reach him at once!"

"Follow me," said the head usher.

The two men in uniform had to fight their way through a mob of people who were leaving Soldiers Field, not staying for the second half of the game. Aisles were jammed. They finally got through behind the head usher to the field box containing the Navy commander and his party.

"Fortunately, they're still here," said the chief petty officer. He slipped a tip to the head usher and motioned to the army pilot. "I'll present you."

"Okay," said Harry, but his interest was elsewhere, as his eyes searched the field. Directly across from him he saw the portable radio platform, on which Numar had spoken, being moved off the gridiron. Betty must be over on that side somewhere.

"Commander," he heard the chief petty officer saying, "this is Lieutenant Harry Hopper from Washington. He's here on urgent business."

"I'll say it's urgent," said Harry, turning and saluting. "Commander, can you loan me your field glasses for a moment?"

Before the astonished Navy official could do or say anything, this young flying officer had snatched the glasses from his hands and was focusing them on some object or person on the other side of the stadium.

Numar and his party were actually in the process of leaving. Plane reservations had been made for them to depart for California at five that afternoon. There was just time to get back to the Palmer House, secure their luggage, and catch the limousine for the airport. Numar was taking leave of President Hutchins, with Betty, the Baileys, Mr. Alex and Mr. Schwartz beside him.

"Sorry you have to miss the second half of this great contest," said President Hutchins, humorously, as the two teams were lining up on the field.

"It is necessary," said Numar. "I have finished here."

"This will be a long remembered occasion," said President Hutchins, "and I, for one, will watch for this great light in the sky."

"It will come," said Numar, quietly.

Big Hank Morrison had secured a police detail and a way was being cleared for them to exit, with a car waiting outside to take them back to the hotel.

"Very fine, Mr. Numar," said Big Hank. "I never heard anything like it. You certainly wowed your audience."

"He certainly did," said Betty. "He even wowed me."

"I'm unconscious," said Sam.

"You've always been unconscious," said Sid.

The Professor and Mrs. Bailey were still beyond speaking.

ACROSS the field, a young flying officer had finally located the object of his search. She was a blonde in a red dress.

"There she is! That's her!" cried Harry, excitedly. He turned quickly and pressed the field glasses back into the hands of the Navy commander. "Here you are, Sir. I'll be back."

A straight line is still the shortest distance between two points. With the aisles so crowded, it would take at least half an hour for an individual to go around the stadium to the point directly opposite on the other side. Harry could not afford any such expenditure of time. He had to be over there now because the girl in the red dress was leaving. There was only one course open—and Harry took it. He leaped out of the field box and started racing across the gridiron.

"Stop that man!" yelled the Navy commander.

Chicago University was kicking off to Notre Dame. The football, spinning end over end, struck the earth in front of Harry and bounced into the arms of a Notre Dame man, and out again. A wall of frenzied U. of C. tacklers, intent on recovering the free ball, executed a converging movement. Harry had eyes only for Betty. He kept them on her as he ran. But ominous things were happening in his immediate vicinity. He was suddenly struck as though by a ten ton truck, and sent reeling.

"Betty!" he shouted. "Oh, Betty!"

He was hit again, but still kept his feet. However, he was running into the vortex of a human tornado. The ball, being kicked around, finally landed directly in front of him. He was hit hard from behind and then on all sides. The force of these blows shot him through the air. He fell on top of the pigskin and both teams fell on top of him. Thus it was, that an army pilot recovered the loose ball in the game between Chicago

University and Notre Dame, and precipitated a technical argument involving the referee and every player on both sides, while he, himself, lay stretched upon the field, dead to the world.

WORLD reaction to Numar's radio message was as varied as might humanly have been expected. This reaction depended somewhat upon the geographical location and temperament of the different earth peoples, as was evidenced by a statement issued from a spokesman for the Far East.

"All Asia will watch for this light in the East as the harbinger of good tidings that we are to be freed, forever, from the rule of the White Man."

Mahatma Gandhi came out of retirement to declare: "The only hope for India is in the heavens. We can do nothing with England, otherwise."

Premier Stalin was reported to have said: "Russia has already seen the light. We are sufficient unto ourselves."

As for Winston Churchill, his rumored comment was: "I hope such light may come but, as for me, I see nothing ahead but blood, tears and sweat."

Word from the White House was terse and to the point: "No comment."

Waldemar Kaempffert, science editor of the New York Times, had this pertinent observation to make: "Of course what Numar predicts is possible enough but not probable. There are, no doubt, great cosmic catastrophes occurring throughout the universe, worlds exploding and burning up at unimaginable degrees of heat, as a part of the inexorable changes always taking place. But we earth peoples have never, so far as is known, been eyewitnesses of any such phenomenon. However, if Mr. Numar's prophecy should come true, it would be startling, to say the least."

Roy Howard, in his Scripps-Howard papers, took a facetious point of view. In a lead editorial headed: "Numar Turns Out to be a Prophet?" he said, "Now we know the Green Man is a prophet. We, therefore, apologize to our readers for welcoming him to this earth. He told us, in this momentous broadcast, that we should look for a light in the East. We see a light in the East every morning and humans have been seeing it for thousands of years—so Mr. Numar is just a little bit late with his prophecy. However, it was a good try. For just a short time, he had us worried, but the moment he announced himself as a prophet, we knew he belonged in the class of the Ballard, 'I Am-ers,' the 'Omnipotent' and the 'Voodoo-ites.'"

The editors of the Daily Worker, with obvious relief, announced to their heterogeneous list of subscribers, "The world can go back to work, now that Numar has spoken. He offered no solace for the workingman, no plan for the bettering of labor conditions or the improvement of relations between employee and employer. We are glad to state that his promised threat to our civilization was piffling indeed. He referred only vaguely to some light that was to appear in the sky and herald the approach of a new spiritual era. We are unimpressed. The capitalists have been predicting this for us for years."

Senator Hoolihan, however, heroically declared to the press that he intended to have Numar's address read into the Congressional Record so that his prophecy might be given official recognition when it came true.

As for the local Chicago papers which, were at the scene of action, the statements of two noted editors are worthy of note.

Colonel McCormick of the Chicago Tribune summed up his feelings in one sentence: "I haven't any evidence as yet—but I strongly suspect a pro-British group is behind this."

Marshall Field of the Chicago Sun seized upon Numar's address as endorsing the "Truth" policy of his paper. "Numar," said Mr. Field, "is a forecaster of the birth of truth on this planet, for which the Sun has long been a pioneer."

And California, not to be outdone, through its Los Angeles Chamber of Commerce, sent a wire of protest to the Green Man: "Mr. Numar," the telegram said, "why give the East all the breaks? What about a light in the West?"

IT WAS a relief to the members of Numar's party to be safely buckled into their seats on the plane. It had been a hectic three days of cross-country travel, scarcely knowing what the next moment would bring in new developments and high-pressure happenings. But now they could sit back and relax as their TWA airliner moved smoothly along under a clear night sky. The stewardess had started making up their berths.

"I wonder what the world is thinking of your talk?" said Professor Bailey, who was seated beside Numar.

"I know what it is thinking," said the man from another planet.

Professor Bailey hesitated. "Is it good?" he finally asked. "Does the world believe?"

Numar shook his head. "No," he said. "The world will not believe until it sees a sign. That is why I came to your earth—to point to that sign. And, when the great light appears…"

"I know," said the Professor. "It's the same with my work. I discover a new star in the heavens and no one will believe me, that is until…"

"Until they find that star for themselves," finished Numar.

Mr. Alex and Mr. Schwartz were having a serious consultation.

"I don't think this Numar is going to go so good in Hollywood now, even if he photographed," said Sid.

"Me, either," said Sam. "Of course we haven't seen the press reports on his act yet—but this…light in the sky business…that's too far away. If people have to wait for something to happen, they lose interest."

"That's right," said Sid. "Now, if he had said that the day after tomorrow, at midnight, we were going to see the heavens lit up, he'd have had the whole world crazy."

"Yeah," said Sam. "Including me."

Sid scratched his head behind both ears. "Well, we've got to salvage something out of this trip." A gleam came into his eyes. "I've got it!" he cried. "We'll do an original story on Numar and put Miss Bracken and Mrs. Bailey in it. Boy…what a drama…what a comedy…what a farce!"

Sam sat blinking. "You're right," he said. "It's got everything and I've got the title for it."

"What's that?" asked Sid.

"The Light That Failed," said Sam.

"That's terrific!" said Sid, "You're in on the deal. I'll register that title at the Hays office as soon as we get off the plane."

"Wait a moment," said Sam. "How can we do this? I'm working for Warner Brothers."

"Resign your position," said Sid. "I'll resign mine. We'll form our own producing company!"

"What'll we do for money?" asked Sam.

"Why did you have to bring that up?" said Sid, and slumped in his seat.

IT REQUIRED some tall explaining and more long distance telephoning for Lieutenant Hopper to get his plane off the deck of the Naval Training Aircraft Carrier in Lake Michigan. That he managed to do it was a tribute to irrepressible youth, a certain degree of human sympathy, and more good luck than any young man has a right to have.

"You can depend upon it, Sir," he had told his outraged Commandant, over the phone. "I'll fly her right in from Chicago…*positively.*"

As he took to the air, this was his firmest resolution, but resolutions, even when made on New Year's Day, last little longer than the fizz on a Bromo-Seltzer. How could Harry help it if the nose of his plane was pointing toward California instead of Texas?

"If I don't hit a mountain peak," he said, grimly, "I'll beat that TWA plane in to Los Angeles and wring Numar's neck the moment he steps off."

Harry arrived, as he had planned, half an hour ahead of the commercial airliner, but he found there were others ahead of him, waiting to seize Numar and visit punishment upon him. The Chief of Police of Los Angeles and half a dozen officers from his department were on the scene, with them were reporters and photographers.

"We'll get the low-down story this time," they said.

"Yes, and we may even get a picture!" laughed a cameraman.

Harry lost no time in giving the police an account of his cross-country chase.

"That guy had the world fooled but not me," he said. "I thought he was a fake from the start, and I've been trying to get my girl away from him. I've risked demotion from the army and everything. Say, can't I prefer charges against Numar for transporting Miss Bracken from state to state?"

The Chief shook his head. "No, what you're talking about is white slavery."

"White slavery?" said Harry. "It's *green* slavery. He's got her mesmerized!"

"We know he's a fake," said the Chief, "And we're not going to let him set up any cult in California. That's unquestionably what he's coming back here to do."

"By Gawd!" exclaimed Harry. "I see it all now—and he's going to make Betty his high priestess."

"We'll put a stop to that," said the Chief. "I've dealt with every kind of a nut there is. We'll expose his tricks and put him in jail."

There could now be heard the far-off drone of a two-motored plane and a TWA airliner was sighted, its silver sides glistening in the morning sun.

"There they come!" cried the police.

All on the ground rushed for the spot to which the plane would taxi, when unloading.

Inside the airliner, Numar suddenly stiffened; a pensive look came in his dark eyes. He turned to Professor Bailey.

"Will you call all of our party to our compartment?" he requested. "Please hurry. We haven't much time."

Wonderingly, the Professor did as instructed. Numar eyed them all, soberly.

"My time on earth is now getting short," he announced. "In leaving you, I have a few things I wish to say."

"Mr. Numar," said Professor Bailey, "You are welcome to stay with us as long as you…I think I'm speaking for my wife as well as myself, when I say we've both become quite…"

"You have each been very kind to me," said Numar. He took some folded slips of paper from beneath his robe and handed to them. "Here are my checks from the Frank Morgan and *Information, Please* programs. I have signed them over to you. As you know, I have no use for money."

Professor Bailey tried to speak and couldn't. Mrs. Bailey was speechless.

Numar turned to Mr. Alex and Mr. Schwartz. "You gentlemen must not feel too badly about not getting me for pictures," he smiled. "I foresee that you will profit from this experience after I am gone."

"He talks like he's on his death bed," said Sam.

"He'll have us crying in a moment," said Sid.

"I think you all should know," said Numar, quietly, "that, waiting at the airport now, to arrest me, are policemen from the city of Los Angeles."

"But you have done nothing," protested the Professor.

"I have disturbed a great many people," said Numar, "I want you to be, prepared for my reception. It will be unlike any I have had before."

"Can we do anything to help?" asked the Professor.

"Yes," said Numar, "I must get to the place in the mountains where my spaceship is waiting."

"Your spaceship!" cried Betty. "You really mean it?"

"Of course he meant it," said Professor Bailey. "I've told you people, I've seen it."

"Then we've *got* to help him some way," said Betty. "I'll figure out something, Mr. Numar. You leave it to me."

The stewardess came hurrying toward them. "Get back to your seats, please," she said. "And fasten your belts. We're coming in for a landing."

THE first to appear in the plane's door, when it opened, was Betty. She looked out at the lineup of police, flanked by newspapermen, and bristled with defiance.

"What a fine reception committee," she said.

"Betty!" cried a familiar voice.

Betty's eyes popped. "Harry?" she shrieked and ran to his arms. "Where have you been?"

"What's that man done to you?" said Harry.

"Which one?" said Betty. She looked around.

A frightened Mr. Alex and Mr. Schwartz were dismounting from the plane.

"There he is again," said Sam.

"He's going to kill somebody!" exclaimed Sid.

"You *know* which one!" Harry was raving. "I'm going to murder him!"

"You hear that?" said Sid.

"I'll see you later," Sam shot back.

Professor and Mrs. Bailey had now left the plane and Numar was standing in the doorway. The police started for him but Harry jumped ahead of them.

"I want first crack at that guy," he said. "Let me at him!"

"Harry!" cried Betty. "Come back...you mustn't!"

But Lieutenant Hopper had not risked his life and reputation for nothing. He was going to get satisfaction or know the reason why.

"Do not touch me," said Numar.

"Don't touch you, eh?" said Harry, advancing up the steps to the plane. "Come down out of that ship, you green monster—I've got a nice little score to settle!"

He took a swing at Numar. The blow was aimed at the Green Man's cheek but some invisible force seemed to repel it. It also repelled Harry. He landed on his back on the ground, rolled over and sat up.

"What happened?" he asked, dazedly.

"I told you not to touch him," said Betty.

The Chief of Police of Los Angeles and his men had been stopped in their tracks. They pulled their guns and covered Numar.

"No more of your funny business," said the Chief. "Or we'll shoot!" He turned to the rest of the party. "Come on, folks, you're all going to take a ride in the patrol wagon. I'm going to find out just what your connection is with this faker."

"The idea!" said Mrs. Bailey. "Us ride in the patrol wagon? What a way to end a fine trip like this!"

"I think it'll be fun," whispered Betty. "I've always wanted to ride in a police car, haven't you, Harry?"

Harry, at the moment, was holding his head and staring at Numar. It is doubtful if he heard the question.

"You can count me out," said Sam. "I've got other business."

"That's strange," said Sid. "So have I."

"Get moving, all of you!" ordered the Chief. "There's the patrol wagon over there." Then, turning to his men, "Sergeant, you ride down with them. "I'll follow with the boys in my car."

"Okay, Chief," said the burly officer. "Hey, you!" he called out. "Where are you birds going?"

"I'm going home," said Sam.

"I'm going with him," said Sid.

"You're getting in this wagon," said the Sergeant. "And no back-talk or I'll clip your ears."

"He means it," said Sam.

"He sure does," said Sid.

They tossed their grips on the floor of the patrol wagon and climbed in.

"My!" said Mrs. Bailey. "I'm glad this isn't happening in LaCanada. What *would* my neighbors say?"

"It's an outrage!" said the Professor. "A personage like Numar to be treated this way."

"Don't worry," whispered Betty. "I've got an idea."

"Be careful," warned the Professor. "You're dealing with the law."

"I'm ignorant of the law," said Betty.

THEY were all in the patrol wagon, which had a small open window in the front. The back of the wagon had no door. The seats were along the sides. Numar sat up forward. Betty placed herself next to him and pulled Harry down beside her. Mr. Alex, Mr. Schwartz, the Professor and Mr. Bailey sat directly opposite. The Sergeant was talking to the driver.

"Yeah, we got the Green Man in there. Strange crew with him, too. That pilot's the only sensible one of the lot. The rest are nuts."

"Beats all how you can always get new damn fools to join something, don't it?" said the driver. "Take my wife, for instance…"

The Sergeant waved his hand. "You can have her," he said. "I've got troubles enough with my own. Let's get going." He sauntered around to the back of the patrol wagon, stepped in and sat next to Mrs. Bailey.

"Nice morning!" he chortled.

Mrs. Bailey eyed him. "What's nice about it?" she said.

A siren sounded and the patrol wagon moved off. Behind it, members of Numar's party could see the Chief and fellow officers following in his car. Both machines swung onto the main highway leading into downtown Los Angeles.

"I hope they send this green guy up for ninety-nine years," said Harry, in a low voice to Betty.

"Oh…you mustn't say that," said Betty. "Honestly, Harry, you've got him all wrong. Didn't you feel what he did to you?"

"Yes," said Harry, glowering. "He crossed me with a right!"

"Why, he never touched you," said Betty. "He didn't raise a finger. That was his electric current…"

Harry put a hand to his head. "What a wallop! I felt it all over. No. What are you saying…electric current?"

"Yes," said Betty. "He kissed me with it once. I can still feel it!" she chuckled.

Harry stared at her. "I saw the pictures," he said. "Do you mean that was on the level?"

"I was almost electrocuted," said Betty.

"You poor kid," said Harry. "I don't see how you stood it."

"Well, anyway," said Betty, "a man like that isn't normal."

"I'll say he's not normal," said Harry. "A man like that shouldn't be walking around loose. I'd sooner grab a high tension wire."

The patrol wagon was doing a good forty miles per hour on its way into the city. The Sergeant, after his one effort to be sociable with Mrs. Bailey, had folded his arms and was staring straight ahead.

"I suppose I could pay Mr. Numar's bail," the Professor was contemplating. "It's a disgrace to think of him being locked up in jail."

Numar, himself, appeared to be impassive. He was sitting, quietly, turbaned-head slightly lowered, and green hands folded in his lap.

Betty kept up her running fire barrage on Harry. "So, you see, Harry—Mr. Numar really isn't the kind of person you thought at all. He doesn't belong on this earth and we've got to help get him off of it, if we can."

Harry's interest was caught; he was studying intently.

"Fat chance we've got!" he said, "with him on the way to jail."

"That's just it," said Betty. "We have got a fat chance. Do you know something, Harry? Mr. Numar can take that electric current of his and shoot it out and stop an automobile."

"He can?" said Harry. "But what good is that going to do him here?"

"You wait and see," said Betty. She turned to the Green Man. "Mr. Numar," she said. "I've got a plan. If you'll stop the Chief's car, and this car, too, I think we can get away."

Numar smiled. "I've been waiting for you to suggest that," he said.

He lifted his head, purposefully. Betty and Harry watched out the back door of the patrol wagon. They saw the Chief's car, which had been following them at a good speed, slow down and stop. At almost the same time, the motor of their own car gave a sharp cough and died.

"What the hell?" said the Sergeant, jumping out to investigate.

Harry stood up and looked out through the little front window. "The driver's got the hood up, checking the motor," he reported.

"You see," said Betty, "how simple it was? Look at the Chief and his men. They can't figure out what's happened, either."

"Gosh!" said Harry. "What a secret weapon..."

Betty grabbed him by the arm. "No, Harry...*you're* our secret weapon. Quick—now's your chance! Run around and get behind the wheel. Start the car up!"

"But it won't go," said Harry.

"It will go now," stated Numar.

A grin came to Harry's face. "I get the picture," he said. "Where to?"

"I'll direct you" replied Numar. He stood up beside the open window.

"Hurry!" cried Betty. "The Chief's coming our way!"

Harry ran to the rear of the patrol wagon, jumped off and dashed around the side. The driver and the Sergeant had the hood up and their heads under it, examining the motor. Harry jammed his foot on the starter. The engine caught on with a roar. The car leaped forward. Driver and Sergeant jumped for their lives.

"What did I do!" moaned the driver.

"Hey, *you!*" yelled the Sergeant when he saw the army pilot at the wheel. He made a grab for the handle of the rear door as the patrol wagon passed and swung onto the step. As he did so, he was met by a determined middle-aged woman who gave him a push. The Sergeant landed smack on the seat of his pants in the middle of the highway.

"Now, how did I ever do a thing like that!" exclaimed Mrs. Bailey.

"I don't know," said the Professor, a big smile on his face, "but I'm glad you did."

"That's worth three hundred and twenty-five a week!" exclaimed Sam. "She could be a second Marie Dressler."

"My baby isn't so bad," said Sid. "She's Scarlett O'Hara on wheels."

Harry was feeding the patrol wagon more and more gas and it was rapidly picking up speed.

"The Chief's stopped a taxi and they're all piling in," reported Betty. "They're coming after us!"

"Turn left at the next cross street," directed Numar.

HARRY took the corner on three wheels, running up over the curb and leaving a shower of oranges in his wake from a sidewalk fruit stand. Pedestrians ran wildly for storefronts. The occupants of the patrol wagon bounced around inside.

"Sorry," said Harry. "I forgot where I was. I've been trying to get this thing off the ground!"

"Turn left again," directed Numar.

Betty put hands to her eyes. "Oh—slow up, Harry! Look out for that building!"

Harry was sounding the siren continuously and motorists were pulling to one side to let the police car pass.

"Must be a riot call," commented a spectator.

It appeared as though Harry's frenzied chase of Numar and his party, from coast to coast, had been for the primary purpose of putting him in training for this maddest of all rides. He needed no head starts or stopped motors to keep him out in front.

Reaching the mountain road, Harry tore up the increasing incline at only slightly reduced speed. He took the patrol wagon around the bends, sometimes appearing to be on the very outer rim, with sheer drop-offs beyond of a thousand to two thousand feet, to the valley below.

"It's a good thing my heart's stopped beating," said Sid.

"It's a good thing I'm unconscious," Sam shot back.

Mrs. Bailey was holding on for dear life. The Professor had lost his glasses several times and had to grope for them as they slid about on the weaving car floor. Now he had them jammed in his handkerchief pocket.

"William…put your glasses on!" said Mrs. Bailey. "You can't see where we're going."

"I don't want to!" said the Professor. He had driven up this mountain road many times, himself, en route to Wilson Observatory, but he was never destined to make better speed this side of heaven.

Harry delivered his human cargo, including the escaping Numar, to the place directed, without mishap. He jumped from his seat behind the wheel and ran around to the back in time to help his passengers as they staggered out.

"Whew!" gasped Mrs. Bailey, her hat on one side and looking otherwise disheveled. "I'm glad that's over—but I wouldn't have missed it for the world."

Professor Bailey, next out, was looking up at the mountainside. "Yes, Mr. Numar, this is the spot where I left the road and met you. My, it seems like an eternity ago."

Numar smiled. "Yet it is only a week of your time," he said.

"Speaking of time," said Harry. "I'm glad you mentioned it—my leave is up tonight."

"Oh, I can fix that," said Betty. "I'll just pick up the phone and call your commander…"

"No, you won't!" said Harry. "I'm in a bad enough jam now."

Mr. Alex and Mr. Schwartz had descended from the car and were looking anxiously down the mountain road.

"No police in sight," said Sam.

"There's things worse than police." said Sid. "This ride, for one!"

NUMAR faced the members of his party. "I am grateful to you all," he said.

Then, turning to Betty and Harry, who were standing with their arms around one another, he added: "Some day, you will tell your children about this occasion...and they will tell *their* children."

"Oh, Harry!" cried Betty. "Then, we're going to be married!"

"I know that already," said Harry. "But what's the Army going to do to me?"

Numar smiled. "You will be punished," he said. "Then sent overseas, to return a hero. I see the President of this country conferring a medal."

"That's not my future," moaned Harry. "That's my past!"

"I must leave you now," said Numar. "You are to remain here. But, if you will fix your eyes above the trees around the clearing, you will see my spaceship as it leaves this planet."

"Now, Nellie," said Professor Bailey, "I want you to look sharp."

"It will just be a flash in your atmosphere," said Numar. "You will have to watch closely."

"Won't we ever see you again?" asked Betty.

Numar gave her a kindly look. "There is an eternity of time ahead. Perhaps we shall all meet again, somewhere."

"Jeez!" said Sam. "Look at my goose pimples..."

"Those aren't goose pimples," said Sid. "Those are *eggs.*"

Numar left the road and started toward the clearing. He turned just once to smile and lift a hand in farewell.

"You will think of me," he said, "when the great light appears."

The little group stood on the road by the mountainside, looking breathlessly off toward the clearing. Far below on the highway could be heard the labored sound of a taxicab motor. The Chief of Police of Los Angeles and his officers were finally arriving. But no one in the party was paying any attention to them now. They were watching the white-robed figure of the Green Man as it grew smaller and smaller and disappeared behind a fringe of trees.

There was a moment of indescribable suspense. Then, suddenly, from up over the clearing, there flashed what appeared to be a blinding silver beam of light. It shot toward them, at incredible speed, then upward and out of sight.

"Gosh...that was something!" exclaimed Harry.

"You see, Nellie," said Professor Bailey.

"My eyes hurt," said Sam.

"That was worse than Klieg lights," said Sid.

The Chief and his officers came running up.

"Where is he?" bellowed the Chief. "What have you done with him?"

"He's gone!" cried Betty. "He just left in his spaceship. Oh, Chief—it was wonderful! Didn't you see it?"

"No, I didn't," said the Chief. "And you didn't, either..."

"GOOD evening, ladies and gentlemen, from border to border and coast to coast and all the ships at sea," said Walter Winchell, on Sunday night's broadcast. "Let's go to press. *Flash!*

"Numar, the mysterious Green Man, has been here and gone—taking his mystery with him.

"In one of the most sensational escapes in history, rivaling Houdini at his best, Numar—seized by the Los Angeles police chief and his aides—played some electrical magic, stopped their automobile motors, then intimidated or influenced a young flying lieutenant and his girl, riding with him, to drive him to his mountain hideout. Members of Numar's party were found later, in a hysterical condition, swearing that they had seen the Green Man take off in his spaceship. Their word, however, is not to be trusted, after their harrowing experience.

"J. Edgar Hoover advised this reporter that Numar definitely had something—just what, he didn't know—but he couldn't be finger-printed.

"Little boy Walter also testifies that Numar actually packed an electrical wallop. But when this Green Man predicted to radio's biggest audience, yesterday, that a great light would appear in the East, this was something we could understand. He was referring to a new, big advertising sign on Broadway's Great White Way. This light is apt to appear at any moment.

"And now, your reporter has a prediction: One of these days, in the not too distant future, the Green Man will emerge from his mountain retreat, explain his hocus-pocus to the world, and claim the fabulous radio, stage and movie contracts awaiting him!"

"WILLIAM! Oh, William!"

Professor Bailey stirred and sat up, placing a hand to the back of his throbbing head. He was cold and it was pitch dark but he thought he had heard his wife calling.

"Oh, William!"

Yes, that was his wife all right. But where was he? Last thing he remembered, he'd been listening to Walter Winchell. The professor got stiffly to his feet. He was outdoors on a mountainside. It was strange—very strange indeed.

"William! Answer me!"

"Yes, dear—I'm coming!"

He stumbled forward, feeling his way in the direction of her voice as she continued to call.

"I can't understand this," he mumbled to himself. "My...the things that have happened!"

His head was still reeling as he reached the road. It reeled even more when Nellie grabbed him and shook him.

"What do you mean, giving me a fright like this? Where have you been? Why didn't you answer?"

"You ought to know," said the Professor. "You were with me. What a time we had...what a time..."

Mrs. Bailey eyed her husband, worriedly.

"What are you talking about? Did you get to a telephone? Is someone coming out to fix the car?"

"No," said the Professor. "That won't be necessary. Numar stopped the motor. It will start all right." He motioned to his wife to get in the car and slipped in behind the wheel.

"Numar? Who's Numar?" demanded Mrs. Bailey.

The Professor put his foot on the starter. There was a cough and the motor came to life.

"You see?" he said.

"Well, for pity's sake," said his wife. "Carburetor must have been choked, or something. All this trouble and worry for nothing."

Professor Bailey drew a great sigh of relief. "You don't know who Numar is?" he asked.

"No," said Mrs. Bailey. "I never heard of him."

"Never heard of him?" said the Professor. "Why you met him. He was a man from another planet!"

"Oh, stop it!" said Mrs. Bailey. "Won't you ever get that speech off your mind? I'm frozen and tired and I want to get home and get to bed."

The Professor backed his car onto the highway and they resumed their descent of the mountain, while up above him—the stars of the universe looked down—and laughed.

THE END

If you've enjoyed this book, you will not want to miss these terrific titles...

ARMCHAIR SCI-FI, FANTASY, & HORROR DOUBLE NOVELS, $12.95 each

D-1   **THE GALAXY RAIDERS** by William P. McGivern
SPACE STATION #1 by Frank Belknap Long

D-2   **THE PROGRAMMED PEOPLE** by Jack Sharkey
SLAVES OF THE CRYSTAL BRAIN by William Carter Sawtelle

D-3   **YOU'RE ALL ALONE** by Fritz Leiber
THE LIQUID MAN by Bernard C. Gilford

D-4   **CITADEL OF THE STAR LORDS** by Edmund Hamilton
VOYAGE TO ETERNITY by Milton Lesser

D-5   **IRON MEN OF VENUS** by Don Wilcox
THE MAN WITH ABSOLUTE MOTION by Noel Loomis

D-6   **ENCHANTRESS OF VENUS** by Leigh Brackett
THE PUZZLE PLANET by Robert A. W. Lowndes

D-7   **PLANET OF DREAD** by Murray Leinster
TWICE UPON A TIME by Charles L. Fontenay

D-8   **THE TERROR OUT OF SPACE** by Dwight V. Swain
QUEST OF THE GOLDEN APE by Ivar Jorgensen and Adam Chase

D-9   **SECRET OF MARRACOTT DEEP** by Henry Slesar
PAWN OF THE BLACK FLEET by Mark Clifton.

D-10   **BEYOND THE RINGS OF SATURN** by Robert Moore Williams
A MAN OBSESSED by Alan E. Nourse

ARMCHAIR SCIENCE FICTION CLASSICS, $12.95 each

SF-1   **THE GREEN MAN**
by Harold M. Sherman

SF-2   **A TRACE OF MEMORY**
By Keith Laumer

ARMCHAIR MASTERS OF SCIENCE FICTION SERIES, $16.95 each

MS-1   **MASTERS OF SCIENCE FICTION, Vol. One**
Bryce Walton—"Dark of the Moon" and other tales

MS-2   **MASTERS OF SCIENCE FICTION, Vol. Two**
Jerome Bixby: "One Way Street" and other tales